THE SILVER CASTLE

DL BARRON

The Silver Castle.

Book cover design by Alejandro Colluci.
Edited and Formatted by Christine Nielson

ISBN 979-8-9985338-0-8 (paperback)
ISBN 979-8-9985338-1-5 (ebook)

dlbarronauthor.com

This book is dedicated to my father, who taught me to love good books. And by good, I mean the kind with lots of action—not the 'boring ones.' That lesson has served me well as a writer.

And to Bram Stoker, creator of not only the most famous vampire in fiction, but an entirely new genre that has endured for more than a century.

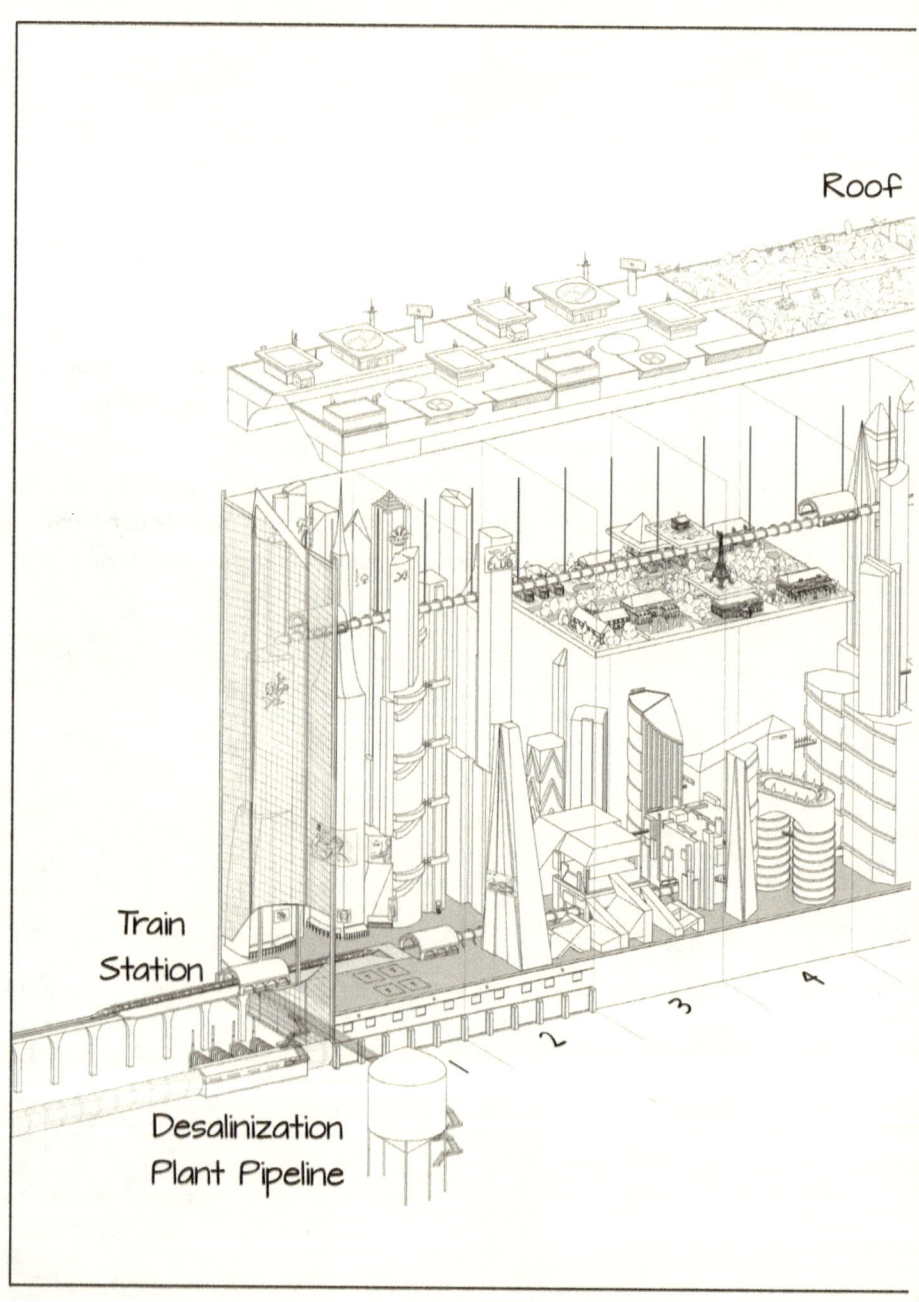

Roof

Train
Station

Desalinization
Plant Pipeline

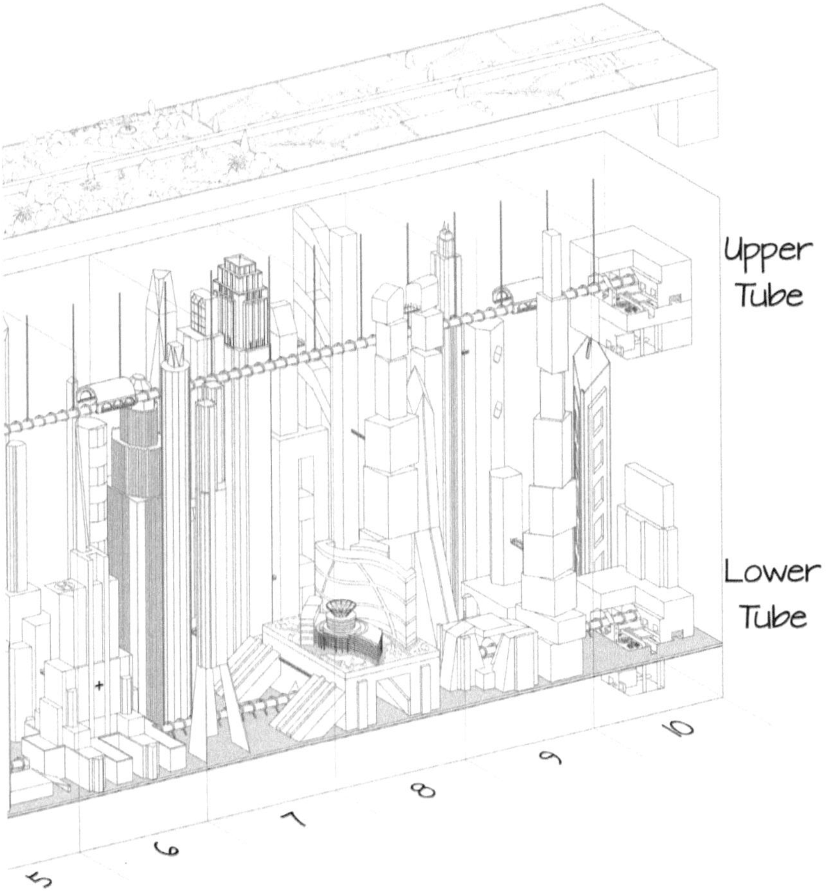

Upper
Tube

Lower
Tube

5   6   7   8   9   10

DRISSIA   Planning & Development

"Mojave Line Project"

CHAPTER ONE

THEY SAY time heals all wounds.

It's a lie. I tried it.

Cactus plants and craggy rock formations whizzed by my circular window. Soon, the train would arrive at the Line. I didn't care about making money, advancing a career, or any of the other more debauched reasons people flocked to the newly built city. For me, the high speed magnetic levitation train offered a lifeline—a move away from the daily reminder of the husband I lost.

The train left Los Angeles hours ago, and my watch told me we were getting close. I kept staring out the window, waiting to see the glint of metal and glass. Instead, I saw nothing but mile after mile of wide open desert.

The blonde-haired man next to me glanced up from his phone and focused his attention out the window. He made eye contact with me and smiled. "Look, we're almost there."

I turned back to the window and finally saw the Line for the first time. Of course, I had seen pictures of it already. The advertisements had popped up everywhere, on billboards lining the freeways and all over social media. But nothing could convey the stunning enormity of the real life structure. The silver facade gleamed like a diamond in the sunlight of the Mojave desert. It was as if a lone skyscraper had been plucked from New York City, stretched out like an accordion, and then dropped into the middle of the wilderness. Cubes of glass poked out randomly from all sides, many filled with bright green gardens. If you squinted hard enough, you could see trees lining the top of the building.

The stark contrast of the giant manmade oasis next to the dirt and rock looked unreal. Now, seeing it in person, I understood the Line's mystical quality, a sense of entering a fantasy world—one that bordered our own but was somehow different.

I finally understood the Line's nickname. The Silver Castle.

I looked away from the window and noticed the man still smiling at me.

"First time you've seen the Castle?" he asked. The pronunciation of 'castle' revealed a hint of a British accent. Or maybe Irish. Hard to tell.

"Yes."

"It's huge. Ten miles long, and they're planning another extension."

His attempt at small talk seemed innocent enough, but I wasn't looking to make friends. After a polite nod, I put my phone in my lap with my left hand on top, prominently displaying the decade-old wedding band.

Either he didn't notice the ring, or he didn't care. Blondie kept talking.

"So what job did they give you?" he quizzed. "I got in as a lawyer. Lots of competition for that one. The waiting list is six months."

That figured. Blondie wouldn't shut up. Just like a lawyer. I kept trying to place the accent. I leaned towards Blondie being a Scot.

Hoping it would end the conversation, I offered a tidbit. "Health care," I replied before turning back to gaze at my new home. The tall building now blocked out the evening sun. Without the glare, I could see the balconies peppering the side facing my window, some large enough to contain entire groves of trees growing alongside lush lawns of grass. Swarms of drones buzzed around the building like insects, making deliveries to balcony landing pads.

Behind me, Blondie kept bugging. "Are you a doctor?"

A voice inside told me to be polite, but I ignored it. After a deep sigh, I replied, never bothering to look away from the window. "Hospice nurse. I watch people die."

We were approaching the south end of the Line, where the train would unload. Giant pipes at least fifty feet tall ran parallel to the tracks, filled with water from the desalinization plant in Long Beach, the lifeblood making it possible for people and plants to thrive in the middle of a wasteland. The south end of the Line contained a water tower and a waste treatment facility to recycle every drop of water used by the city.

Behind me, Blondie fell into silence and I allowed myself a quick smile. Never failed. Everyone was afraid of death. They ran at the mention of the word. I was like that, too, until I had to spend years with Alex in and out of more facilities than I could count. Now those places felt like home.

A deep booming voice rang out over the intercom on the train. "Welcome to the Silver Castle Station, also known as the end of the Line."

Next to me, Blondie, along with many of the other passengers, chuckled at the announcer's attempt at humor. Silently, the train slowed down then came to a stop with a slight jerk. The mag lev train had more than lived up to its reputation. It was the smoothest train ride of my life.

Not surprisingly, Idrissia had built the train, just like the Line. Idrissia started as an oil company, but now they had their hands in just about every type of business—technology, pharmaceuticals, weapons. One day they showed up, bought a piece of the desert, and somehow took control, creating their own private city. They owned everything out here.

I reached under the seat and removed my backpack. In my head, I checked off the long list of things I needed to accomplish on my first day in the Castle. The Idrissia videos showed welcoming attendants at the train station. Time to find out if that was real, or if all of it was just a sales pitch to get desperate people out into the desert.

Blondie made one last effort before he filed out of the train. "I hope you like it here. I'm Celwyn, by the way."

His persistence began to grow on me, and I forced a terse smile.

"Thanks. Good luck to you with the lawyer stuff." I paused. "And I'm Mel."

"I hope to see you around, Mel." He turned his back and I watched him blend into the mass of people making their way out of the train onto the station platform.

Stretching my legs brought an immediate sense of relief. I threw the backpack over my shoulders and followed Celwyn, who was at least six feet and tall enough to completely block my line of sight, out through the sliding train doors onto the metal landing that was connected to a giant concrete platform carved into the South end of the city. Once I stepped out of the train, the oven-like heat of the Mojave desert washed over my face like a wave.

Celwyn waited for me to catch up. "You need to go that way." He pointed towards a row of kiosks manned by Idrissia employees in black jackets. Above the kiosks, a sign read 'Welcome Center: New Residents.'

"Thanks."

"I meant what I said, Mel. Maybe I'll see you at the Joshua Tree Saloon?"

The look of anticipation in his deep green eyes made me pause for a second. Then sanity flowed back into my brain. No chance I was going to meet a stranger for drinks in uncharted territory.

"Bars aren't really my thing."

"How about at least connecting on the Idrissia app? Can't hurt to have someone you know in the Castle in case you need something?"

It had been a long time since I had run into such persistence. I finally relented. "Fine, but I don't know what you're talking about. What app?"

"You have the Idrissia app right? Show me your phone."

I sighed and pulled up the Idrissia app on my phone. Celwyn touched my phone and swiped a few times.

"See, you have a user name, and there is a social media function for residents. Now that I know your name, I can message you."

"That doesn't mean I'm going to respond."

"Of course not," he replied, then bowed as if I was royalty. "Welcome to your Castle, m'lady," he said with a grin.

I watched Celwyn until he disappeared into the horde of people moving towards the entrance to the towering glass structure. I yearned to follow him into the city and explore my new home, but I couldn't. Not yet.

Like those on the train, the attendants at the welcome center lived up to Idrissia's promises. As I approached the row of kiosks, an older woman waved me down. "Honey, you look like you're new. Come on over here and let me help you. Give me your name and I'll look you up."

"Melanie Sanger."

A name tag on the woman's jacket said her name was Sheila from Texas. A quick glance down the line of attendants revealed that all of the Idrissia name tags included a home state or country.

Sheila typed on the keyboard and waited impatiently, staring at the screen. "Ah. Found your luggage. Do you have your ticket?"

I pulled out my phone and showed the electronic claim tag. Sheila smiled and went back to typing. In a few seconds, a man in a black Idrissia uniform pushing a cart full of luggage approached from the rear of the train.

Michael from Canada handed me my suitcase, then continued to dole out bags to the others waiting beside me at the welcome center. Sheila grabbed a trifold map from a stack next to her computer, unfolded it and slapped it down on the counter in front of me.

"Alright Melanie, let's get you into the Castle. Your apartment is at this address." She wrote some numbers on the top of the map. "The Line is divided into grids, like city blocks. There are ten blocks that make up the Line, and you are in number eight. Take the Tube through Broadway to Grid Eight, and then scan the code with your phone. The app will take you straight there. With me so far?"

I nodded.

Sheila pulled out a black plastic credit card. "This is your I-card. First thing you need to do is scan that code on the back with your phone. If you lose the card, you have it on your phone. Don't lose both of them, got it?"

My curiosity got the better of me. "What happens if I lose both?"

A look of surprise flashed over Sheila's face, then it darkened.

"Don't you know? They take security real serious around here. You don't go anywhere without scanning your code. If you get caught without one—" she began to stammer. "Lots of freeloaders trying to sneak in. If they think you don't belong here—"

I took the card and smiled. "Don't worry. I'm sure I'll be fine."

Sheila collected herself and resumed her speech. "Like I said, your apartment is in Grid Eight. Your job is on the medical level. The career center is in Grid Six near the Hospital. If you show up tomorrow at eight, they'll get you set up." She pointed at the bottom of the map. "Here is the contact information for the Idrissia help center. If you have any questions, just call them. Day or night, they always answer."

I gathered the map and placed it in a pocket on my backpack. "I think I'm all set. Thanks, Sheila."

The entire process had taken less than five minutes. Everywhere I looked, people moved with a purpose. Most of the visitors from the train had already left the kiosks and entered the city, leaving the Station nearly empty. At the rear of the train, forklifts unloaded cargo too important to transport over the highway. Employees moved containers onto giant platforms, then lowered them into a network of warehouses and smaller docks below us bustling with the loading and unloading of trucks.

Suddenly, a shout caught my attention and I turned towards the entrance to the city. One of the doors flung open and a disheveled woman sprinted into the Station, running straight towards the train. Behind her, several uniformed men, whom I assumed to be police officers, chased in pursuit. Others wearing the same black uniform seemed to materialize from various points around the terminal, all converging on the woman.

Before she could reach the train, a female officer stepped out of one of the cars and pointed a handgun at the woman. "Stop!"

The crazed woman's momentum slowed before she reached the edge of the platform. She recoiled suddenly as if struck by some unseen force, then began to sob, melting into the shadows lining the concrete floor, curled up into a fetal position. Silence descended on the Station. The woman crawled backward, away from the train, covering her eyes with one arm, squinting at the bright desert sun. Officers in full riot gear carefully approached the woman from every direction, and her cries turned into angry shouts in a language I didn't understand.

I moved forward, straining to get a closer look. The young woman stood up and pushed long brown hair away from her face. Dark, lifeless eyes flashed wildly against pale skin that appeared to be a light shade of gray. Her mouth snarled and she bared her teeth.

The woman lunged like an animal towards one of the officers. An electric bolt shot out of a taser gun, knocking her to the ground. Momentarily dazed, she kept shouting the same foreign words repeatedly until the female officer from the train reached her side. Within seconds, the officer secured her hands with zip ties. Three more officers scooped up the young female, secured a gag in her mouth, then escorted her out a door at the back of the terminal.

"Bless her heart," Sheila said. "I hope that poor girl is alright."

"What just happened?"

"Drugs. Even way out here, that stuff finds a way in. Idrissia will clean her up."

I nodded to Sheila and headed towards the Silver Castle. With the distraction handled by the officers, people again moved freely through the rows of glass doors marking the entrance to the city I would now call home.

Inside me, I felt something stir, a feeling I thought I had lost.

Excitement.

CHAPTER TWO

EVERY ADVERTISEMENT for the Castle focused on Broadway, and for good reason. The centerpiece of the city stretched the entire length of the Line and functioned both as the main transportation artery and the largest hub of commerce. Broadway split the Line into two halves, supplying a healthy amount of natural sunlight into the middle of the Castle through a pointed glass atrium atop the building that spanned the entire length of the Castle.

I walked along what resembled a brick paved street, admiring the shopping area adjoining the Silver Castle Station. Above me, giant LED screens rotated through advertisements for every type of product imaginable, along with popular restaurants and clubs along Broadway. Crowds of people pressed beside me, moving in an orderly fashion in every direction.

At the first intersection, a black sign with silver lettering hung above the busy street. The logo for Idrissia, an oversized 'I' in the shape of a skyscraper with a horizontal line connecting the logo to the rest of the letters, marked each level and grid section. Ahead of me, I saw my immediate destination—one of the interior train stations that would take me to my apartment. The clear plastic tube stood empty.

Above it, a digital sign counted down the minutes until the next arrival.

Within a matter of seconds, a *whoosh* sound announced the approaching train, and the doors on the side of the plastic tube opened. All the people exited, and I followed the waiting crowd inside, scanning my resident card to open a small metal gate.

I sat down on a comfortable plastic seat inside the gleaming car made of stainless steel. It quickly began moving again, silently gliding through the tube spanning the length of Broadway. Silver Castle Station marked the southernmost end of the Castle, or Grid One. Looking up at the map above the sliding doors, I realized that the trip to my home grid would be a long one. Each grid had multiple stops, and I lived in number eight.

Around me sat a number of people carrying luggage, clearly new arrivals to the Castle like me. Apparently they also had destinations in the rear of the city, so they all settled in, pulling out their phones to keep them occupied. People filtered on and off the train at each stop, some wearing Idrissia work uniforms, others dressed casually. I heard more than a few languages I couldn't understand, but I quickly learned that everyone, regardless of language, referred to the internal train as the 'Tube.'

Once the Tube made it past Grid Five, the passengers inside the car dwindled to just those of us with luggage. Outside the car, the bright LED signs and colorful buildings lining Broadway turned into a boring mixture of plain cookie-cutter buildings housing commercial businesses at street level with apartments on the top floors.

An older woman with gray hair sitting two chairs down shook her head. "Looks like they put us new folks out in the boondocks." She looked up at the screen showing the Tube's progress. "I still have two more grids to go. Anyone else going to be my neighbor in seven?"

Everyone else in the car nodded, and a few raised their hands.

The gray-haired woman looked at me. "Are you in seven?"

I shook my head. "Nope. They put me in eight. Hopefully I'm not out there by myself."

"Don't worry. The Castle is the safest place in the country. My son and his wife have been here for two years. They came early so they are in Grid Three, but they love it. I couldn't take San Francisco any more, so I moved here to be with them. I got tired of people bothering me on the streets. I couldn't even take a walk with my dog." She pointed to a crate at her feet where a well-behaved weiner dog slept peacefully.

"I didn't know they allowed dogs here. Where do you walk him?"

"Each neighborhood section has a park on an outside ledge along the side of the Line, and there's always the roof. As long as you don't mind heights, it works pretty well for walks."

One of the other new arrivals on the train snickered. "You better make sure to keep that dog close. I heard they kick people out if their dogs get loose."

The old woman scowled at the man making the comment, then pulled the crate a little closer to her feet.

Grid Seven finally came up on the computer screen, and everyone in the car rose to their feet except me. The weiner dog grunted as the old woman lifted the tiny kennel and carried it through the sliding doors, out onto Broadway. Here, near the far north end of the Line, Broadway lacked the luster and extravagance of the south side. The wide boulevard outside the Tube had little foot traffic. Unlike the earlier stops, where the din from the streets rushed into the car immediately upon the opening of the doors, the exit of of my fellow travelers brought nothing but silence from outside.

When the Tube resumed its northerly trip through the bowels of the Line, I had the car completely to myself, swooshing by bland office buildings and apartments, many of which looked to be newly constructed, all awaiting new arrivals to the Silver Castle. Sitting in silence, I studied the interior of the car, amazed at its cleanliness. Not a single piece showed wear or damage, and the light gray walls and bright yellow seats appeared freshly painted. Every train car I had seen in Los Angeles had been filled with trash, graffiti, and worse, but the Tube somehow remained pristine. I wondered how Idrissia pulled it off, imagining cleaning teams descending upon the Tube each night, like the workers at Disneyland who scoured the parks after closing time.

The trip to Grid Eight took nearly half an hour, but my stop finally arrived. I stood up, threw on my backpack, and rolled my suitcase out into Broadway. I plugged the address into the navigation app on my phone and studied the route. Looked like I needed to go up.

I followed the instructions on the phone until I found the closest elevator shaft. One of the black Idrissia street signs hung beside the entrance—Grid Eight, Elevator Eight. I smiled. That would be easy to remember.

Thankfully, no one entered behind me, and I pushed the button. The elevator lurched upwards upon command. Through the glass window facing the street, I watched Broadway and the Tube fade out of sight below me.

When the door opened, I saw an unexpected sight—another Tube. I studied the map given to me by Sheila and realized there were two trains stacked upon each other through the center of the Line. One ran north to south along the fifth floor, or Broadway, while the other ran along the same route above it on the fortieth floor. The open Atrium housing the Upper and Lower Tubes allowed sunlight into the Line through skylights clearly visible only six floors above me.

I began to sweat as I made my way through Broadway towards the smaller street leading to my apartment. Close to the top of the city, the building's temperature control struggled to overcome both the rising hot air and the radiation from the windows. If it felt like this in my apartment, I was going to be upset.

Finally, after twists and turns through rows of buildings that all looked the same, I came to the one identified by Sheila. I placed my card against the scanner on the door and heard a click. I entered the foyer of the apartment building and immediately met a few of my neighbors.

A man and woman sat on a couch in a large sitting area near a television screen. On the other side of the main floor, a middle-aged woman sat at a desk typing on a computer.

She peered around the screen and smiled. "You must be Melanie?"

I nodded, a bit surprised she knew my name.

Sensing my surprise, she held up a computer tablet with my photograph on it. "I've been expecting you. You're the only one moving in today. I wanted to say hello and make sure you got settled."

"You really didn't have to do that. I think I'm good."

"I make sure to personally greet every new resident." The woman smiled and pulled up a QR code for me to scan. "Scan this code. Everything you need to know is on the link. Trash disposal is at the end of your hallway. If you need maintenance, call them directly. And if you need anything else, well, that's why I'm here."

I scanned the code and made the trek across the foyer to a maze of hallways. A family appeared from a corner to my right and I moved my bag to avoid a small boy who never slowed down as he ran past me.

The excitement started to build as I neared my new home. I followed the signs down hallways lined with perfectly clean beige carpet. This was it.

The card reader by my door clicked, and I turned the doorknob to enter my apartment. The room felt like an icebox, and I immediately knew I could make it work. The size wasn't much, but what it lacked in space it made up for in comfort and quality. Stainless steel appliances and white solid stone countertops filled the small kitchenette connected to the living space. The fully furnished living and bed rooms lacked windows, but each room had a LED screen built into one of the walls, covering it completely.

I placed down my bags and located the remote control sitting on the kitchen counter. I pushed the button for 'television' and a channel guide began scrolling down the wall in the living room. I pushed another button for 'window' and a series of questions appeared. I plugged in my floor number and Grid coordinates, and a high definition view of the Mojave desert materialized. In the distance, the mag lev train sailed down the tracks towards Barstow. I flipped through the other window options before finally deciding on a view of the stubby Castle Mountains to my east.

Who needed real windows? I had every imaginable view at my fingertips. Exhausted, I fell into my perfectly comfortable bed and closed my eyes.

CHAPTER THREE

I MADE my way down to the first floor a little before seven in the evening, following a now familiar path. After nearly two weeks, the organization of grids and floors in the Castle felt familiar and reliable, a marvel of civic engineering where the trains ran on time and the elevators always worked.

My day shift counterpart, Deirdre, sat at a large half-circle shaped work station, splitting her attention between a computer screen and a tablet lying in front of her on the wood paneled desk. The young woman's bright purple scrubs stood out against the neutral beige color dominating the surroundings of the hospice ward.

"Saul's been asking if you're working tonight." She glanced at me briefly then went back to checking boxes furiously on the tablet. "Don't be getting too close with these people in here. You gotta keep a distance. They're dying, you know."

She finished swiping on the tablet then handed it to me. I quickly reviewed the conditions of each of the twelve patients in my section and signed my name. By the time I looked up, Deirdre was already walking towards the elevator.

"Have a good night!" I shouted.

She never turned around, but instead raised her arm and waved. "Girl, it's Friday night. Broadway is going to be hopping."

The mental image of Deirdre dancing in one of the many night clubs on Broadway made me chuckle. I forced myself to get serious and began working on my list for the night. Preparing meds always came first, followed by patient checks. A small cart sat next to the nurse's station, already overflowing with the patient medications and supplies I would need to treat the twelve men and women on my end of the hall.

The hospice sat behind the hospital on the third floor of the Castle, and behind the hospice was the morgue. Like every other aspect of the Castle, its medical facilities were brutally efficient, pushing patients along the sterile hallways based on the severity of their condition.

As I pushed my cart into my own hallway, I saw a neighboring nurse in the distance starting his rounds. Three more nurses just like him were busy tending to their own wards in the rest of the hospice outside my line of sight.

On the night shift, in the deep quiet of the night, we were the masters of our domains—the keepers of the souls in our wards. The other nurse waved at me, and I casually nodded my head back in his direction. I hadn't yet gotten to know any of the nurses on the other wards. Idrissia prohibited us from leaving our wards unless someone called for help, and that almost never happened. Certified nursing assistants (CNAs) offered the first line of defense and circulated the hallways regularly. It would take a full-blown crisis to get another nurse off their ward.

The first room on my rectangular path loomed to my right. "Nurse. Coming in."

A distinguished elderly man sat upright on the bed, his gaze fixed to a large flat screen television hanging from the opposite wall. "I've been waiting for you, Melanie. I've been binging *Lost*. Have you seen it? It's a great show."

"Yeah, I watched some of it years ago. They *lost* me around season two."

"Clever girl. I see what you did there."

I smiled and placed medicine into a cup. Saul's mental acuity certainly remained intact, even if his body was failing him. Liver spots and wrinkles marred his friendly face, and a pale complexion revealed he had not seen the sun for months. But where age clouded many patients' eyes, Saul's were still a clear, crisp blue. "I looked at your chart. Your numbers are holding. At this rate, they may have to move you back the other direction in the hallway. Here. Take this."

Saul took the pills and washed them down with a cup of water. "I appreciate the kind words, but we both know I'm dying. Soon. Nonetheless, I have decided that the best way to cheat death is to find a good television show to binge. It gives me something to live for."

"You're definitely getting your money's worth out of Idrissia's Netflix subscription. Let me know if you need any recommendations."

Saul had somehow outlived every prognosis given to him by the oncologist. At a hundred and twenty-one days, he also enjoyed the longest tenure in the entire hospice, by far, and had become something of a celebrity, fighting off an exotic and highly deadly form of blood cancer. I quickly discovered that Saul liked to talk, and I liked to listen. Twelve days working in the Castle and Saul had already become the closest thing to a friend I had in the place.

"I want to walk again tonight." He paused the television. "The doctor said I could do a lap around the hallway if I feel up to it. Will you walk with me?"

"Of course, but I have to do my rounds first. I'll check on you around midnight, but I'm not going to wake you up." I smiled warmly as I finished taking Saul's blood pressure, then made some notes on his chart on my tablet. "Deal?"

"Yes," Saul replied. He hit the button to start the television program and laid his white curly hair back down on the pillow. Quickly, his attention returned to the show, and I left his room.

The other patients in my ward were not so talkative. Unlike Saul, they had given up the fight.

For most people, death doesn't come quickly and painlessly. They suffer until they decide they've had enough. The signs are clear—first the patient stops eating, then it's only a matter of days. My job was to keep patients comfortable until gone, but for some reason, I struggled to accept that role. It just seemed like giving up. So I took my daily victories as I could, knowing full well that I would always lose the war.

That night as I made my rounds, I made a mental note of who I thought would be the next person to pass away. The exercise, although morbid, had become part of my routine back in Los Angeles. I might be the last person this human being saw in their life, and I felt obligated to ensure their last memory would be an act of kindness, no matter how small.

Ms. Thompson had already stopped eating, and I knew her time in the ward grew short. I knocked on the door to her room. "Nurse. Coming in."

She rested in the bed on her back with a breathing tube placed in her nose. The steady beeps from the machine next to her bed chirped at a quick and erratic pace.

I replaced the saline bag hanging on the IV pole next to her bed, and she opened her eyes. "How are you doing, Ms. Thompson?"

She cleared her throat. "Fine. Can I have some water?"

I handed her a cup of water with a straw, and helped her sip until she waved it away. "You going to eat something tonight?"

A shake of her head gave me the answer I expected.

"Any family here in the Castle?" I asked.

Another shake of the head.

"Is there something you need? Want me to help with a letter or anything?"

Same response. Negative.

Frustrated, I looked around the room. A framed photograph sat on the bed side table. A white cat with patches of black on its face posed in a park next to a wall of glass. I picked up the frame and showed it to Ms. Thompson.

"What's the cat's name?"

At the mention of the animal, the woman's attitude brightened. "Cheyenne. She's a Siamese."

"She's beautiful," I said. "Do you mind if I ask what happened to her?"

"Had to give her up. They won't let you keep animals in the

hospital." She looked down and a tear formed in the corner of her eye. "That picture is all I got."

"I'm sure Cheyenne misses you as much as you miss her." I placed the frame back down on the table and a plan formed in my mind.

"You get some sleep, Ms. Thompson."

After finishing my rounds, I returned to the nurse's station and worked on reports until nearly midnight. A few minutes before the agreed time, I returned to Saul's room, pausing outside to listen for the television. Hearing nothing, I wondered if he had fallen asleep.

I slowly pushed open the door and found Saul sitting in a chair next to his bed. He wore a worn leather jacket over his hospital gown and had slippers already on his feet. A walker sat next to the chair.

He rose from the chair carefully and grasped the handle of the walker with both hands. "Shall we take a walk?"

"I wish I had your energy. You know it's past your bed time, right?"

"Look around," he said. "There is no night and day in this damned place. I sleep when I'm tired, and right now I'm not tired. I prefer to take a walk."

By this time, Saul had made his way to the door, moving at a slow but steady pace, leaning on the walker as it rolled in front of him. His chart said he had once been six feet tall, but the combination of age and sickness had taken its toll, leaving him hunched over and diminished. He seemed giddy to escape the confines of his room, and a broad smile spread across his wrinkled face as he walked past me out into the hallway.

"Midnight. Funny how when we're young, we think of the middle of the night as a scary time. My mother used to say only bad things happened in the middle of the night. Now, each turn of the calendar is a cause for celebration. The birth of a new day."

I thought about Saul's point for a moment, then cracked a smile. "I guess I never looked at it that way." It sounded morbid, but I had always found the dying to be the most interesting. I wasn't sure the reason, but my prevailing theory was that people lost their inhibitions and said what they wanted. No point in being coy on your deathbed.

Saul stopped. "And how do you look at it, Melanie? You find

yourself here in the middle of the night surrounded by the dying. Are you a glass-half-alive or a glass-half-dead kind of woman?"

"Man, Saul, you cut to the chase, don't you?" I paused in thought, my fingers absentmindedly playing with the small silver cross I wore on a delicate chain. "Well, I guess I agree with you. I've never been afraid of working at night. Been doing it a long time. And as for being around the dying, I've always felt that everyone deserves to be surrounded by someone who cares at the end. It's not just a job, you know. It's a calling. Most people will never appreciate why I do what I do."

"It is special," Saul agreed. "God puts us in people's lives for a reason, Melanie. Don't ever forget it." The walker began rolling again, and Saul plodded towards the first turn in the rectangle that made up my end of the hospice ward.

"So, how is *Lost* going?" I asked.

"Just finished it. I appreciate an abstract ending more than most, but it was unsatisfying."

I choked back a laugh. "I tried to warn you."

"At this point, it's more about the journey. Each show is a mystery to unravel." Saul stopped at two large doors along the wall on one side of the hallway. "Speaking of mysteries, have you ever wondered what is on the other side of those doors?"

A bright red metal arm spanned the windowless steel double doors, crossing through slots on each side. At the far end, a padlock latched the arm into place. A reinforced metal kick plate covered the lower half of each door.

"That's the morgue," I said softly. "Whatever is beyond those doors is not a mystery you or I can solve, Saul."

"Hmmph." He began moving more quickly. "You know the last nurse wouldn't walk with me, so I walked by myself. One night I heard scratching on the other side of those doors. When I got close, the scratching stopped, like whatever it was knew someone was listening." He turned and looked into my eyes. "I get chills every time I walk by those doors."

Saul's fearful look made me pause for a moment, then I quickly brushed the concern out of my mind. "Probably someone doing maintenance work on the other side."

He looked at me. "In the middle of the night?"

I shrugged. "Like you said, night and day doesn't mean much in here."

Saul turned the corner, and soon the doors were out of sight behind us.

"So what's your next show? Make sure to pick something with a lot of seasons."

Saul shook his head vigorously. "No. I prefer quality over quantity. If you only had a limited amount of time, would you fill it with boring drivel?" Saul answered himself. "No, of course you wouldn't. You would do what I'm doing. Watching the greatest shows you missed over the years."

"Fine. What great show is next on your list?"

We finally turned the last corner of the rectangle and ended at Saul's door. As he followed the walker into the room, he turned to me and smiled. "*Sherlock* is next. I love my mysteries after all."

I left Saul to his television. For the rest of the shift, I waited patiently to see if my patients would win their nightly battle with death. Not all passings were gentle, or quiet, and they all stayed with me. I remembered each one. But that night my patients all lived until the sunrise, and I left my shift with twelve souls intact.

CHAPTER FOUR

THE ELEVATOR DOOR opened and I stepped out into the night air. It was the last of of my three days off and I decided to go for a run on the roof. Of course, the problem with the night shift is it messes up your sleep cycles. Even when I wasn't working, I ended up sleeping during the day and remaining awake all night. There aren't a lot of things to do in the middle of the night—at least legitimate ones—so I ran. A lot.

I picked up the habit in Los Angeles, and figured if I could avoid getting attacked in my old neighborhood, I would be safe at the top of a skyscraper in the middle of the desert. But I wasn't stupid. I touched the outside of the pouch that hung from my waist where I could feel the outline of a small can of pepper spray.

A slightly overweight Idrissia security guard smiled at me from his post near the elevator bank located in the middle of the rooftop. "Scan your card," he instructed.

I walked over and swiped my phone to reveal my unique QR code. The code scanned with a beep and a light turned green on the console. "Ms. Sanger?" the guard asked.

"Yep."

"I'm Quint." He pointed to the badge on his vest. "I haven't seen you before. First time up here at night?"

I nodded.

"I thought so. We don't get a lot of runners at night, but we have a few regulars. It's perfectly safe, but I recommend you stay on the path. It's well lit and I can see you on the cameras in case you twist an ankle or something." He turned and pointed to a wall of television screens behind him with differing views of the rooftop.

"Thanks. Good to know." I swiped the phone screen and music began playing. I adjusted the fit of the thin headset which wrapped around the back of my head and ended in a disk on each side, clinging tightly to the skin below my ears. The music piped in through bone induction, leaving me the ability to hear ambient noise. I watched enough true crime to know how many crazies prey on women running alone. No way I would allow someone to sneak up on me.

I unzipped the pouch on my hip and placed my phone inside. Quint nodded at me as I left the sheltered alcove near the elevator and moved along a gravel path leading through a row of manicured hedges. I had never been to New York, but they say the Castle's rooftop gardens are bigger than Central Park—and they took up only half of the rooftop space. The other half of the roof contained communication antennas, drone and helicopter pads, and industrial equipment used to power the giant city. That part was off limits, at least to people like me. For now, I planned to explore the world renowned Idrissia gardens, which contained nearly ten thousand acres of dirt and was heralded as the largest elevated agricultural project in the world.

Even at night, the gardens took my breath away. The main path began at a stunning waterfall originating from an opening in a miniature Greek-style temple, flanked by white columns. I followed a stream of clear flowing water lined with flowers and sculpted topiaries. After a few minutes, a stunning dogwood tree with white blossoms blocked my forward progress at an intersection. To my right, a stone lined trail led towards a gazebo bathed in artificial light. I turned left, following the running path towards the perimeter.

After about half a mile, the carefully constructed flower gardens melted away and any illusion of being on solid ground left my mind.

The wind increased and I tightened my thin jacket. Ahead, I saw a moonlit desert and the faint outline of mountains in the distance.

A small sign marked the start of the perimeter trail. I paused to appreciate the view, then picked up the pace as I turned north. The desert to my left remained constant, but the decorative gardens on my right soon gave way to more utilitarian plants. I passed what seemed to be a mile of towering corn stalks that eventually transitioned into a shorter crop that grew close to the ground. Suddenly, I felt exposed, like a scarecrow jutting out from the middle of a field.

The path made a sharp turn and I increased my speed. For some reason, every time I ran, my mind wandered back to Alex. This time, I tried to fight it. I came here to start over, so I worked to push those thoughts out of my mind.

But the image of my husband, dying in my own hospice, fought its way to the front of my consciousness. He died alone on a Tuesday. It was my day off, and I was exhausted, so I went home to sleep.

It's the simple things we regret.

I made my way along the narrow width of the Castle. The view changed, and out in the desert I saw the faint lights of a town, miles away, glowing like a distant porch light on a darkened street. One more turn and the perimeter path would lead me back to the guard quarters.

The cool night air filled my lungs and my mind relaxed. For some reason my thoughts turned to Deirdre.

How did she do it? How was she always so...happy?

I yearned to have a small piece of what she had—to be excited to wake up in the morning, to look forward to doing new things. And to meet someone new.

I groaned. That last part would be hard, but that's why I came to the Castle.

The path made a right angle. I crossed the halfway point of my run when a nagging feeling began welling up inside my stomach. I felt a presence. The primal feeling of fight-or-flight filled my senses and adrenaline surged through my body.

I slapped the button on the side of my headphones to turn off the music and began sprinting, listening intently for sound. The wind filled my ears as I picked up speed, too afraid to stop.

This is the safest place in the world the woman on the train had said. Safe enough for her to be up here in the middle of the night walking her little weiner dog? Alone?

Safe enough for me?

If someone was following me, I knew I wouldn't have any help. Quint sat in his chair literally miles away, separated by cornfields and a fake forest. I glanced upward at a light pole that contained a video camera and felt my confidence rebound. Hopefully he was keeping an eye on my progress. Nothing else for him to do at this hour anyway.

As soon as I passed the camera, the uneasy feeling in my stomach returned with a vengeance, but I kept moving. The path turned again, and I faced the long return trip along the dark rooftop path towards the elevator. Without stopping, I fumbled to unzip the pouch on my waist and searched inside until I felt the familiar shape of the can of pepper spray. I flipped open the top of the can with my thumb and held it close to my body with my finger on the trigger.

My head rotated on a swivel while I backtracked towards the cornfields. I saw no one, and began to wonder if I was somehow overreacting, or perhaps experiencing an anxiety attack. I tightened my pony tail and kept moving.

The path finally reached the corn fields and I stopped.

The temperature dropped and I felt a blast of cold air, like opening a freezer door. Something rustled in the rows of cornstalks lining the path on my right.

"Crap, crap, crap," I muttered to myself. I had seen enough horror movies to know to be afraid of cornfields, and what could be hiding inside of them. In the dark, I wouldn't be able to see anything until it was right on top of me.

I crouched down and surveyed my surroundings. If I stayed here, I would be exposed, but I could at least see a threat coming a mile away. If I moved forward, I would be at the mercy of anyone lying in wait in those fields.

I took a few deep breaths and waited.

Be patient. Calm down.

Something flickered up ahead and I saw a light moving towards me. Part of me thought it was Quint, but I squeezed the can of pepper spray tightly in my right hand just in case. The light got brighter and the silhouette of a figure appeared.

The figure called my name. "Mel! Mel!"

I stood up, expecting to see Quint, but a much slimmer profile came into view, illuminated by a small flashlight fixed atop a pistol. He stopped about twenty feet away and I realized it was Celwyn.

Why was he here?

His blonde hair hid underneath a cap, and black tactical clothing replaced the dress clothes from the train. He spoke my name again, and the accent confirmed it. It was definitely Celwyn, and he was pointing a gun at me in the dark in the middle of the night.

Slowly, I raised my can of pepper spray. "Stand back!"

He lowered his gun and the flashlight. "I'm not here to hurt you, Mel. I'm here to save you."

"Save me from what? Where's Quint?"

"If Quint was the guard at the elevator, he's dead." Something rustled in the cornstalks behind Celwyn, and he whipped around and raised his gun. With his back turned, he began to shout instructions. "Listen carefully, it is *not* safe up here. We are not alone, and the only way you don't get killed by what is in that cornfield is if you go back with me right now. Make a decision."

Things were happening so fast. The feeling in my stomach intensified and I wasn't sure if it was because of the man pointing a gun at me or because of what might be in that cornfield. But my mind kept coming back to a single question that needed answering before I could make a decision.

"I will go with you if you answer one question. How did you know I was up here?"

He turned around briefly and smiled. "Because I'm tracking your phone, of course." His eyes returned to the cornfield. "Not in a creepy way. I need you to help me with something and I didn't want you to get killed before I could talk to you."

"Help you with what? And why would you think I would get killed?"

"Dammit, Mel. Are we really going to do this right here? I need to get you off this roof. If you follow me, I'll take you to the most public place on Broadway and tell you whatever you want to know." The cornfield rustled again, and the tops of the stalks moved in the distance. Something big and fast moved in our direction.

Celwyn motioned for me to follow him as he began walking slowly along the field back towards the elevator.

I froze.

He motioned again, this time more urgently. "Please?" he whispered.

This time, I followed. He quickly picked up the pace, keeping me on his outside towards the edge of the building while he split his attention between the dark path ahead and the cornfield on our right. The rustling seemed to be following us and I looked back to see stalks falling. Something moved in a straight line towards us.

Celwyn stopped and gently pushed me to the ground. "Stay behind me."

He raised his gun and calmly knelt into a shooting stance between me and the field. A circle from his flashlight shone on the stalks, and we waited.

The seconds ticked off, and I could hear my heart beating like a freight train.

The temperature dropped like before and the rustling stopped. Silence gripped the rooftop like a glove.

That's when he came at us.

A man leaped from the cornfield and flew towards Celwyn. The flashes of light from the gun and the quick jerky movements of the flashlight created a strobe effect, making it impossible for me to see what was happening. The man crashed into Celwyn and knocked him to the ground.

I scooted back towards the edge of the railing that lined the rooftop. The railing prevented any further retreat, leaving me caught between the unfolding fight and a steep drop to the desert floor. My right hand still gripped the can of pepper spray. I raised it in front of my face like a shield, keeping it between me and the man from the corn field.

Celwyn rolled away from a downward hammer strike and

25

transitioned quickly back to a standing position. In that brief moment, the man turned and lunged toward me. I kicked wildly with both feet, scooting backwards until my body smashed into the railing.

The gun flashed two more times and the man staggered. The light from the gun briefly shone on the man's face and his eyes locked with mine. I panicked, dropping the can of pepper spray without even using it. Then I froze, shocked at what I saw. The thing attacking me wasn't a man. It was something else entirely.

Another *pop* sound rang out from Celwyn's gun, and the side of the man's head exploded with the impact from the bullet.

I screamed.

The thing's eyes blinked out, but the lifeless body kept moving towards me. I came to my senses and rolled to the side as the flailing torso collided with the railing and careened off the edge of the building, disappearing into the night.

In the glow of the flashlight, I thought I saw a smile cross Celwyn's lips before he turned to me and offered his hand.

I took it.

CHAPTER FIVE

I SAT DOWN HEAVILY and took deep breaths, trying to compose myself while I scanned the Joshua Tree Saloon.

A vista of neon plants lined the wall—a row of the signature cactus plants with a 'Y' shape that ended in tufts of sharp green cactus needles. Celwyn arrived with a whiskey in each hand. My legs felt wobbly and my hands shook.

Everything had been a blur on the roof, and my mind only now began to slowly process what had happened.

"You're lucky to be sitting here." He handed one of the glasses to me and raised his own toward the middle of the table. "To your health," he toasted with a strangely confident smile.

I took my drink but ignored the toast. My hand still shook. "Not funny. I almost died up there."

He shrugged. "Wasn't intended to be a joke. Not everyone survives a run-in with a shade. Thought you might want to celebrate."

I shuddered at the reminder of the thing I had seen for a brief moment, right before Celwyn blew its brains out. At first, I thought it was a man. Now, I didn't know what I thought. The skin was gray, like the woman on drugs at the train station, but tight and weathered—almost like leather. Its eyes were pitch black and soulless like a shark.

"Fine, I'll take the bait. What is a shade?"

Celwyn leaned across the table, green eyes intense. "Are you sure you want to know, Mel?" He looked around the bar. "Look at them. They're living it up, courtesy of Idrissia. Sure, every once in a while someone gets randomly murdered in the middle of the night, but we can chalk that up to a crazy person high on some new designer drug."

He sat back in his chair. "That's what they tell themselves so they can sleep at night. Is that what you want?" He paused. "Or do you want to know the truth?"

"I think you're full of shit. And the last person I would ask for the truth is a lawyer—assuming that part on the train was even true."

"I'm not really a lawyer. I hate 'em too," he said emphatically. "But I can play a damned good one." He paused and leaned forward. "I'm not here to practice law. I'm here to stop the creation of the things you saw last night. I promised I would tell you the truth, so there it is."

He finished the drink and placed the empty glass on the table.

I just stared at him. "Cut the crap and just tell me what that thing was out there."

"I told you. It's a shade. That's what we call someone who is not yet in control of the parasite. They are essentially mindless animals. With time, some may evolve into what you would call a vampire."

The whiskey stung as it came out my nose. It sounded like a cross between a laugh and a snort. I couldn't believe he said that word with such a straight face. "Did you just say 'vampire'?"

Celwyn looked annoyed and began scanning the room. "Idrissia police forces will be here soon. You scanned your ID at the guard station before your run, and your face will be all over the cameras. Once they find the guard's dead body, you'll be the first person they want to interview. With your scan on the Tube, and facial recognition at the door, that will lead them here."

"Good," I replied. "I would hope they would investigate one of their people being killed. I have nothing to hide"

"Listen. You can't tell them about me or this conversation. More importantly, I need you to do something for me. I need you to get me into the medical wing next to the hospice. I believe Idrissia is experimenting on shades here in the Castle."

Instinctively, I shook my head. "Why would I do that? Even if I could, which I can't, I would never let you into a medical facility. I barely know you. How do I know you wouldn't hurt someone?"

A grimace of pain crossed Celwyn's face. "Because if you don't help me find out what is really going on, my people are going to assume the worst. They'll destroy this place and kill a lot of innocent folks. I would prefer that not happen, and I suspect you would also prefer not to die."

At that moment, I realized I was having drinks with a terrorist. True, he had saved my life, but it had all happened so fast. Maybe he staged the whole thing.

My mind raced. All I could think about was stories of charming men who had convinced women to help them carry out heinous acts of destruction. Now, I sat right in the middle of one of those stories, and I discovered a newfound appreciation for the complexity of the decisions those people must have faced.

Before I could respond, a crowd formed at the door of the Joshua Tree Saloon. Three men in the black Idrissia police uniform and a stern-looking woman in a dark jacket peered over the faces of onlookers, searching the small Broadway bar. The woman made eye contact with me, and all four began immediately moving towards my table.

I looked up to say something witty to Celwyn about not talking about mass murder on a first date, but his chair was empty. He was gone.

––––––

SOMEHOW I MADE it to the ripe old age of forty two without ever seeing the inside of a police station. That streak ended today.

The stern-looking woman in the black jacket sat at a small desk, glaring at me from behind her utilitarian pair of glasses. Detective Serrano had made it clear that the short walk from the Joshua Tree to the Broadway police station would either be voluntary or in handcuffs. I chose to cooperate. That was me. Always the rule follower.

The desk in the interrogation room was the first thing I had seen in Idrissia that wasn't neat and organized. Stacks of paper and red accordion file folders sat unevenly on the surface in front of the detective.

Serrano picked up an electronic tablet and showed me a photograph of a guard whose throat had been ripped apart. Blood covered much of the face, but I knew it was Quint. I had seen the body before exiting the roof. I also knew that I would have suffered the same fate if Celwyn hadn't shown up.

"Someone did this to one of our security officers a few hours ago up on the roof. You were the last person to see him alive." She placed the tablet down on the table in front of me so I could see the photo in gruesome detail, then studied my reaction.

I thought about how crazy my story would sound. I also knew that if I told the truth, it would be impossible to avoid mentioning Celwyn. But, like I said, I'm a rule follower, and the words started flowing out of my mouth.

"I was attacked on the roof. I assume whatever attacked me killed the guard. There was another man, Celwyn. I met him on the train into the Castle last week. He fought it off and saved my life."

Serrano listened intently to every word, and paused before speaking. "You said 'it.' He fought 'it' off. What did you mean by that?"

I exhaled sharply. I had tried to avoid the crazy part, but she cut right to the hard questions. "I don't know. It was dark. And it all happened so fast. I barely got a look at it, but it just looked not quite... *human*." I looked down, hoping to feign confusion. "I don't know how to describe it."

I stared at the table for a few seconds, then slowly made eye contact again with the detective.

Serrano wasn't going to let me off that easy. "Take a breath and slow down. Tell me everything you remember."

"Like I said, it was dark, and it happened fast, but I saw it for a minute. It had gray skin and dead eyes. It lunged at me, and Celwyn shot it with a gun. I moved out of the way and it went over the edge." I paused as a memory floated into my mind. "There was a woman. At the train station when I arrived a few weeks ago. Her skin was gray, too. I heard someone say she was on drugs. The thing that attacked me was much worse. Like an animal. Different, but maybe the same?"

I thought I saw a flash of recognition cross Serrano's face, but the stern mask quickly returned. She leaned back and studied me again. "And this guy, Celwyn. What was he doing up there?"

I finally reached the limits of my rule-following nature. So I lied. "Don't know. Didn't have time to talk. He fought it off, we ran to the elevator, and then parted ways once we made it to the Tube. I was too scared to be alone at home, so I went to have a drink. Safety in crowds, you know."

Serrano nodded and began writing. "So the person—or 'thing' in your words—who killed the guard disappeared. Another man named Celwyn was on the roof. Also disappeared. All we have is you and a dead body."

The words hit me like a slap. Stupid cops. That's what I got for trying to do the right thing and cooperating.

"Look, I know it sounds weird, but it's the truth. I didn't kill that guard—"

"His name was Quint. He had a family."

"I know. He told me his name," I said defiantly as I glared back at Serrano. "Why would I randomly kill an armed guard I've never met in my life while in the middle of a run? You can't be serious."

"Talk to me outside." She got up from the chair opposite mine and waved me towards the door.

I followed her through the small police station. It was now early morning, and the quiet from earlier in the night had been replaced by the buzzing sounds of activity. A photograph on the wall caught my eye, a picture of a stern middle-aged man in a black pinstripe suit. He stood alone along Broadway, arms crossed, surrounded by Idrissia officers. He posed as if he owned the place.

"Who's that?" I asked.

"Tarek Malik, CEO of Idrissia. He built the Line, but he's never around. I guess when you're that rich, you have lots of toys to play with."

"He looks more like a gangster," I said. "I guess it's the suit."

"Well, that gangster and his father are in charge of this city. No politicians out here. Just Idrissia."

Everywhere I looked, officers stood around talking. A couple of white cardboard boxes filled with breakfast burritos lay open on a table off to the side of the large office space.

"You hungry?" Serrano asked. "You've been up all night."

"No. I'm used to it. I work the night shift."

"Right." She kept walking, and I followed her out of the station to the still neon-lit streets of Broadway. Once outside, she turned around and stopped. "Look, Ms. Sanger, I don't think you killed anyone. You and I have something in common. I run at night, too, so I knew Quint. He liked to eat, but he was pretty tough. We found two casings and his weapon lying beside him. No offense, but you don't seem like the type to dodge bullets."

My tension relaxed a bit. Finally, some common sense.

"One more thing. I was there at the station when you arrived. I helped catch that woman. We catch them and Idrissia hauls them off for med checks and we never see them again. It seems like the numbers are picking up lately, and the people are...more violent." She looked directly into my eyes. "If you see gray skin again, you run to get help. Understood?"

I nodded. "Thanks."

"Don't thank me. Officially you're still the only suspect in the murder of an Idrissia security officer. My advice is to talk to a lawyer." She handed me her card.

Good thing I knew one...sort of.

"And if you run into Celwyn again, call me. Better yet, have him call me directly. I would like to talk to him."

Too bad he was a witness.

We shook hands and I headed towards the Tube. My stomach rumbled, objecting strenuously to my decision to refuse a tortilla-wrapped breakfast from Serrano. I decided to stop to eat at a trendy Idrissia taco stand before running an errand—one that could not wait.

CHAPTER SIX

WORKING IN A HOSPICE BUILT PERSPECTIVE. For the dying, death was the one misfortune that would not pass. It couldn't be overcome or ignored. For those loved ones who remained behind, death was a trauma that would forever leave an emotional scar.

I considered myself to be an expert on the subject, and had long ago realized that every day untouched by death was a good day. Anyone who said differently was a liar, or a fool.

After a few hours of sleep, I awoke with a newfound determination to block out the events of the previous night. Instead, I needed to focus on what mattered—my patients.

I stepped off the elevator out into the third floor hallway. I had barely reached the entrance to the hospice ward when the automatic doors swung open. Two large males in scrubs wheeled out a gurney topped with a blue plastic bag. My heart sank.

"Who was it?" I turned and walked with the closest medic while they wheeled the gurney towards the elevator.

"Ms. Thompson," he replied. "One of yours."

Whatever composure I had mustered immediately evaporated. Apparently, my day could get worse. And it just did.

The medic studied my pained look with credulity. "You new or something? You can't let this get to you. They're all going to pass. If you can't handle it, maybe this job isn't for you."

"No, I know. I'm fine. It was just...I had something for her. Timing sucks."

He shook his head. "They ain't got no time. If you got something to say, don't wait. Eventually they'll all end up in the basement."

I paused. "Wait. Where are you taking her?"

"Basement. That's where the morgue is." We reached the elevator and his partner hit the down button.

"But I thought the morgue was next to the hospice."

He shook his head again. "Nope. Definitely basement. No windows. I guess it's easier to keep cool."

"So what's next to my ward?"

The man looked around nervously, then leaned in towards me. "Officially, that's temporary cadaver cold storage. But that's just to keep people out. Unofficially, I hear it's some type of top secret anti-aging therapy for rich people. I knew a girl who worked in there." He motioned for his partner to wait for him in the elevator before he continued. "She had to sign these crazy contracts, hand over your unborn children type of thing, but my friend liked to drink, and one night we—well, you know. Anyway, there's a bunch of people frozen in cryo in there. Typical crazy Idrissia stuff." He walked into the elevator. "You better get to work. It's almost shift change."

As I wearily made my way back down the hallway towards the hospice, I thought of the gangster photo of the Idrissia CEO that I had seen in the police station. Somehow the idea of rich people frozen in cryo didn't seem that farfetched.

I hadn't even clocked in and I already felt exhausted. Making it to the morning was going to feel like an eternity.

Of course, Deirdre met me at my ward with a smile on her face. "For a minute, I thought you were going to be late. I was about to start causing a scene." She smiled. "I've got places to go. People to see."

That smile was infectious. I couldn't help but return it weakly. "I've been doing this a long time. I know the drill and wouldn't leave you hanging." I picked up the tablet. "Let's do the walk through. What's new?"

"Thompson passed. You also got a new one. Mr. Nguyen. Wife is still here." Her smile disappeared. "And Saul got some new blood numbers. Not good. Figured you should hear it from me."

"Does he know?"

"Yep. The doctor told him earlier and he didn't take it so well. Saul kicked him out of his room after asking to see his medical license."

I wondered how much bad news I could get in one day. I had just made it to work, and I had twelve hours to go in a place full of dying patients. I meekly nodded my head to Deirdre. "Understood. I'll talk to him."

Deirdre glanced down at her watch and the beaming smile returned, her pristine white teeth nearly blinding me. "Hey, I've got a friend I think you would really like. He's cute. What do you think about me giving him your number?"

"I appreciate the offer, but I'm good. Not really wanting to jump into anything right now, you know?"

Deirdre shook her head. "How about you come with me next week? We are both off on Friday. You can come dancing with me and I'll make sure my friend shows up." She smiled mischievously. "You don't have to go home with him, just talk to him. What do you say?"

"I'll think about it. I really will."

"You need to get out there and meet people. It's not healthy for you to only hang out with folks in here who are dying. You need to meet some people who are living. And one more thing—promise me you'll take off that ring. You did your duty and took care of your husband, and now you have to take care of yourself."

"I'll think about it." I couldn't muster a stronger promise, even though I knew Deirdre was right. The idea of removing the wedding band still felt like a betrayal. The whole 'til death do you part' thing just didn't sit right with me.

"Don't think about it too long. Life is short." She adjusted her hair in the mirror on the wall behind her. "I'm out of here. See you tomorrow." Within seconds, Deirdre had fled from behind the lengthy curved desk that doubled as mission control for the ward.

Before starting my daily routine, I removed the cell phone from my pocket. I clicked on the last photograph in my camera roll. A white cat named Cheyenne stared back at me. It had taken me a little time to track down Ms. Thompson's cat, but my persistence had paid off. When the old single woman went into the hospital, the Siamese cat went into a kennel and then eventually a shelter out on the outskirts of Grid Six.

I was always a dog person myself, but I had nothing against cats. Same thing I guess—people get attached to pets. Part of me wondered if Ms. Thompson would have made it one more day if she knew what I planned. But none of that mattered now. I was just beating myself up over something out of my control. I needed to let it go.

My finger hovered over the screen, then swiped left. I clicked one more time and the photo disappeared. Time to get to work.

After loading up my cart, I began making my rounds. The first room on my ward housed the new patient, Mr. Nguyen. Ms. Thompson's body wasn't even cold and the room had already been filled. Idrissia efficiency at its finest.

I knocked and announced myself. "Nurse." I opened the door and walked over to the side wall. I neatly wrote my name on the white board after scrubbing out Deirdre's chicken scratch.

In the bed, a man slept on his side with a blanket pulled up to his ears. In a chair next to the bed, a short woman sat facing the man, whom I assumed to be her husband, stroking his black hair. She looked up at me as I entered the room.

Her clothing immediately caught my attention. Most people spending the night with a loved one in a hospice dressed for comfort. Ms. Nguyen, however, wore a power suit ensemble that looked like she came from a business meeting. She had kicked off her high heels and her stockinged feet sat on a makeshift ottoman made from a small table she had moved towards the chair.

"I'm Mel. Shift change," I whispered. "You doing all right?"

"Yes," the woman replied softly.

"Good. If you need anything, just push that button." I pointed to the remote control device hanging beside the bed with a large red button at the top.

The woman waved at me dismissively and turned her attention

back to her husband. As I left the room, I could hear quiet but beautiful singing behind me.

I steadily made my way around the ward, doling out medicine, exchanging small talk and writing my name on white boards. Anxiety built in my mind as I turned the final corner back to my station. This night, I reversed my normal pattern, leaving Saul's room for last. Deep down, I hoped he would be asleep.

The sound on Saul's television could be heard in the hallway as I approached his room. I knocked on the door out of habit, but there was no way anyone inside the room could have heard anything over the sounds of explosions and bass-thumping music. Inside, Saul sat upright in his bed eating deep purple-colored grapes from a clear ziplock bag.

"It's a bit loud, don't you think?" I walked over to the white board and went through the required motions.

Saul remained transfixed on the television. "If I haven't gone deaf yet, I fear the hearing aid industry may never see a dime of my money."

"Fair enough, but there are others to consider. Your neighbor may be trying to sleep." I approached him with a small cup containing pills. "You have a water to take these?"

He grabbed a small carton of chocolate milk and downed the pills with a long swig. Without comment, he lifted the remote from his bedside and lowered the volume on the television hanging on the far wall. "Satisfied?" he asked.

"Actually, yes. Thank you." I took back the empty paper cup and threw it in the trash can. "So, *Fast and Furious*, huh? I have to say I'm a bit surprised by the selection. What happened to quality control?"

"I've moved on to guilty pleasures. Saw the 1970 Dodge Charger in the trailer and I was hooked." Saul smiled. "I had one of those, you know. Not a fancy version like the one in the movie, but I had a Charger. I took it to car shows on the weekends, usually just at parking lots." A look of grim acceptance replaced the smile. "But those days are over."

"So what happened to the Charger? Did you sell it?"

"Sold it along with everything else. Won't need a car at the Line. That's what my wife said. Now I've lost both."

"Well, you still got me," I said. "I ain't much but if you're up for a walk tonight let me know."

Saul shifted uneasily in his bed. "I think I'll take a pass tonight. Feeling tired."

I thought about whether to mention the test results. The rational voice inside my head told me to mind my business, but as Saul's friend I desperately wanted to cheer him up. Maybe seeing his spirits improve would somehow make my day seem like less of a disaster.

"Saul, I know about the test results. It's just one data point. People go up and down."

He shook his head. "Healthy people go up and down, Melanie, not people who are dying."

"It will be midnight soon. The dawn of a new day, remember? Look, you made all those cancer doctors into liars and outlived every patient in this hospice three times over. You're still here, and it will take a while to make it through all of those *Fast and Furious* movies. What are they up to now? Twenty?"

A smile finally crossed Saul's mouth, and his wrinkled cheeks stretched widely. "Thank you, Melanie. I needed that." He looked down at the grapes in his hand and laughed in a deep, melodious chuckle I had never heard him make before.

"What's so funny?"

"I'm eating these black grapes because they are filled with anti-inflammatory properties. The day I was diagnosed with cancer, I changed everything in my life, hoping that one of those changes would allow me to live longer. Isn't it ironic? I smoked a pack a day for twenty years and now I'm eating grapes to somehow hold off death." He placed them on the table beside his bed. "I hate grapes."

I didn't know what to say, so I just listened and nodded. During my short time in the Castle, Saul had seemed invincible. It sounds stupid, but the thought of him dying didn't seem possible even though he was a patient in a hospice. I let my guard down and we had become friends. That had been a mistake, and I realized Saul was going to die just like everyone else in my ward. Soon.

"Is there something I can get for you?" I asked softly.

"Yes, you can, Melanie. Another midnight." The chuckle returned.

"That's in God's hands, Saul, not mine."

He nodded. "I know. But I figured I'd ask anyway." He picked up the bag of grapes and extended his hand. "Want a grape? They are good for you, I hear."

My lips spread into a smile.

"Don't be bashful. You have a beautiful smile, Melanie. You should show it more often."

"You know this is a hospice, right? People die here." As soon as the words left my mouth I regretted them. My smile evaporated, replaced by guilt.

Saul sat quietly for a moment.

"I'm sorry," I stumbled. "You know what I mean. I'm not Deirdre. The job—it's just tough, you know?"

Saul nodded, satisfied with my answer. "You know, if I was a younger man, I would take Deirdre dancing myself. That's all she talks about. And you. She talks about you."

"Oh really? What does she say?"

"Well, we have discussed how she invites you dancing and how you always refuse to go. We both feel that you need to move forward with your life, meet someone new."

"Oh, you both feel that way, hmm? Well, I guess that settles it. Do I have a say at all in this extremely personal decision?" I shot Saul a mean look.

Saul ignored my mounting frustration. "Of course, Melanie. But look, we both know I won't be here long, and I don't have time for patience or subtlety. Some things need to be said." His voice softened. "I have only known you a short time, but I can tell you are an amazing woman. You deserve to find happiness." He looked around the room. "The days and nights fly by in this place. I see you investing your time in me, and I know that when I'm gone, you'll find another and another to fill that void. But these relationships aren't *real*, Melanie, because they are, by definition, destined to end quickly before you become too attached." Saul took a deep breath and sighed. "I think you fear deep attachment. I think you fear a relationship where you will become deeply invested over time, and one day, when you least expect it, something will rip that person away unexpectedly. And it will hurt, but that's life, Melanie. And it's worth experiencing. Take it from an old man on his death bed."

I stared at Saul, unsure how to respond. I felt angry to be judged. I barely knew this old man. But deep down, I knew everything he said rang true. And that made me angry, too, for a different reason.

"I—I've got some work to do." I turned the cart around and headed for the door.

Saul reached towards the remote and increased the volume. The room filled with the sound of revving engines as two cars raced through a city on the screen behind me.

I closed the door and returned to the nurse station. Saul's words kept repeating in my head. Why did I care so much what he thought of me? He's dying. People say mean things at the end of life. I shouldn't take it so personal.

That's what I got for getting so close to my patients. I needed to stop doing that.

I took a seat and surveyed the screens spanning the length of the desk. A modern nursing station that more closely resembled NASA mission control than a hospital, simultaneously displaying information on all twelve patients in my ward. My trained eye focused on the vitals for Mr. Nguyen. His heart rate was slowing.

I watched as the number on the screen dropped. A red light began to flash and I leaped out of my chair. That was the first and only night Mr. Nguyen slept in my ward.

CHAPTER SEVEN

DEIRDRE ARRIVED EARLY for shift change. Funny how her mood at the start of a shift never seemed to match her excitement at the end. That worked out well because our moods matched this morning. We talked briefly about Mr. Nguyen, and I left.

I thought briefly about giving her grief over her talking about me with Saul, but decided against it. I just wanted to go home.

The Tube ride was a blur, and I walked the familiar route through Grid Eight to my apartment on auto pilot. I didn't take the time to shower, instead choosing to collapse, fully dressed, into my bed.

My eyes opened a few hours later to blinding light coming from my fake Idrissia window. I must have left the video screen on when I fell asleep, and the sun had finally risen high enough in the sky to flood the camera filtering images onto my wall with light. I looked down at the scrubs still on my body and groaned. Now I would have to throw away the sheets.

I picked up my cellphone and saw a text from Celwyn: *What did you tell the police about me?*

I bit my lip and typed out a message: *The truth. They want to talk to you, too.*

In a few seconds, I received a response: *I wish you hadn't done that. I can't talk to the police.*

Why not?

Complicated.

You mean because they may not like the idea of you threatening to blow up the city?

You don't understand. I'm the only one who can save your life along with everyone else in this place.

I'm not going to help you. Leave me alone.

I threw my phone down on the bed and rubbed my eyes. What was I doing? I had hoped to start a new life here. I had believed the commercials. Now, two weeks later, a monster had tried to kill me, I was being investigated for murder, and a terrorist was threatening to kill thousands of people if I didn't help him commit who-knows-what type of crime.

Slowly, an idea formed in my head.

I could just leave, get back on the train and return to Los Angeles. It sounded so simple.

I dropped everything to move here, and I could do the same again. I could live anywhere I wanted. A small quiet town in Montana sounded nice right now. A real mountain view, not a fake one through a fancy television screen built into the wall.

Deirdre might have to work some overtime, but Idrissia would hire a nurse to replace me. I briefly thought about Saul. He would be the only one in the Castle I would truly miss. I regretted I would not be there to see his final midnight.

The more I thought about leaving, the more I became convinced things were too complicated here and running away made the most sense.

I looked around the small bedroom and quickly started choosing a few important items to throw into my backpack. I had to be discrete. Just a trip back to Los Angeles to visit some friends. No luggage. That would raise too many questions.

I brought up the Idrissia app on my smart phone's screen and reserved a ticket back to Los Angeles on the next mag lev train. Before clicking the button to purchase a ticket, I momentarily paused, wondering if I had been flagged by the police because of the investigation into Quint's death.

What if they wouldn't let me leave? Were they monitoring my messages?

My finger hovered over the button, waiting for me to take the final step to secure a one-way ticket out of the Silver Castle. I took a deep breath and touched the screen. The screen went blank, and the next two seconds seemed like an eternity. Finally, a white box appeared with a QR code for my ticket. Success!

For the first time in days, I felt a sense of confidence. I was taking back control of my life. And it felt good.

I showered and changed into clothes comfortable enough for travel. I slung the backpack up onto my right shoulder and strolled through the lobby of my apartment as if I was going out for a walk. I even smiled at the overbearing manager as she waved at me when I passed her office.

The train car was nearly empty when I entered the Upper Tube at Grid Eight. The car glided without noise southward towards Silver Castle Station, making only one stop at each Grid. Unlike the Lower Tube, which remained full at nearly any time of day, the Upper Tube functioned as an express train and enjoyed much less use. Most suspected it only existed as a personal benefit to the residents of the Heights—the ritzy neighborhood tucked into the top levels of the Castle.

Grid Four housed the priciest real estate in the Castle. Before construction even started, Idrissia had sold out the Heights, a neighborhood of exclusive penthouses lining the Upper Tube. Rich celebrities and business moguls jumped at the opportunity to own a unique vacation home inside the country's new desert marvel.

On both sides of the Tube, private landing platforms and garden-covered verandas whizzed by the train, stacked nearly to the top of the sun filled Atrium. Up ahead, the centerpiece of the Heights came into sight—La Scala Bridge.

A staircase of rectangular garden-filled platforms spanned from one side of the Upper Tube to the other, climbing upward and then back down again. Each step appeared to hang suspended in the open air of the Atrium, supported by a staircase connecting each step to the one above and below it with cleverly masked engineering. The highest step hovered over the Tube, lined with white Greek columns formed into a replica of the Parthenon. Beside it, each step contained a miniature version of a famous historical landmark, starting with the pyramids of Giza on the left, and ending with the Eiffel Tower on the right.

My phone buzzed.

It was Celwyn. "Where are you going?"

I looked around the train car. Was he following me? How did he get my number?

"Don't call me again," I whispered then hung up.

The car arrived at Grid One, and the door effortlessly slid open. I walked out of the car and found an elevator to take me down to Lower Broadway. Once there, the crowds picked up and I merged into a stream of people.

My phone buzzed again. Then again.

I ignored it.

The police station where I was interrogated by Serrano loomed to my left. I walked to the other side of the street and increased my pace until I passed through the row of glass doors and breathed fresh air.

The air smelled like rain—not the kind that brings flowers in the spring, but the steamy kind that comes out of nowhere in the summer. Dark gray thunder clouds rolled over the mountains. In the distance, vertical lines poured water from clouds onto the thirsty desert.

On the tracks, the mag lev train sat still, its doors held invitingly wide open. I smiled and walked confidently towards the closest access point, ready to scan my reservation and take a seat on the marvel of technology that had brought me to this nightmare place and would soon deliver me to salvation.

I placed my phone atop the scanner and waited. Nothing happened.

Then all hell broke loose.

A red light on the podium began flashing and a siren above me wailed like a fire engine. The door to the train shut automatically with a whooshing sound.

The passengers around me retreated as if I had a contagious disease, leaving me standing alone in the middle of the station. An attendant ran towards me from a nearby door to the train, shouting at the top of his lungs. "Stop. You can't get on the train!"

Thank you, Captain Obvious. I shook my head in disgust and started walking briskly back towards Broadway, trying to casually blend in with other members of the crowd mulling on the platform. But it was too late.

Like before, Idrissia police officers seemed to materialize out of the corners of the station and bounded across the platform towards me. *Crap. Crap! How could I be so stupid?* I was going to be arrested twice in one week.

I nearly made it to the row of glass doors when Serrano exited, flanked by two other police officers. She glared at me and I froze.

"Hello again, Ms. Sanger." She pushed up her glasses and motioned to an officer on her left. "I can't believe you tried to run. Now, we're going to have to talk again." She nudged an officer. "This time, we'll use the cuffs."

The officer grabbed one of my arms roughly, then placed the the other one behind my back before applying a thick zip tie. He pulled it against my skin and yanked it tight until it dug into my wrist.

Relieved of my backpack, I followed Serrano back through the glass doors and into the crowded streets of Broadway. People made way for the police, and I hung my head low to avoid the stares of onlookers as I made the walk of shame back to the police station. Here and there, people held up their cell phones recording the procession. You would think I was some kind of notorious criminal.

Serrano held open the door to the police station, and I looked her in the eyes when I passed. I couldn't hide my anger. "What kind of messed-up place is this? I was the one attacked and now I can't leave?"

The officers on either side pulled me through the door while Serrano held her ground, emotionless. I finally realized that protesting would get me nowhere. My plan was doomed from the beginning.

I couldn't run away from this hellhole.

THIS TIME, I sat alone in the interrogation room for at least an hour. Thankfully, my hands were free of the zip tie restraints, but those hardware store torture devices left a painful red mark on both wrists. My phone was gone, along with my backpack, leaving me with nothing but my thoughts to keep me company. I imagined scenarios ranging from being thrown into prison to being brutally murdered.

About the time I began seriously considering the possibility that I might never leave my windowless ten-by-ten room, the door opened. A tall, distinguished man entered, followed closely by Serrano. His tanned, wrinkled head was shaved clean, and a neatly trimmed mustache and beard framed his face. He wore a well-tailored black uniform with an Idrissia logo on a patch over one shoulder. The uniform reminded me more of the military than the police department, but his chest lacked any markings or insignia other than a small white pin on his lapel shaped like a dove.

Both of them sat down across from me at the table, and Serrano waited for a nod from the older man before speaking. "I'm sorry for the delay," she said. "I was waiting for my colleague to arrive before we talked again."

The man watched me with cold blue eyes and my mind again wandered to the thought of being murdered in the room. I mustered up the courage to speak. "And who is your colleague?"

The man cracked a thin smile. "I am Captain Paloma. Pleased to meet you, Ms. Sanger." His pronunciation was crisp and perfect, but I could tell English was not his first language.

He extended a gloved hand across the table, and I nodded politely and shook it. His strong grip lingered for a bit too long before releasing my hand.

"I understand you were a witness to a murder of an Idrissia security officer and were interviewed by Detective Serrano only yesterday. Surely, you understand how it must look for you to decide to run away?"

"Honestly, I don't care how it looks. I just want out of this claustrophobic nightmare. If I'm going to be getting attacked every time I step out of my home, I'll just go back to LA. So, what's the deal? Am I under arrest?" I was tired and angry. If I wasn't going to be arrested, I needed some sleep before going to work. And it didn't help that there was something about Paloma that rubbed me the wrong way.

The smug smile returned to Paloma's face. I still didn't trust him.

"You are not under arrest. In fact, Idrissia sent my team here to bolster the security of this facility and I am deeply apologetic for your negative experience. I assure you it will never happen again."

"It was a bit more than a negative experience," I replied.

"Yes, well, I understand there was a man who assisted you, and I would very much like to speak with him." Paloma turned to Serrano. "What was his name?"

"Celwyn."

"Yes, that was it." He turned around and there was no longer a trace of the smile. "How do you know Celwyn?"

"I told her. I met him on the train when I first arrived. Never saw him again until the roof. He saved my life. I thanked him then he disappeared."

"It is fortuitous that he would appear at the very moment you were attacked. Perhaps he was following you, or had some sort of...*interest* in you. Did he say why he was up there on the rooftop?"

I felt myself blushing. "No. He didn't. Maybe he also likes to run at night."

"Hmm. Perhaps." Paloma rose from his seat and leaned his hands against the chair, staring at me. "First, let me say that I don't believe you're a killer. The reason I am here is to restore security, and I don't think that arresting you will serve that purpose. That said, you are a material witness in an open investigation and will not be allowed to leave Idrissia's jurisdiction until the investigation is closed."

I shook my head, frustration building. "So I'm stuck here? You won't let me leave?"

"It's temporary, I assure you. Indeed, helping us speak to Celwyn could greatly accelerate the completion of our investigation." He paused, then stepped out from behind the table, glaring at me from only a few feet away. "Are you sure you have told us everything about this man?"

Nervousness bubbled up like a tidal wave, and I fought to keep it together. I held Paloma's gaze without looking away or blushing. "Yes. I don't know what else I can tell you. I have nothing to do with this guy."

For a few seconds, he watched my face, processing every blink of an eye, measuring my breathing. I finally looked back at Serrano. "Look, I have to go to work tonight. I need sleep."

It was Paloma who responded. "Lying to me is a bad idea, Ms. Sanger. Celwyn is a dangerous man and he will likely get you killed. If this man contacts you again, I strongly suggest you reach out to Detective Serrano and follow her instructions." He looked at me while he pointed to Serrano, then his thin smile returned. "You are free to leave, Ms. Sanger. You can pick up your things at the front desk."

CHAPTER EIGHT

BY THE TIME I sat down on the leather-cushioned seat inside the Tube, I wanted nothing more than to sleep. My escape attempt had failed miserably, leaving me with the harsh realization that I needed to be at work in a few hours. I had barely slept and hadn't eaten a thing since morning.

The lights of Broadway whizzed by my window before turning into colorless building facades. My eyes drooped and I could feel the rhythmic movement of the train car lulling me to sleep. For a moment, I felt the sweet release of time and space before being suddenly yanked back to consciousness by something hitting my foot.

"What?" I opened my eyes quickly and scanned my surroundings to learn the source of the rude bump that had interrupted my much needed nap.

Celwyn sat on the seat next to me, his hands folded across his chest. "Straight ahead. Don't look at me."

I groaned and closed my eyes again. "Not a problem. I'm going back to sleep. Just go away."

"What did you tell them about me?"

"Don't worry, I'm not stupid. I left out the crazy stuff. I told them that you saved my life and then you ran off. They're looking for you,

you know. I don't know how you avoid them with all the surveillance in the Castle."

"They rely too much on technology. It can be fooled."

Intrigued, I opened my eyes and looked around the car. A tiny camera in the corner of the ceiling pointed right at the back of my head. I spoke to Celwyn without facing him. "They're watching me, aren't they?"

"Of course. With the AI-controlled facial recognition tools, they can find you anywhere in the city within sight of a camera."

"But why can't they see you?"

Celwyn smiled and pointed to a small metal clip hanging on the front of his black t-shirt. "Disruptor. Creates an electromagnetic field that blocks facial scans and wreaks havoc with cameras. All they will see is a small distortion in the video transmission."

"I hope it's working because I met some guy at the police station and he's looking for you. I don't think he's local to the Castle, and he was... intense. The other detective barely said a word, like she was afraid of him."

Celwyn squirmed in his seat and his face darkened. "What was his name?"

The lack of sleep had done a number on my short term memory. "I don't remember. It's been a long day."

"Think. Please." He paused and waited while I searched my memory bank without success. "Forget the name. What did he look like?"

I had less trouble with this question. "Older guy, bald, plain black military uniform with a small pin on the front. A bird maybe."

"The pin," he said. "It's a dove." Celwyn stroked his chin with one hand while exhaling sharply. "His name is Paloma."

"Yes, exactly! I remember now."

"This is bad." His eyebrows furrowed. "I can't stay here any longer. It's not safe." He slowly moved his hand and placed it atop my own. "You need to leave, too. Come with me."

I jerked back my hand and exploded. "I'm not going anywhere with you. I don't want to ever see you again. Whatever game you're playing, go play it on someone else."

"You don't understand, Mel. Paloma is one of my kind. He hunts shades. If he's here, something isn't right. It means whoever hired him is concerned about an outbreak, and the first place he will lock down is—"

"The facility you want to get into next to the hospice."

"Exactly. My work here is done, and once I report what is going on, the response will be—" He looked down. "Swift."

The video screen above the doors announced the upcoming stop at Grid Six.

"This is my stop," Celwyn announced. He stood up and turned to me. "Mel, that's not the worst of it. There are more shades roaming the Castle beyond the one you saw on the roof. The parasite is like a virus. Left unchecked, it will multiply."

I shook my head. "Stop. Enough."

"No. You have to listen to me!" The train car slowed. "If there are shades in this Castle, there will also be vampires, and they will not hide in the shadows forever." He looked at me sternly. "You don't want to be around when that happens."

"I'm not a vampire hunter, I'm a nurse. And right now, I need some sleep so I can go to work tonight. Goodbye, Celwyn." I closed my eyes and did my best to block out his words.

The truth seemed irrelevant, and he might as well have told me aliens had landed. Even if Celwyn was right, what could I do?

The door hissed and I felt the blast of warm air from the outside. It hissed again and the train began moving northward through the Line. I opened my eyes and Celwyn was gone.

———

BY THE TIME I got back to my apartment, it was already late in the afternoon. The commute to work would require me to travel all the way down and across the Castle, and once I did the math, it was clear I wouldn't be getting much sleep.

I tossed my backpack onto the bed and threw myself down beside it. Staring at the stretched nylon bag, I realized that everything important to me could fit into a backpack. That saddened me, but at the same time it felt strangely liberating.

My mind slowly reviewed the contents of the backpack, its main pocket mostly filled with clothing and a few toiletries. My laptop, of course, was inside a small side pocket along with a folder filled with photographs and documents. Paper, like photographs, had been rendered obsolete years ago with cheap and easy access to digital files and cloud storage, but I held onto a few important things over the years.

Other than my wedding ring and my small cross, I didn't have much from my time with Alex.

But I kept one more thing.

I unzipped the small pocket on the front of the backpack and removed a stainless steel Leatherman multitool. It resembled a pocket knife, but a host of concealed gadgets cleverly unfolded from inside the handle, including everything from a screw driver to a bottle opener. My name was etched into the side of the handle—a birthday gift.

Alex had big plans to take me camping in the Sierra Nevada mountains in eastern California. With him, it was all about the gear, and he wanted me to be prepared. I humored him on a few trips, but sleeping in a tent never appealed to me. Needless to say, we never camped for long, but the nights in a sleeping bag were memorable.

The sides of my mouth turned up into a wide grin at the thought of him approving of my keeping the knife. Somewhere up there, he's saying *I told you so. You never know when you might need to fight a vampire.*

I placed the knife down on the end table and rested my head on the pillow, content in my decision. Going forward, if I left my apartment, I would keep Alex's knife with me, concealed in my pocket.

When I closed my eyes, however, I didn't find peace. Instead, my mind returned back to the face of the shade who tried to kill me on the roof. There was no emotion or hint of life reflected in its features, only a cold hunger for death.

Then I remembered Celwyn's warning—a shade could evolve into a vampire, and they were far more dangerous.

I shuddered at the thought of running into something worse than a shade. The fear built inside me until it became almost overpowering, and the room felt cold. Eventually, the fear subsided and I felt the warmth return to my body. I realized that I had faced death hundreds of times, with both strangers and my husband.

Death was an old friend. I understood it.

After that moment, I slept more soundly than I had in days, even if only for a few hours.

CHAPTER NINE

ON THE WAY TO WORK, I realized everything in Idrissia had changed during the span of my short nap. Soldiers wearing the same nondescript black garb as Paloma patrolled the stops along the Tube. A young man in body armor politely asked me to scan my card before I was allowed to enter the elevator down to the medical level, and once I arrived on my floor, the scene resembled a war zone.

I made my way through another checkpoint and craned my neck to get a look down the long hallway past the hospice entrance. A command center blocked my progress, and a crowd of soldiers holding assault rifles stood in front of a barrier hastily constructed out of dark green storage containers with military markings on the side.

"Ma'am, do you work here?" One of the soldiers approached me, no doubt noticing my unwelcome curiosity.

I fumbled for my card and held it up. "Yes. I'm a nurse." I continued to play dumb. "What's going on? Why are you here?"

"There is a threat of a terrorist attack. Idrissia called in extra security."

"Oh my god, that's horrible," I replied. "Are we safe?"

I could see the confident smile through the plexiglass shield on his helmet. "You're in the safest spot in the Line. We got an army down here." He turned and casually walked back toward the other soldiers standing by the barrier.

Once inside the hospice, Deirdre immediately flagged me down. I could always count on a smile from Deirdre at shift change in the evening, but today it was gone, replaced by a look of concern.

"Girl, I'm so ready to get out of this place. I heard the soldiers are all over Broadway, too. Did you see them on the way in?"

I nodded. "Yeah. They're everywhere."

"So crazy," she replied. "When I got to work this morning, everything was normal. A few hours later, the soldiers showed up in the hallway and people on social media started talking about the Castle being under attack by terrorists."

"I don't know what's going on, but you be careful, Deirdre. Might be a good night to stay home. You know what I mean?"

Deirdre hugged me gently. "You sound like my mom. I'll be fine. Besides, some of these soldiers are cute. They've got to have down time, and I bet they'll hit the clubs on Upper Broadway. Those are the best ones."

Deirdre's 'mom' comment caught me off guard. And it stung. Alex and I had decided to wait to have kids. We got busy with life, one thing led to another, and then the cancer diagnosis took all the wind out of our sails. Alex said that having a child wouldn't have been fair to either him or the child, and I, of course, agreed. But seven years later, Alex was gone—along with my chances of ever having a child.

It hurt, and not a day went by that I didn't second-guess our decision.

I forced a smile for Deirdre. "Those soldiers can't handle you." I grabbed her hand. "I mean it. Be careful. And one more thing..." I paused. "I think I'm ready to take you up on your offer. If all this blows over, and you still want me to tag along, maybe we can go out next week."

"You're going to really like my friend. He's cute, Mel."

"One step at a time. I'm just going out, okay?" I looked down at the electronic tablet for my shift sitting on the desk and quickly changed the subject. "Anything I need to know tonight?"

"Nobody admitted today. Everyone stable, except..." Deirdre looked up from the notes on her screen. "Saul. He isn't doing so good."

At first, I grimaced, but then I steeled myself. Deep down, I knew I would be no more successful at preventing Saul from dying than I had been in escaping the Castle, or controlling the spiraling danger unfolding out in the hallway. But, I was a nurse, and this was my ward. If I had anything to say about it, Saul would survive the night.

We finished our shift change hand-off and Deirdre left through the doors out into the hallway. I could imagine her flirting with the soldiers outside, and it almost made me smile. Almost.

My fingers moved quickly, preparing the medications and other supplies I would need for my rounds. The entire time, I wondered what Saul would be watching on his television. He never failed to surprise me with his choices.

Today, I started my rounds with Saul's room, determined to lift his spirits. I approached his closed door and knocked before announcing myself. "Nurse!" I shouted.

Silence greeted me from inside.

I pushed open the door and found Saul in his bed, sitting up reading a book. The television was dark. "Good evening, Saul. Whatcha reading?" I went over and wrote my name on the white board and prepared Saul's medications.

"The book of Exodus," he replied. "Chaplain dropped by to meet with me today and left the Bible." He looked up. "I asked for him."

The last part had the intended effect, but I maintained a happy face. "Huh. You two must have had a rowdy discussion."

Saul shook his head. "Apparently, there are no rabbis in the Castle. Nothing but interfaith ministers who are apparently short on theology and hand out Bibles like party favors. Charlatans all of them. That man couldn't have had a rowdy disagreement over anything. Believe me, I tried."

I handed Saul his medicine and watched him wash it down with a swig from a straw sticking out of a small carton of chocolate milk. After rearranging the pillows behind Saul's head, I sat down in the chair next to him. "I'm worried, Saul."

He nodded in agreement, then sighed. "Melanie, it's just my time."

"No. Not about you. About me."

Saul looked confused. "What do you mean? You know about my test results—and calling the chaplain."

"Stop the pity party. You're going to die of old age in this place. The only reason they haven't released you is because the doctor doesn't want to admit he was wrong and you were right. Trust me, I have bigger problems."

Saul scowled. He clearly wasn't expecting this approach.

"I'm afraid I'm in trouble, Saul. And I don't have anyone else to talk to. No family left, and the few friends I have are back in Los Angeles. You're the only one who will listen to me. Will you do that for me? Listen?"

"Melanie, of course, but I don't know that I'm the right person to help you with this...problem, whatever it is."

"There's only one way to find out. I have to finish my rounds, but I'll circle back. How about we go for a walk at midnight?"

Saul exhaled sharply and rested the Bible in his lap. "I don't know, Melanie. I haven't walked in days."

I remained quiet, staring hopefully at Saul's face. He returned my gaze and the tension became palpable as no one dared blink.

He finally shook his head in an apparent surrender to my request. "I will try. Either way, I look forward to hearing about your dilemma and providing whatever advice I can give."

I smiled. "Good. And by the way, there is no try. Do or do not. Surely you've seen *that* movie."

After making my way outside, I breathed a sigh of relief. If anything could keep Saul alive a few more hours, it would be curiosity. He loved his mysteries, and I just served up a big one.

For the next few hours, all I could think about was Celwyn and Paloma. Who could I trust? Clearly, they knew each other. That much was certain. Was Paloma here to stop Celwyn from destroying the Castle? Celwyn did threaten to kill everyone, after all. Or was Paloma in the Castle to clean up a vampire problem as Celwyn had claimed on the train?

The more I thought about it, the clearer the answer. Could I believe Celwyn was a dangerous terrorist? Yes. Could I wrap my mind around an entire army being called in to protect the Castle against vampires? No.

I finished my rounds and sat down at the desk to finish my data entry. Vital signs from each patient flowed across the multiple computer screens spanning the length of the desk, each one providing real time signals, along with a twenty-four-hour history. I never quite understood the necessity of manually inputting data on my handheld tablet if it was already being monitored electronically, but those were the types of things nurses were forced to do. I guess it was a way to make sure we were paying attention.

Saul's numbers continued to get worse. Blood pressure and oxygen saturation had fallen off a cliff in the last few days. His body was systematically shutting itself down. It was only a matter of time, and he had precious little of it left.

Speaking of time, I glanced at my phone. Almost time to check on Saul. I laid down the tablet and walked towards Saul's door, hoping my friend could find the strength to take one more walk around the ward.

Tonight, like he had done so many times in the past, Saul completely shattered my expectations. When I arrived in his room, he was sitting in the chair beside his bed, casually reading from his Bible with one leg crossed over the other knee. A slipper hung precariously from the foot dangling in front of him, ready to fall if he made any sudden movement.

"Good evening, Melanie. I've been waiting for you."

"I'm right on time." I looked at my phone. "And...it looks like you're ready to take another walk."

"I fear I have few, if any, left, Melanie. Now stop teasing me. I'm not getting out of this chair until you tell me about your problem."

I pulled another chair out of the corner and sat it directly in front of Saul. "Saul, some of this may sound fantastic, but I promise everything I am going to tell you is true."

He closed his Bible and placed it on the bedside table. "Of course."

"There are soldiers outside the hospice guarding the medical level. They arrived today, and the Castle is filled with them. I am afraid something bad is going to happen."

"What kind of soldiers?" Saul asked. "Army? National Guard?"

"No. Idrissia. The private kind."

He nodded, and I continued. I told him the entire story, starting with the attack from the shade on the roof and ending with my failed escape attempt. He listened intently, never interrupting me once, hanging on every word.

I finally finished and paused to get his reaction. "So what do you think?"

The old man stood up slowly and leaned against his walker. "Melanie, you were right. That is the most fantastic story I have ever heard. We definitely need to discuss." Saul looked at me defiantly. "But first, I want to see the soldiers. Take me to the doors and let me look out into the hallway. This is the most excitement I've had in decades."

I rose. "I can't let you leave the ward, Saul. You know that, right? Just a peek out the windows."

He nodded. At that moment, the blood pressure cuff began tightening around his arm, and he froze.

Saul's numbers had been dropping all day. If the systolic dropped below eighty, the wireless sensor on his band would signal an alarm at my nursing station. And most people couldn't stand, much less walk, with that level of blood pressure.

We both held our breath until the cuff eased its pressure, and the small screen built into a device outside the cuff began flashing green. A few seconds later, the number appeared: 110/70.

I relaxed and shook my head. "I don't know how you do it, Saul. That's the best number you've had in a long time."

He started moving again. "I'm not dead yet. By the way, did I tell you that I served in the Israeli Defense Forces? It was required back in those days if you wanted to be a dual citizen."

The door closed behind me as we walked into the hallway. "So what did you do in the IDF? Did you see any fighting?"

"Mechanic. Worked on anything with a motor. And, yes, I saw enough fighting to know I didn't want to be any where near it when it was happening. So, the official word is that these soldiers are here to protect us from a terrorist attack, hmm?"

I nodded. Saul kept talking as we slowly moved down the hallway where it dead-ended at an intersection. On the right, a set of double doors offered a rear exit from the hospice ward leading to the elevator. To the left, the ward continued its rectangular circuit.

We reached the double doors exiting the hospice and Saul stood on his tip toes peering through the glass. "I don't see anything."

"They're staged towards the left, down the hallway."

"I'm opening the door," he said. He turned and bumped the push bar with his hips and the door clicked open.

"Saul!" I shouted. "You can't go out there. I'll get in trouble."

"I'll just take a peek." He wedged his walker in the door frame, and carefully stuck his head over the threshold out into the hallway. He remained silent and motionless, while I waited, hoping none of the soldiers would spot the white hair poking out the door.

After almost a minute, I decided I had gambled enough with my career. "Saul!" I hissed. "Close that door."

He grabbed the walker and backed towards me, letting the door close in front of him.

"So, what do you think Saul?"

"I think the soldiers are *not* here to stop a terrorist attack." He looked straight at me. "Melanie, I believe your friend is right."

I froze. "What did you just say?"

Saul began moving the other way to continue his route around the hospice. "You heard me, Melanie. I believe we're dealing with vampires."

CHAPTER TEN

I STOOD in shock long enough for Saul to get a head start down the hallway inside the ward leading away from the exit. My feet finally started moving and I caught up to his side. "So you believe Celwyn is telling the truth?"

"Did he save your life up on the roof?" He paused and waited for my answer.

"Well, yes. Yes, he did," I replied.

"Does your gut tell you he is a good man?"

I hesitated, thinking about Saul's question. "Yes, but it's not that simple. People lie, you can't always tell—"

Saul cut me off. "You saw this thing he called a shade with your own eyes, did you not?"

"Yes. I-I can't forget it."

"Hmmph." He began walking again, nearing the locked emergency doors on the back wall of the hospital ward. "You don't want to believe Celwyn because you're afraid. You're afraid to admit vampires exist."

"Aren't you?"

"No," he replied confidently. "I have seen incredible goodness and love in my lifetime, but I am equally aware of the darkness. To fight against it, you must have the courage to first admit that evil exists.

Otherwise— " He faltered and caught himself on the walker. "Otherwise, it has already won." When he spoke again, his voice was broken and weak. "When I was young, back in Israel—" He cleared his throat, and I thought I saw a tear welling up in one of his eyes. "I have seen things, too, Melanie. Terrible, evil things that I also can't forget."

He stopped in front of the emergency doors and pointed with one hand. "I told you I was right. Whatever is behind those doors is evil, and I felt it since I arrived. Your friend was correct, we are not safe. Those men out there from Idrissia are not protecting us. They are guarding what is behind these doors."

At that moment, the hallway around us plunged into darkness. Seconds later, dim red emergency lights flickered into life around the hospice ward. Loud beeping sounds erupted around me, as medical equipment in patient rooms shifted onto temporary battery power.

"Crap. Power's out. We need to get you back to your room, Saul."

Saul slowly began the process of turning his walker around. Before he could make the full rotation, loud popping sounds emerged from outside the hospice. First, the pop sounds were sporadic, but then staccato sounds filled the air, blending into a steady stream of loud noise.

"Gunfire!" Saul shouted. He picked up his pace, shuffling his feet across the floor.

We made it back to the exit doors where Saul had earlier spied on the soldiers. Smoke now blocked visibility through the windows, and all I could see through the glass were sporadic flashes of light. I quickly turned the lock in the middle of the right hand door, and felt the internal mechanism slide into place. I prayed the other nurses would be able to lock down their own access points to the hallway.

Saul had already turned the corner, and was in sight of his room when I heard the sound of grinding metal from behind me. Smoke from the gunfire outside had seeped under the exit doors and slowly filled the dark hospice hallway.

Time stood still. Blinking red lights and chirps assaulted my heightened senses. I fought back panic. All I could think about were the patients in my ward, scared and alone, wondering what was happening.

I strained to find the source of the faint grinding noise in the dark before finally noticing a bulge in the emergency doors lining the back wall.

An uneasy feeling rumbled in my stomach and I felt bitterly cold, just like on the roof before the attack. There was another crashing sound, and the red bar blocking the pair of doors bent inwards. The two slots locking the solid steel bar in place over the double doors broke off and flew into the wall on the opposite side of the hallway. One of the steel kick plates curled upwards from the floor, making a terrible screeching sound as an opening emerged between my ward and whatever lay on the other side.

Through the opening, I thought I saw a gray hand bending the metal. Instinctively, I reached my right hand in the pocket of my scrubs and took hold of the Leatherman. I held it in front of my body and flicked the knife blade open.

Deafening sounds of gunshots, screams, and crashes filtered under the mangled door into the hospice hallway. I waved frantically at Saul to keep moving towards his room, then took a step forward, determined to protect my patients from whatever tried to make it through from the other side.

I made it to the emergency doors and stood a few feet away from the opening, watching for movement. The kickplate on the damaged door began to bend upward again, enlarging the hole. Now that I was close, I could clearly see a gray hand pushing and twisting the metal from the other side. Without hesitation, I plunged my knife into the hand, so deep that I felt the impact of the tip on the metal door grasped by the hand.

The hand withdrew, dislodging my knife, then disappeared through the opening.

I listened, but the noise on the other side of the door had subsided. The sound of my heart beat immediately filled my brain, fueled into overdrive by adrenaline. For what seemed like an eternity, nothing but eerie silence and mechanical beeping filled the smoky darkness.

Then the hallway exploded around me.

Both of the emergency doors flew off their hinges. I dove to get away, then flattened my body against the tile floor of the hallway.

Above me, chunks of steel turned into deadly projectiles. A flat sheet of steel that once formed part of a door landed on top of my back, pinning my upper body. I struggled to move, then something grabbed one of my feet and yanked me out from underneath the wreckage, throwing me down the hallway like a rag doll.

The impact on the floor knocked the breath out of me, but I forced myself to stand while raising my knife. Somehow, it had remained in my hand through the explosion.

Even in the dark, I recognized what stood before me as another one of the creatures I had seen on the roof. This one had long, straight black hair and appeared female, or at least had been a female before turning into a shade. She wore a tattered hospital gown and an IV needle stuck out of her muscular arm. Although her eyes displayed the same soulless shark-like stare, the cold eyes didn't flash the desperate aggression of the other shade. When I looked her in the face, I saw a dash of a pink color instead of the ugly gray, the subtle signs of a calculating intelligence, and, for a moment, what almost seemed like a rugged beauty.

I wondered if this thing was a vampire.

Any sense of curiosity disappeared once it opened its mouth and snarled. Its jaw extended to twice the size of a human, and I saw rows of jagged blood-soaked teeth that looked as if they had been used recently to tear open flesh. It leaped in my direction, and I did the only thing I could.

I ran.

Luckily, the shade had thrown me far enough to get a solid head start. I was always more of a long distance runner than a sprinter, but in a pinch I could be fast. The shade made up ground quickly behind me, while Saul peeked out of his room at the end of the hallway.

"Get away from the door!" I yelled.

I flew through Saul's open doorway and tried to slam the door behind me. The heavy wooden door nearly made it back to the door frame when it suddenly stopped its progress. I lowered my shoulder against the door and planted my feet, pushing against it with all my weight.

But the door didn't move. Instead, it began opening inward, revealing the shade on the other side.

It slashed at me with its fingernails through the gap in the doorway, forcing me to shift my position. I could feel my feet sliding along the floor behind me. The shade was far stronger than me, and I was rapidly losing leverage.

From behind me, Saul rushed forward holding the IV stand like a spear. He poked the end through the doorway, striking the shade in the face. "Get back! Get back!"

I loaded tension in my legs, then rammed the door with my shoulder, hoping to take advantage of Saul's distraction. The door moved. Maybe an inch.

Keeping one hand against the door, the shade grabbed the IV stand with its free hand and threw it back into the room. The stand and Saul went tumbling towards the bed.

With the makeshift spear out of its face, the shade redoubled its efforts on the door, flinging it open, pushing me into the wall behind it. The beast strutted into the center of the room, and turned its head, looking for me.

I let go of the door, and the eight-foot barrier slowly closed, revealing my position. By this time, I had retrieved the knife from my pocket and flashed open the blade. The weapon was small, but it was all I had.

The shade wasted no time, lunging towards me with lightning quick speed. It pinned me against the wall and snapped at my neck with its teeth. It would have torn out my throat except I somehow managed to stab the shade's arm with my knife, which loosened its grasp, allowing me to squirm far enough away to protect my carotid artery.

But the shade still bit me.

Its teeth sank into my shoulder blade, making a wet crunching sound. I screamed so hard my throat felt like it was on fire. I thought I was going to black out, but instead the pressure on my shoulder relented and the shade released me from its grasp.

I dropped to the floor, fighting to remain conscious while blood streamed from my shoulder. Behind the shade, Saul repeatedly slammed his metal walker into the thing's back. "Let go of her, you bitch!" he shouted in a raspy voice.

Throughout the entire fight, the shade had never said a word. Not even a grunt. Just like the one on the roof, it kept coming without any display of anger, pain, or emotion of any type. That's why what happened next broke my spirit, sapping whatever strength remained in my injured body.

It laughed.

A hauntingly melodic female laugh. It laughed right before it slapped away the walker and sent it flying into a wall. It laughed again right before it attacked Saul and sank its jaws deep into my friend's neck.

I knew at that point this was no shade. Everything Celwyn said was true. This was a full-fledged vampire.

And she was going to kill me, right after she killed Saul.

CHAPTER ELEVEN

THE VAMPIRE DROPPED Saul's limp body to the ground, and turned to face me. Blood ran down her chin, and through my hazy vision I thought I saw a smile. Somehow, I knew that she wanted me to see what happened next.

She wanted me to see her take Saul's life.

The vampire turned her back and reached for Saul. Before she could touch him again, the door to the room burst open and an Idrissia soldier in a combat helmet entered, spraying bullets from an assault rifle at the torso of the vampire. The soldier moved forward and, in one fluid motion, dropped the gun and drew a sword from a scabbard on his back. He spun the blade in a downward arc, and a second later the bloody severed head of the vampire lay on the floor of Saul's room next to her still-twitching body.

I took one more look to ensure it wasn't a dream, then promptly fainted.

———

WHEN I WOKE UP, I found myself resting in Saul's chair. Saul laid on his back in the bed beside me with a blood-soaked hand towel covering his neck. Celwyn stood at the foot of the bed, dressed in an Idrissia soldier uniform. The plexiglass face shield hung open on his helmet.

"I'm so happy to see you," I mumbled weakly. "I take back everything I said. You were right. About all of it."

He shook his head and pursed his lips. "Mel, I'm so sorry. I wish I had gotten here sooner." He raised his rifle, grabbing it from a sling hanging around his neck. He pointed it at both Saul and me, and a pained look crossed his face. "Bloody hell, you're both bit."

My shoulder ached. Celwyn hadn't even dressed my wound. I looked over to Saul, and his face had grown pale. His complexion was turning gray.

I exhaled sharply with the realization of what Celwyn meant. "We're infected. You're not going to save us. You're going to kill us."

Celwyn shifted nervously. "I have no choice." He nodded towards Saul. "This one is already turning gray. You can see it."

"How long do we have?" I asked.

"Everyone's different. Some can only fight off the parasite for minutes. Some last hours."

"Then why haven't you killed us already? Why make us wait? That just seems...cruel."

Celwyn began pacing around the room. "Where I come from, we have a code. I don't kill unless I have to. And right now, under my code, I don't have to. Everyone gets a chance, Mel. You have a *chance*. There are some—precious few, but some—who are immune."

I looked down at the back of my hand. Under the caked blood, the tanned skin retained its normal flesh color. "I don't have a mirror. How am I looking over here?"

Celwyn stared at me for a few seconds, then looked away. My heart sank.

"Celwyn. Tell me! My skin. How does it look?"

His gaze returned. "You look fine, Mel."

I remained confused. "So that's good news right? It's been a while since I got bit. Maybe I won't turn."

Celwyn looked away again. "Perhaps."

"So how many people do you know who have survived a bite?"

"None," he replied. "It's statistically…improbable. You would have a better chance of being struck by lightning. Twice. In the same day."

"No! Don't do that. Don't give up on me. I choose hope. I choose to believe that I'm going to live." I turned to Saul. "He gave his life for mine. I want that to mean something."

I stood carefully from the chair, the movement pulling on the bite wound in my shoulder, and stepped over to the bed to touch Saul's forehead. Raging heat and a pounding heart rate. "Saul, can you hear me?"

"Be careful," Celwyn hissed. "He's almost gone. And when that happens, you know what I'll have to do."

"Well, he's not gone yet," I snapped. I turned back to Saul and his eyes fluttered open. The pupils had darkened and were dilated, but a hint of the old man's bright blue eyes remained.

"You're alive, Melanie. I'm glad."

"Thanks to you, Saul" I replied. I found his hand and gave it a squeeze.

He smiled. "I want to tell you something, Melanie. I want to tell you the reason why I made it so long in this place, even when the doctors thought I should already be dead. I stayed alive because I didn't want to die. Every day, I willed my body to survive." A light in his eyes blazed brightly. "One more midnight, Melanie. It's all about one more midnight."

I started crying. "One more midnight, Saul. You made it. You can stop now."

Saul shook his head. "No. No. You don't understand. I can feel it inside me. I'm getting stronger. I know I shouldn't want it, but I do. I still want to live, Melanie. Don't do this." He returned the squeeze on my hand, and it felt firm.

"He's losing it," Celwyn said.

The radio on his helmet crackled to life with Paloma's voice. *"Clear out the hospital floor. Evacuate survivors to Broadway. If they can't walk on their own, follow the protocol. Put them down. Repeat. Put them down."*

Celwyn opened the hospital room door and looked outside. "We have to go. Now."

"So you're not going to kill us?" I asked.

He glared at me. "I'm not going to kill you, not yet, but him—I'm going to kill him." He walked towards Saul with his rifle raised at eye level.

"No!" I shouted. "If anyone is going to kill my friend, it should be me."

Celwyn lowered his rifle and stroked the stubble on his chin. "Do you even know how to use a gun?"

"It's not that hard. Point and shoot," I replied.

He shook his head and handed me a pistol he removed from a holster on his belt. He chambered a bullet and handed me the weapon. "When you're ready, just pull the trigger." He pointed to his temple. "Twice. Right here. Understand?"

I took the pistol and nodded. Celwyn walked to the open door and turned to watch.

"Can you give me a little privacy?" I put my hand on my hips and cocked my head in frustration.

Celwyn shook his head. "We don't have time to play games. Real soon, that's not going to be your friend lying there in that bed. If you don't kill him, he *will* try to kill you. Or worse, he'll try to kill the next person that he finds. Can you live with that?" He walked outside the room and closed the door behind him.

I walked back to the side of Saul's bed and pointed the gun at his head. He stared back at me with black, soulless eyes. He began rambling in a language I didn't understand, the same language spoken by the woman at the train station when I arrived.

Tears welled up in my eyes. *I can't do it. I can't kill my friend.*

My finger relaxed from the trigger.

Saul writhed in the bed, as if fighting a hidden demon. He turned to face me, then howled.

This wasn't my friend.

"I'm sorry, Saul." I stared at his eyes, looking for any trace of the friendly soul I knew. I thought I saw a flicker of recognition and hesitated, but then the image was gone. I pulled the trigger. Twice. Then I left the room.

I slipped into the hallway and handed the still-warm pistol back to Celwyn. He took it cautiously, staring at my face.

"It's done?" he asked.

I nodded.

He waited by the door, listening for noise. He looked at me with distrust, then placed his hand on the door to Saul's room.

In the distance, I heard voices and the pop of a rifle. Celwyn's radio crackled again. "*Hospital evacuated. Heading into hospice now.*"

He looked down the hallway towards the other wards in the hospice, then back to Saul's door. "We have to go. Paloma's men are coming."

I grabbed his outstretched hand and followed Celwyn through the smoky corridor leading away from the hospice. The only thought racing through my mind was that at that moment, Celwyn was probably planning to put two bullets in my temple, just like he had instructed me to do to Saul.

I wasn't sure if I was following him to safety, or to my death.

CHAPTER TWELVE

CELWYN LED the way with a small flashlight attached to the top of his rifle. The checkpoint outside the hospice had been ripped apart, and everywhere I looked, bodies of dead Idrissia soldiers littered the floor.

"Where are we going?" I asked.

"I came here to see what they were up to," Celwyn whispered. "And I'm not leaving before I find out the truth."

We followed the trail of carnage down the long corridor past the elevators. I took a quick glance towards their dark, open doors. "How are we getting out of here if the elevators don't work?"

"The same way I got in." He moved methodically forward, scanning left and right with the light.

Occasionally, I saw a dead body with the distinct gray color of a shade. At least the soldiers killed a few of them.

But not many. It was obviously a lopsided fight.

I'm not sure why we were whispering, but I followed Celwyn's lead. "How can you tell if it's a shade or a vampire?"

Without turning around, Celwyn replied. "You'll know. A shade is like an attack dog. A vampire is…something entirely different. They're smart, and look more like a normal human."

"Can they talk?" I paused. "Or laugh?"

Celwyn stopped in his tracks. He lowered his light and turned to face me. "The female one I killed back there—you heard it speak?"

"She didn't speak. Not exactly. But I thought I heard her laugh. It sounded...beautiful? Is that crazy?"

"No, that's not crazy. What's crazy is you fought off a vampire with a pocket knife and an old man's walker. It may not have been fully mature, but that thing was on its way. Heavens, Mel, you're lucky to be standing here."

Celwyn stepped through the gaping hole that once served as the doorway into the secret facility located next to the hospice. The setup looked identical to the other medical wards along the floor. Nurses' stations served as a central nerve center for surrounding patient rooms. The video monitors were smashed and bullet holes riddled the walls behind the same type of curved desk where I sat every night.

A pile of bodies rested on the floor behind the desk. Blood splatter painted the walls. A few of the dead wore soldier uniforms, but most of them wore black scrubs. The hospital employees wore blue, and we wore purple in the hospice, but I had never seen that color in the Castle.

Celwyn pointed to the bloody scene behind the desk. "They put up a fight here."

I nodded. "How many shades do you think attacked?

"To do this type of damage? A lot. Maybe hundreds."

We kept moving, and I followed Celwyn into one of the patient rooms. It could have been one of mine from the hospice. It looked the same, down to the whiteboard still inscribed with the name of the nurse on duty before the attack.

But in the place of a bed, the room held a body-shaped pod hooked up to a small kiosk filled with computer equipment and video monitors.

All of it had been smashed to pieces.

I approached the open pod and quickly realized it lacked the top cover, which had been removed. Inside, there was a narrow strip of white bedding. Loose hanging wires and IV tubes led out of the pod through small openings and connected to a pole hanging beside the bed. Celwyn rushed towards the pod and began taking pictures of every inch of it with his phone.

"Look at the IV bags," he said. "What are they?"

I looked at the bags hanging on the pole, some still filled with a red liquid, and a feeling of unease settled into my mind. "Blood. This was a setup for a transfusion."

"Yeah, I can see that. But what type of blood? You're the nurse here. Is it plasma? Platelets? What is it?"

I studied the long list of numbers and letters printed on the bag. "I-I don't know. The yellow one...maybe it's a cryoprecipitate? Frozen plasma. It looks fancy. The red one is definitely red blood cells—RBCs."

Something clicked in my mind. A distant memory. Saul.

"Actually, I've seen this stuff once here in the Castle. On a chart. A patient of mine with blood cancer had treatments before they moved him into the hospice. Not the same thing, but close."

I walked over to the whiteboard. "At least they followed standard procedure on medications in this place." I pointed at words on the board. "This drug is a sedative. A heavy one. This person was basically in a coma."

Celwyn now stood behind me and took more pictures with his phone before placing it back into his pocket. "Thanks. Let's look through a few more rooms."

I caught him staring at my face. "And? Any change?"

"You're still you." He left the room and the light went with him.

I hustled to follow.

We made our way through several more of the wards, and they all looked identical. Outside the rooms, the medical staff had been slaughtered alongside the soldiers trying to protect them. Inside, only empty pods remained.

Near the end of the facility, the layout finally changed. Much larger patient rooms were set apart, each taking up a corner of the ward. Celwyn opened the door of the closest one and entered, shining his light around the room.

Inside, two broken pods sat in the middle of the room instead of one.

Celwyn laughed. "His-and-her guest suite. Nothing but the finest at Idrissia."

I located the whiteboard and found the names of the patients. "Celwyn. Look here." I waved him over to me. "Recognize the name?"

He whistled. "He's that billionaire who owns the LA football team, right? The one who is always dating celebrities?"

I thought about some of the names I had seen on the whiteboards. Many of the names had seemed familiar, but I couldn't place them at the time. This one, however, I knew.

The hospice medic's theory about an anti-aging clinic returned to my mind. I turned excitedly to Celwyn. "These were all rich people. They were paying to become vampires."

"Yes," he said calmly before walking out of the room. "And it's madness. Pure madness."

I matched his quick stride back through the length of the facility. "Why is it so crazy? I mean, what rich person wouldn't pay for a longer life?"

"Mel, I understand the draw. Believe me, I do. The madness is not on the part of those who paid to be in those pods. The madness is in the one who created this lab experiment."

"I don't understand."

"If you had the power of a god, would you enjoy your dominion or create competing gods? What happened here changes everything, and it can't remain a secret."

We finally made it back to the corridor outside the facility. Celwyn ran away from me towards a door marked 'Maintenance.' He opened it slowly and flashed the light inside.

"Wait here," he said before disappearing through the doorway.

I sat alone in the smoke-filled corridor, surrounded by blood and destruction. My thoughts kept going back to my own bite and the fact I had not yet turned. It had been more than an hour. Saul had turned quickly, but maybe that was because of his age.

I was younger, and, no doubt, stronger. Or at least that was what I kept telling myself.

But if I wasn't going to turn into a shade, I needed to get the wound on my shoulder cleaned to avoid infection. Soon. Even with the benefit of the pain killers I had picked up from one of the nurse stations, my shoulder still throbbed with pain.

The maintenance door opened, and Celwyn stuck out his head. "All clear. Let's go."

"Celwyn." I pointed to my shoulder. "If you aren't going to kill me, I need to get this dressed. We need to find someplace safe...and clean."

He nodded. "I have a place in mind."

I ducked through the door and found myself in a network of metal stairwells and catwalks. Idrissia did everything bigger and better, and emergency stairwells were apparently no exception. Unlike the narrow stairways in skyscrapers that simply went up and down, the Castle contained a vast network of internal catwalks and stairs traversing in every direction. Each Grid contained a series of emergency access tunnels used for infrastructure construction and maintenance. It was a hidden frame around which the Castle's walls were built. The backbone of the city.

And it was dark. Boy, was it dark.

On the metal catwalk in front of me, the bodies of four uniformed Idrissia soldiers lay on the ground, ripped to bloody pieces. A body hanging over the railing to my right was missing a head.

"This is how the shades ambushed the lab," Celwyn said. "Paloma got the lab secured, but didn't have enough time or men to lock down the Maze."

"The Maze?" I asked.

"That's what the people here in the city call this place. Fitting, right?"

"Well, I can barely see my hand in front of my face, so I'll take your word for it."

Celwyn knelt down and began rummaging through the gear on the dead soldiers. "Here." He tossed me a combat helmet along with a rifle with a flashlight secured to the top. I placed the helmet on my head and slung the rifle strap around my neck. Celwyn surveyed my new look with approval and pushed the button on top of my flashlight.

With double the illumination, I finally got a good look at the Maze, or at least what I could see of it. Every direction looked identical—

metal stairwells and catwalks as far as my light could shine. "I hope you know your way around this thing," I mumbled.

After relieving a dead soldier's kit of a few rifle magazines, Celwyn stood and pointed the light forward along one of the catwalks. "I've been using it for weeks. We need to go straight this way until we hit the Tube. The Maze is divided into two halves with a break in the middle for the trains. We'll have to get out in the open to cross the Tube." He stroked his chin. "That will be the most dangerous part."

Celwyn took off ahead of me, and we settled into a steady but brisk pace with him leading me across the Maze. Occasionally, a clanking sound of metal or the groan of the giant surrounding structure caused me to wonder if we were alone in this open but narrow space. In the depths of the Castle, every sound carried, and we might as well have been walking through a canyon.

Somewhere in the darkness to my left, I heard the sound of grinding metal. I turned my light to track the noise and Celwyn stopped me. He placed a hand on my rifle and slowly pointed it back towards the floor of the catwalk.

"We're getting close to the Tube. Lights off." He switched off the light on his rifle and touched a panel on the side of his helmet. The plexiglass on the front visor lit up with a pale green glow.

"Night vision," he said. "Now turn off that light or you're going to blind me."

I found the same panel on the side of my helmet and tapped the button. My vision suddenly improved by tenfold and the light emitted by the flashlight seemed brighter than the sun. I squinted my eyes, then turned off the flashlight.

The catwalks and stairs around me glowed with a soft green light and I got an even better look at the enormity of the Maze. In front of us, a giant wall loomed from below us to what I presumed to be the top of the Castle over forty stories above our heads. To both my left and right, a lattice work of connecting pathways led along the wall, connecting each of the floors by staircases.

"This night vision is incredible. Why didn't we do this sooner?" I asked.

"These batteries won't last. It's not a toy, and we need to save it for when we need it most."

We finally neared the edge of the wall marking the end of the Maze, and Celwyn sprinted ahead. More dead soldiers lined the catwalk at the base of the wall. One of the soldiers lay face down, with a torn uniform, missing both a helmet and shoes.

Celwyn turned the body over, and even in the pale green glow of the night vision, I could see the gray complexion of a shade. He rushed to the side of another dead soldier and felt the forehead. "This was recent. They're not even cold yet."

"What about the shade?" I asked. "It's wearing a uniform. How?"

"Probably one of the men from back at the lab. Got bit and turned." He stood up straight. "That's the problem with fighting shades. Our side loses people, while the other side gains them. It's not a fair fight."

I followed him along the wall, passing doors that would presumably lead us out into the open atrium that housed the dual-stacked Tubes. Celwyn read the Grid numbers on signs at each door before finally locating the one he desired.

"This one," he announced. "Grid Six." He stopped and looked at me before checking to make sure a bullet was chambered in his pistol. "I don't know what is on the other side of this door. Paloma will be watching the Tube since it's the main artery through the Line, and we will be out in the open until we get to the other side. We have to move quick, you understand?"

I nodded. "I can keep up."

"Good," he replied. He opened the door and dashed through it, into the open Atrium on the other side. I followed behind him, suddenly appreciative that I had decided to take up running instead of yoga.

CHAPTER THIRTEEN

DIM, natural light greeted me on the other side of the door, and Celwyn tapped the side of my helmet, disabling the night vision. "Save those batteries."

I lifted the plexiglass visor on the helmet for good measure and took advantage of the early morning sunlight pouring through the Atrium to survey my surroundings. We found ourselves standing in the shadow of something huge above us, partially obscuring the light.

Celwyn pointed above our heads. A row of train cars sat idle, stalled within the Tube. We had entered the Maze on the third floor, and exited into the Atrium on the same level, two floors below the Tube that traveled through Broadway. An area that normally would have been full of life remained eerily quiet, just like the train.

"No one around," I said. "You think it's safe to cross?"

Celwyn crouched motionless behind a support beam for the Tube, scanning the Atrium for signs of movement. "I don't think it's safe. But I also don't think we have a choice. My place is on the other side. We have to get through the Atrium."

I pointed up with my finger, hoping that the new day would bring some relief from the horror of the night before. "Sun's up. Does that mean the shades will stay away?"

"Maybe." Celwyn kept scanning for movement. "Too many shadows in here right now. The sunlight won't be a deterrent until mid-day when the sun is directly overhead. They're definitely out there. Let's just hope they're focused on something else until we get across."

The minutes ticked off, and I sat waiting for Celwyn to decide it was safe to leave our hiding place below the tracks. Finally, he stood and waved at me to move forward.

Inside the Atrium, the metal catwalks leading out of the Maze joined into a wide bridge that crossed to the other side. Like the structures in the Maze, the hexagonal lattice pattern on the floor of the bridge contained holes in the middle of each hexagon, meaning that we would be visible to anyone either above or below us as we crossed the Atrium.

Celwyn set off in a light jog, systematically swiveling his gun in front of his face in a clockwise pattern, first checking up then down and around, before repeating the cycle every twenty feet or so. I could barely keep up with him, even without the fancy tactical movements, so my effort basically consisted of an awkward running motion, cradling the assault rifle in one arm. Occasionally, I glanced above or below our floor, mainly hoping to see something I hadn't seen since the attack—normal people living in the Castle.

Where did they all go?

We made it across the bridge, arriving unscathed on the other side of the Atrium. There, I got the answer to my question. Sounds of talking filtered down from the Broadway level above us. Celwyn ducked beneath the solid Tube platform and crouched down, blending into the shadows. I did the same, resting beside him.

He placed a finger in front of his closed lips then pointed upwards. I nodded.

The sounds of footsteps on the metal platform by the Tube station broke the silence. Once they were close, the clanging of footsteps merged with bits and pieces of unintelligible conversations into a chaotic noisy mess. I couldn't tell how many people were above us, but I guessed a small crowd based on the time it took for them to pass over our heads.

Before the crowd made it past earshot, one voice shouted above the rest. "From here on out, we just follow Broadway back to Grid Five. That's the safe zone." The announcement from what I assumed to be an Idrissia soldier was followed by a round of murmuring that gradually faded as the group headed away from us down Broadway.

I prepared to stand up when Celwyn grabbed my arm tightly, making sure I didn't move. His eyes remained fixed on the underside of the Tube, a long cylinder stretching through the center of the Atrium two floors above us. I sat in silence, waiting to see what caught his attention. I felt a sense of unease, then I saw it, too. Something moved along the bottom of the Tube, hidden in the shadow of one of the idle train cars.

A figure crawled underneath the train car, leaping in and out of the structure supporting the Tube, and then back up onto the underbelly of the translucent cylinder, being careful to remain hidden from anyone walking along Broadway. More dark figures followed, massing underneath the Tube below the shadow of a train car.

"We have to do something," I whispered.

"Bloody hell," Celwyn replied. "They're all going to die." He looked down and shook his head, deep in thought. "Fine. Follow my lead." He rose to his feet and closed the visor on his helmet. "And don't hesitate to use that rifle."

He sprinted to the nearest stairway and began climbing, taking two steps at a time. I clamored up the stairs behind him, trying my best to not get left behind. In less than a minute, Celwyn reached the landing platform two floors above us on Broadway and shot several rounds from his rifle into the air.

"You're under attack!" he yelled. "Under the Tube!"

My head rose above the platform in the stairwell just in time to see the shades pouring out from underneath the train. Wave after wave of the creatures leaped onto the street from underneath the long, hollow tunnel like cockroaches fleeing a hiding spot. I lost count after the third wave, but there had to be at least twenty of them.

A football field away, a group of men and women, along with a few children, were being escorted by a squad of Idrissia soldiers. The shades moved quickly, charging into the crowd of people, creating a swirling cloud of chaotic screaming and fighting. Celwyn had already closed at least half of the distance before stopping and resting the barrel of the rifle on his knee. He began releasing carefully aimed bursts of fire, targeting the shades as they became visible in the melee.

I arrived at his side, out of breath, with my wounded shoulder killing me. In front of me, all I saw was a confusing mass of screaming people running in every direction. The shades had once been people, so they still retained some semblance of clothing, albeit bloody and tattered. As they slashed their way through the crowd, it became impossible to tell the injured from the attackers. It was all just a loud, bloody blur of motion.

Away from the Tube, a few remaining soldiers tried to form a protective formation around the children and any others lucky enough to have avoided the first wave of assault. They huddled in the center of Broadway in a protective swath of sunlight.

The other soldiers fired at anything moving in the crowd, desperately trying to hit the fast-moving targets that were quickly decimating their ranks.

Celwyn took out a shade with a head shot from his rifle, and the others stopped moving and looked in our direction. One of the shades barked a string of guttural commands and half the attackers broke off from the main group and charged up Broadway, straight towards us.

Without pausing or looking in my direction, Celwyn shouted, "You can start shooting any time now!"

I had never shot an assault rifle. In fact, the first time I had ever shot a gun of any type was a few hours earlier in Saul's room. But I was a fast learner, especially when faced with monsters seeking to tear out my throat.

My rifle sputtered to life beside Celwyn. The noise of the two guns, working together, nearly deafened me. I kept it simple, aiming for the torso, hoping to slow them down. Celwyn consistently dropped shades with head shots, and for a moment I thought we made a good team.

But as the shades flew down the street at breakneck speed, I realized the math wasn't on our side. Celwyn stood and began slowly backtracking as he shot, buying a few precious seconds while seeking the protection of sunlight. We were thinning the shades' ranks, but the gap between us kept closing.

They would be on us in seconds and some would make it through our barrage of bullets.

I fought back the overwhelming urge to turn and run. Instead, I held my ground and kept shooting. "Celwyn, what do I do?"

"You fight, Mel. You fight until you can't fight anymore," he shouted.

Celwyn's rifle went silent then fell to his side, held in place by the sling. In its place, a sword appeared from a scabbard on his back.

Three shades survived the gunfire. That number dropped to two as the one in front immediately lost his head due to a vicious swing from Celwyn's blade. The next one lunged for my throat and knocked me backwards. As I fell, I angled my rifle upwards and held down the trigger. Bullets ripped into the black Idrissia uniform of the shade, disrupting its momentum and allowing me to twist away from the grasp of its outstretched arms.

I landed on my backside and sat up to see the injured shade crawling in fits and starts toward me, a dark substance pouring out onto the ground from gun shot wounds in its chest. I gathered my composure and aimed the rifle at its head and pulled the trigger. *Click...click.* Nothing happened.

Panic overtook me as the shade latched onto my closest foot with both hands, digging its claws into my ankles to counter my attempts to squirm away. I repeatedly kicked the face of what appeared to have been a woman at some recent point in the past, and let loose a loud primal scream. I'm not sure where it came from, but it felt good to release the pent-up emotion.

I dug in my pocket and grabbed the Leatherman knife. I flung it open and plunged the blade into the side of the shade's head, right above its ear. I jerked the tip out from the skull and repeated the process, again and again, until the shade stopped moving and I stopped screaming. I kicked the body into the sunlight and the skin began to smoke right before it dissolved.

While focused on my own existential threat to survival, I lost track of Celwyn. Once the tunnel vision wore off, and my heart slowed to a mere drum beat instead of a full symphony of percussion instruments, I noticed he wasn't doing so well in his own fight with the remaining shade.

The shade had to be at least three hundred pounds and loomed over Celwyn while they both struggled for control of the sword. Celwyn tugged on the hilt sticking out of the beast's chest while the shade rained down punches with hands that looked like cinder blocks. Celwyn's sword plunged all the way through the shade, emerging from the giant's back, right below the shoulder blade. The two danced around the landing platform, with Celwyn refusing to release his weapon and the shade fighting to keep the two of them out of the sun.

Celwyn caught my attention. "My pistol!"

I searched the ground and saw Celwyn's pistol lying a few feet away. I recovered it quickly and rose to my feet, struggling to aim at the shade.

Between grunts, Celwyn shouted again. "Point! Shoot!"

"If you want me to shoot, then stop moving!" I held the pistol in front of me, attempting to track the chaotic movements of the enormous shade as it fought with Celwyn.

Celwyn released his grip on the sword and threw a powerful front kick that landed inches below one of the shade's knees. Physics and gravity took over as the leg buckled and the shade staggered to catch its balance. In that moment, I finally had a stationary target. I aimed at its head and squeezed the trigger.

And missed.

Apparently, shooting accurately with a pistol is much harder than with a rifle. I kept pulling the trigger and kept missing until a bullet finally grazed the side of the shade's head. The impact dazed the monster and forced it to turn its attention towards me. Celwyn then snaked underneath and grabbed the hilt of his sword with both hands. He pulled it out cleanly from the shade's enormous chest with a loud sucking sound then promptly pivoted and sliced the blade cleanly across the shade's neck.

The giant dropped to its knees, still grasping at Celwyn with his arms. Celwyn wasted no time in attempting to separate its head, but it took two more strikes of his sword to cut through the monstrous muscles.

After finishing the job, he leaned on his sword, clearly exhausted, and faced me. "You still in one piece?"

"I think so," I replied.

We both turned to survey how the soldiers on Broadway had fared in their battle with the remaining shades. Mounds of bloodied bodies littered the ground, both shade and human, either dead or dying. Standing back, away from the carnage, a single remaining Idrissia soldier stood in front of two young girls and an old woman, the only survivors of the attack.

"Oh my god," I stuttered.

Celwyn muttered something unintelligible that struck me as cursing. "God won't help us," he replied. "I assure you, we're on our own."

He pointed to the pistol in my hand and I returned it. Next, he secured his sword in its scabbard and began making his way towards the survivors.

God won't help us. We're on our own.

I followed him.

CHAPTER FOURTEEN

CELWYN IMMEDIATELY BEGAN TALKING to the lone surviving soldier, while I walked over to the two young girls. Both of them had straight blonde hair that fell below their shoulders. The younger girl hid nervously behind the older one, who looked to be no more than ten years old. Both of their faces contained a look of terror that one should never see on a child.

My heart broke with each approaching step.

An old woman carried a bright yellow backpack with stripes like a bumblebee. She stood beside the girls, staring towards the dead bodies with a glazed look in her eyes.

"You're safe now," I said as I approached. "We're going to get you out of here."

The younger girl bolted from behind the older one and attached herself to my legs before bawling uncontrollably. I removed my helmet, knelt down, and held her tightly in an embrace. Her hair smelled like a pillowcase after a long nap, and for a moment I closed my eyes.

"What's your name?" I finally said, breaking the embrace.

The girl fought back her tears, took a few deep breaths, then sniffed twice before finally speaking. "Emma."

"Is that your sister, Emma?"

She turned around, then looked up at me again. "Yes."

The older girl walked towards me and stopped beside Emma. "My name is Alexandra, but you can call me Alex." She looked up at me with determination. "Our mom is dead. We're going with grandma to the Silver Castle Station. They say it's safe there." She looked around. "But I don't believe them."

My heart skipped a beat. "Alex. That's a...great name, Alex. I once knew someone—a special someone—with that name."

"Are you a soldier?" asked Emma. "Are you going to take us to the Station?"

I looked at the helmet in my hand and the rifle hanging on my hip, then turned back to the girls. "Yes. Yes, I am a soldier." The words felt like a lie, but the girl didn't need to know about my insecurities. And I had, in fact, just shot a gun, so it wasn't really a lie. The last question, however, proved much tougher to answer. So I chose to ignore it.

I glanced up at the grandmother. She hadn't moved. She remained fixed on the grim scene displayed in the street. I followed her gaze, and Celwyn motioned for me to join him.

"I'll be right back, girls. Stay here with your grandma."

Emma's lip began to quiver, but Alex grabbed her and whisked her away.

I met Celwyn and the other soldier, whom I now realized was a woman.

She stared at my shoulder, soaked with blood from the vampire fight in Saul's room. "Is that a bite?" She turned to Celwyn nervously. "What about her? You said we have to—"

Celwyn lied. "Not a bite. That was hours ago, and look at her. See? No gray skin. That's how you can tell."

He turned towards me. "Mel, there are a few still alive, and we need to...you know. And Gloria here doesn't think it's a good idea for the kids to be around when that happens." When Celwyn said the soldier's name, she nodded at me.

"I'll take them away for a little while, if you want." I looked around Broadway. "Maybe one of these buildings is open."

"No. No. You're not taking the girls anywhere. Gloria's taking them to the Station, and we'll do what needs to be done here once they're gone."

Gloria nodded.

"But, we're in Grid Six. That's a long way."

Gloria finally spoke. "There's a squad at Grid Five right on Broadway. Everything's secure behind that point, but the bastards are scared to come out here and get us, so we have to go to them."

I shook my head in disgust and motioned to Celwyn that I wanted to talk privately.

"Give us a minute," he said to Gloria.

As we walked away from Gloria, I peeked at Emma and Alex over my shoulder. Emma sat on the floor rummaging through the bumblebee backpack. The grandmother still seemed oblivious as to what had occurred.

"They're not going to make it," I whispered to Celwyn. "It's like a half mile to Grid Five."

"We don't know that. And besides, Paloma will have us both arrested on sight."

"What if we just go with them until we can see the other soldiers? Then we break away. It doesn't sound like they're going to come after us if it means going past Grid Five."

Celwyn rubbed the side of his face. "I can't risk it, Mel. I have to get these pictures back to the Knights. They have to know what happened here."

"But what about the girls?" I felt my voice getting louder. "I can't just *leave* them."

He walked further away and I followed. "There are over thirty thousand men, women, and children in this city, Mel. And they're all going to die."

"What are you talking about?" I hissed.

"There is no 'safe zone.' Paloma's consolidating control so he can tie up loose ends. Do you really think Idrissia is going to just let all of these people tell the world about how they were attacked by vampires in their brand new beautiful utopia?"

I didn't want to believe Celwyn. I didn't want to believe anyone could be capable of murdering children. "But that's mass murder. They wouldn't do that." I paused. "I mean, even if they wanted to do it, they would get caught. People would ask questions. How would Idrissia explain it?"

Celwyn flashed me a frustrated look. "C'mon, Mel. Don't be naive. Earthquake? Terrorist attack? Anything's better than vampires. The shades may have taken out the power on the medical floor, but they couldn't have disabled the entire Castle's power or jammed cell phones. Paloma's probably taken down all communications except for his radios. Think. Why would he do that?"

I looked back at Emma and Alex. I never had my own children, and it pained me every day. Now, I suddenly had these two beautiful girls, without a mother, looking to me for protection. I couldn't bear the thought of sending them away.

"We could take them with us," I said softly. "I can protect them."

"No, you can't. And neither can I." Celwyn grabbed my arm. "Listen to me. There are millions of little kids like that out in the world. You've seen what these monsters can do. Now imagine they're running loose in every major city in the world. We can stop that from happening. *You* can stop that from happening. But to do that, we have to make sacrifices."

My heart filled with rage. "Why should I listen to you? You're no better than Paloma. Remember what you said to me in the bar? If I didn't help you, your people would bring down the Castle and kill everyone in it?"

Celwyn shook his head in frustration. "That's different and you know it. I don't want *anyone* to die. I just risked my life to give these girls a chance to live one more hour, even if I don't even believe it's much of a chance."

He turned to Gloria and shouted. "Gather them up and get them over to Grid Five! I'll take care of the clean up!" He pulled out his pistol and loaded a new magazine into the grip before turning back to face me. "And you. Make a decision. Are you going to help me save the world? Or throw in the towel and play mother for a day, or whatever time you get, before Paloma kills them all?"

"You're a real asshole."

"Yeah, I know," he said sadly. "Fighting vampires will do that to you."

"I'm going to at least tell them goodbye."

Celwyn softened. "Don't be long."

I walked over to the two girls. Emma had a small yellow blanket in her hands that she had removed from the bumblebee backpack. "I guess you like yellow," I said to the young girl.

"It's her favorite color," Alex replied. She looked at me intently. "You're leaving us, aren't you?"

The words sliced through my heart. "Yes. I can't stay with you, but the soldier will take you to the safe zone. You'll be safe there."

Alex turned to Emma. "I told you she wasn't coming with us." The young girl looked down dejectedly.

"Do you know where your parents are?" I asked.

Emma looked up at Alex. The older girl grabbed her sister's hand before she spoke. "We were staying with Grandma and had to leave in the middle of the night. We don't know where they are."

"I'm sure they're waiting for you in the safe zone."

Emma brightened while Alex frowned at me.

"Yeah. I'm sure you're right," Alex replied. She bent down to help Emma tuck the blanket back into the bumblebee backpack, fully acting the part of a big sister. A protector.

Gloria approached and silently helped the grandmother collect the girls. Once that was done, the four of them began the journey down Broadway toward Grid Five, clustered tightly together with Gloria in the middle. They had barely made it a few yards when Emma stopped and turned, then waved her little hand at me to say goodbye. I smiled and returned the wave.

It didn't take long before Alex grabbed her little sister and twisted her arm to catch up to their grandmother, but I savored every second watching the girls. I imagined I would see Emma and Alex again, and that everything would be alright, but deep down, I feared Celwyn was right—I feared I would never see them again, and they would never leave this place.

And my heart sank.

When I could no longer see the gold tint of the Atrium's sunlight on the girls' hair, I turned to Celwyn. "They're far enough. Do what you need to do." I wiped the tears from my eyes with a sleeve from my scrubs and turned away from Celwyn's bloody business.

Behind me, I could hear him walking through the bodies lying on the ground and periodically firing off two shots from his pistol. After a few minutes, he joined my side.

"You lied to Gloria. You said I wasn't bit. I guess that means you're finally convinced you won't need to do that to me?"

Celwyn nodded. "I'm not going to kill you. And she didn't need to know you were bit. It would have just given her false hope. Some of the ones I killed were her friends—other soldiers—and they were already turning."

I was too tired to argue any further. The pain from my injured shoulder, and the exhaustion from a lack of sleep, left me almost delirious. The only thing I wanted to do was sit down and close my eyes.

"How far is your place?" I asked. "I'm running on fumes."

Celwyn began searching for a maintenance doorway to access the other half of the Maze. "We're close." He quickly located an entrance, kicked it a few times, then shot off the lock with his rifle.

Through the doorway, I saw the now-familiar pitch black nothingness of the Maze. Celwyn lowered the visor on his helmet and tapped the side.

I did the same to mine, bringing up the night vision's green glow.

"And then you can rest."

CHAPTER FIFTEEN

THE MAZE on the other side of the Atrium looked identical to the earlier section we crossed. Celwyn led the way across catwalks and down stairwells until we reached another maintenance door. I detected a faint source of light bleeding underneath, which offered a welcome sight.

"Home sweet home," Celwyn said. He placed his index finger on a small pad mounted on the door frame and I heard a clicking sound in the dark. He opened the door and we entered a single room apartment lined with cinder blocks, illuminated by LED lights hanging from the ceiling. The first thing he did was switch the lights off except the one hanging over the center of the room.

"Backup battery generator came on over night," he said. "It's getting low, and once it's done, we won't have any electricity." He pointed to the only other door in the room besides the one we used to enter. "Bathroom is there. I recommend a shower before you sleep. The water will probably be cold, but you need to get that wound clean before we patch it up."

I nodded. The thought of water running over my body, regardless of temperature, seemed intoxicating at this point. And Celwyn was right about the shoulder. It needed to be cleaned first, then sterilized before bandaging.

"You've got quite the bachelor pad," I joked. "Not what I would expect from a fancy lawyer."

Celwyn shot me a dirty look, then began removing his gear, starting with his helmet, followed by his rifle sling and sword. The pistol remained fixed in its place on his hip.

He placed his things on a table that lined one side of the small room, its surface already containing an assortment of guns, knives, and electronic gadgets I didn't recognize. Perpendicular to the table that doubled as an arsenal was a desk with a computer and six video monitors stacked in rows of three. One of the monitors displayed myself and Celwyn in the apartment, while the rest appeared to be fed by security cameras outside the apartment, each showing a different view of the surrounding Maze bathed in the same soft green glow as the helmets' night vision.

The only other pieces of furniture in the small, spartanly decorated room were an unmade bed along the wall to my left, and a metal dining table in the middle of the room with two industrial-looking chairs. Against the wall behind the dining table, a mini refrigerator sat on the floor, with a stainless steel microwave stacked on top.

Celwyn rummaged through a duffle bag thrown haphazardly under the arsenal table and produced a black t-shirt and pants. He threw them at me, along with a microfiber belt. "They're going to be big on you, but they're clean. And anything is better than that bright purple stuff you've got on now."

"Thanks." I took the clean clothes and entered the small bathroom. First, I removed the hodgepodge of medical supplies I had taken from the hospice and stashed in my pockets. My necklace with the small silver cross and my clothes were next.

Peeling the sticky, blood-caked scrubs from the wound on my shoulder felt like being stabbed.

With the benefit of lights and a mirror, I finally got a good look at the wound, and it wasn't as bad as I expected. The upper and lower indentations from the bite stood out clearly on my skin, and the surrounding area had already turned a darker shade of purple than my scrubs, but luckily the material had offered a layer of defense that had prevented the vampire's bite from sinking deep into the tissue. The teeth had managed to puncture the skin in a few places, but not deep enough to require stitches.

The wound hurt like hell and would probably leave a mean-looking scar, but I would be fine.

I turned the lever on the shower and prayed for hot water. After a few seconds, the water made it to lukewarm then stalled out on any further increase in temperature. I decided that beggars can't be choosers and dived under the stream of water. The powerful stream stung my shoulder initially, but after a bit of maneuvering, I found an angle that lessened the impact, and I just stood and enjoyed the feel of the tepid water on my tired body.

In my relaxation, I stared at the drain. I wondered if this would be my last shower. I wondered how I could possibly make it out of the Castle, given all that had happened.

And I wondered whether Emma and Alex were still alive.

With every passing moment, the warmth evaporated from the stream of water until the cold finally shocked me out of my zen state of worry. I jumped out of the shower and quickly dried myself off with a towel before suiting up in the pants provided by Celwyn. With the help of the belt, and some rolling up of the cuffs, I actually got them to fit.

Now came the hard part. I looped one bra strap over my shoulder and allowed the one for my wounded side to hang down over my arm. I stared at the supplies on the countertop and quickly realized it would be impossible for me to clean and bandage the wound with one hand.

I needed Celwyn's help.

My stomach turned over, and my heart raced. Somehow, the thought of walking out of the bathroom without wearing a top struck more fear into my heart than the prospect of fighting vampires. Of course, I knew it was silly and childish to be nervous, but that didn't change the way I felt. I took stock of the woman staring back at me in the mirror. Some would say I was attractive, and my curves had largely survived the onset of middle age without softening into flabbiness. I had always been strong, and the thought of not being able to run a marathon seemed tantamount to admitting life had passed me by—a fate I simply couldn't imagine.

I pulled my long black hair back into a ponytail and admired the image. If soldier-chic was a thing, I imagined this would be what it would look like. I quickly gathered the supplies on the countertop and paused when I reached for my necklace.

Deirdre's words filtered back into my head, challenging my dogged insistence on honoring a long-dead obligation. I could hear her yelling at me, *This man took you back to his apartment. He likes you! You shouldn't push him away.*

Did I like Celwyn, too? Sure, but I barely knew the man. I *needed* Celwyn to protect me, nothing more. Without him, I wouldn't last an hour alone. And if he felt a connection between us, I didn't see the harm in playing along, or more accurately, I no longer saw a benefit in pushing him away like I first did on the train.

I looked down at my wedding band, then back to the necklace. A new thought entered—a compromise of sorts. I slipped the wedding band over one end of the necklace, closed it, and placed it in my pocket. Close, but not forgotten.

"Coming out," I announced. "I need some help with the shoulder."

Celwyn rose from his seat in front of the surveillance system monitors and turned to face me. If he was surprised by my lack of clothing, he didn't show it. "Sit down at the table," he ordered. He followed me over with a small black bag in his hand.

"I've got what I need." I showed Celwyn the bandages and alcohol wipes I had taken from the hospice.

He chuckled. "My med kit is … better. Trust me. Just sit down, I've done this more times than I can count."

The metal chair felt like it was coated in ice as it pressed against my exposed back. I leaned forward and watched Celwyn remove a number of items from his black nylon fabric bag.

He moved expertly, removing a thin white package the size of a laptop computer then tearing off the end. He studied the bite mark on my shoulder for a few seconds then removed a bandage from inside the package. He cut the bandage in half with a pair of scissors from the bag, replaced the remaining piece inside the package, and resealed it by sliding a finger across the opening.

"You ready?" he asked.

I nodded. He placed a flesh-colored bandage across my shoulder, pressing it down firmly on both sides of my collar bone. Celwyn's hands lingered on my shoulder, holding the bandage in place. I felt a surge of adrenaline and the nervousness returned. I hadn't been touched by a man since my husband died, and his hands were strong.

He looked down at me and flashed a knowing grin. "This is the good stuff." He continued smiling as a warm gel seeped down into the abrasions on my shoulder, and the pain instantly subsided.

"Wow. I mean, *wow*. That feels great."

"Now, watch this." He removed another small silver packet from the medical pouch that had a lid on one end. He opened the lid and slowly dripped water over the edges of the bandage. The bandage immediately constricted, tightening against my shoulder like a second skin, making it nearly invisible.

Celwyn returned the packet to his medical bag and zipped it closed.

I touched the bandage with my fingers, rubbing around the edges, marveling at the smooth texture. "I guess I can finish getting dressed now?"

"That's up to you," he replied. "But I'm done."

I felt my face blush. "I think you've had quite enough of a show from me today." I lifted up my bra strap, then pulled the t-shirt from Celwyn over my head. It fit like a potato sack, so I tied up the ends into a knot slightly above my waist.

Celwyn walked slowly back to the chair at his desk, watching the screens for any sign of movement. "Get some sleep. When night falls, we are headed to the roof so I can send these pictures out on my satellite phone."

"Send them to who? And why are you now patching me up when a few hours ago you were threatening to put two bullets in my head? I think I deserve to know what's going on."

After an uncomfortable moment of silence, Celwyn turned around in his chair. "You're right, Mel. You deserve some answers." He looked away from me and ran his fingers through his hair, starting at his forehead, and ending at the base of his neck. "Especially since you survived a bite. You have no idea how special you are."

"Then tell me. How did I survive the bite?"

Celwyn stood up and began pacing. "No one really knows how or why, but a small percentage of people are naturally immune to the parasite—and I mean small. One of these monsters can rip out your throat, but it can't turn you."

He paused and looked me in the eye. "Or me. We're mother nature's defense to this evil scourge. The vampires think they're the apex predator, but they're wrong, Mel. They're very wrong. People like us—you and I—we're the hunters."

CHAPTER SIXTEEN

"ME? A VAMPIRE HUNTER? C'MON." I tried not to laugh at Celwyn. "I'm a forty-two-year-old hospice nurse. The only thing I hunt down are eyeglasses misplaced by dementia patients."

"Whether you accept the responsibility or not, it is what you are." He walked over to the arsenal table and removed a sword from the scabbard lying on top. "I'm a Knight of the Holy Order of Carpathia. Ordinary people like you and I have fought these monsters for thousands of years, first in the mountains of Romania, then across the world, wherever they run and hide to spread the parasite."

He leaned the blade of the sword against one arm and showed me the hilt, wrapped tightly in graying leather cord. The hilt ended in a pommel of metal engraved with the head of a wolf atop a flowing serpent tail.

"This was my grandfather's sword. It's a Scottish claymore, and it was given to me after my training. I was twenty-five when the Knights found me. Like you, I laughed at the idea that vampires existed, and that I had some role to play in fighting them. But seeing the truth, like you have now seen, makes an impression that's hard to forget. And I took up the call, just like my grandfather. It's kind of a family thing."

Celwyn's voice broke as he talked about his grandfather.

"Was your father a Knight, too?" I asked.

"No," he replied softly. "No, he was not." He placed the sword down. "I never even knew him. My mother dropped me off at an orphanage in Wales when I was a baby. I think she wanted for me to avoid this life—for obvious reasons. She's dead now, and I still ended up as a Knight."

I pointed to the wolf's head on the pommel of the sword. "What's the deal with the wolf?"

He paused. "It's the Draco – the 'dragon wolf.' The symbol for the Order. It's a reminder that Knights hunt in packs, like wolves." He traced his hand down the blade of the sword. "Vampires are very dangerous, Mel. Impossible for one Knight to kill. You learn to fight as a team, or you die quickly."

"So where is the rest of your pack—your team?"

Celwyn scratched his chin and sighed. "I'm here for…personal reasons."

As he talked, I noticed movement out of the corner of my eye on one of the surveillance monitors sitting on the desk behind him. A figure came into view on the top right screen, peeking over the top of a metal stairway. In the dark, I thought I saw a tuft of white hair.

"What are you looking—" Celwyn stopped mid-sentence, then whirled around and stared at the monitors. The figure was gone.

"Did you see something?" he asked.

"No. I thought, maybe, something was there, but I looked and it was gone."

He turned and studied me for a moment. "Did you feel something?" he asked. "Maybe a sense of unease in your stomach, a tingling on your neck? Anything like that?"

"I don't think so. Why are you asking me that?"

"Because hunters can sense shades. A vampire is harder to sense because the parasite is weaker, and under control, but even then you can feel them if they're looking to feed."

"Cool…so you're telling me I have spidey sense for vampires?"

He looked at me blankly, confused by my question. "I don't understand."

"Never mind," I answered. "It's a comic book thing."

We both stared at the video monitors in silence, watching for movement on the surveillance cameras pointed at the Maze outside the apartment. I finally relented and looked at my watch. It was nearly noon and I had accumulated only four hours of sleep in the last forty eight hours. "You mind if I take the bed?"

Celwyn remained fixed on the monitors. "No. Go ahead. I'll stay up and keep an eye on things." He sat down at the desk and settled into a comfortable position.

I thought for a moment. "I trust you, you know. You can lie down in the bed, too."

Celwyn turned. "Thanks. I appreciate the offer, but if I lie down I'll fall asleep. And one of us needs to stay awake."

My exhausted self didn't have to be told twice, so I crawled into the narrow twin bed and pulled the wrinkled comforter up to my ears. Within seconds, the warm darkness of sleep took hold. As I drifted off, I couldn't help but return to the familiar image on the surveillance camera.

It couldn't be Saul, could it? Perhaps it was my guilty conscience playing tricks on me for lying to Celwyn about killing my friend. Or maybe fear that Saul, or whatever monster he had become, was following us, waiting to attack us the moment we set foot outside.

My sleep was restless and short.

Far too short.

———

A CRACKLE from Celwyn's helmet radio brought me out of what seemed to be a ten-minute nap. "How long have I been sleeping?" I blinked repeatedly, trying to keep my eyes open.

"You've been out for seven hours. It will be dark soon and we need to get up top." He moved to the arsenal table and began placing items into a backpack. "How's the shoulder?"

I slipped a hand through my shirt to touch the bandage and confirmed everything remained in place. The elastic remained tight, and if I didn't know better, I would have thought I had nothing but a scratch covered with a band-aid. I still felt no pain from the wound.

"It feels…it feels great, actually."

"Good. Don't mess with it, even if it itches. In a couple of days, that bandage will disintegrate and you will barely have a scar."

"I love your optimism," I replied as I rolled onto my feet. More sounds of talking buzzed from the helmet sitting on Celwyn's desk. "What's going on?"

"They're getting reinforcements tonight. Helicopters are flying in more troops for Paloma, so we will have company up on the roof. We'll need to be careful."

"What about the people in the city? Is everyone safe?" I kept the conversation to the moment at hand, but something in Celwyn's voice told me he and Paloma had a history. A complicated one.

Celwyn looked at me. "You mean the girls?"

"Yeah, them and everyone else."

He shook his head. "I don't know. Best I can tell, after the attack last night, they moved as many people as they could back into the first five grids and set up a defensive perimeter. They kept the people moving and are now holding only the first grid."

"That's a lot of people in such a short space. They must be packed like sardines."

Celwyn resumed loading his backpack. "There aren't that many people left, Mel. Maybe a few thousand at most from what I hear on the radio. Most of them didn't make it behind the perimeter before Paloma's people retreated."

I held out hope that Emma and Alex had made it to Grid Five before the soldier's retreat. I knew deep down the girls were still alive. I couldn't explain it, but I felt it. "The girls made it," I said defiantly. "Wherever Paloma has the survivors from the city, that's where they will be."

"I'm sure you're right," Celwyn said. "I'm sure they're fine." He affixed the scabbard of his sword to a special slot on his backpack and slung it over his shoulders. "It's time to go."

Celwyn walked towards me, holding several items he removed from the arsenal table. "I have a few things for you," he said. He clipped a small device like his on the front of my shirt, securing it on the collar just below my neck.

"Why do I need one of those? The power is out."

"If Paloma turned the electricity off, he can turn it back on. And if that happens, we don't want him to see us with all those cameras." Celwyn leaned over and hooked a small cannister of pepper spray onto the side of my belt. He smiled at me. "And I know you like this stuff."

"One more thing," he said. "Where's that knife of yours?"

I removed the Leatherman from my pocket and showed it to Celwyn. He took it from my hand and slipped it into a sheath that he strapped to the opposite side of my belt from the pepper spray. He stepped back to look at me. "There. Do you still feel like you're *just* a nurse?"

"Actually, yes," I replied.

He picked up my rifle and helmet and handed them to me. "How about now? Still a nurse?"

"Yep."

He stomped away. "You're hopeless. By the way, make sure that rifle is loaded. There are extra magazines on the table."

I fumbled with a magazine until Celwyn eventually took pity and showed me how to load the rifle. He then removed the magazine and placed it on the table.

"Now you do it."

This time, I loaded it correctly, and he gave me a nod of approval.

"Before we go back out there, there are some things you need to know. First, shades are pack animals. They follow a leader, either the strongest of the pack or a vampire if one is around. If you can take out the leader, they'll be confused, which gives you the advantage. You can't think of them as people, or you'll hesitate." His eyes steeled with resolve. "That's not someone's mother or father. It's not someone who can be saved. They're infected. They're monsters."

"How do you know...I mean, how do you know they can't be saved? You said that some can overcome the parasite, take control again. What if they didn't become vampires? What if they returned to being a normal person?"

Celwyn shook his head. "You can't deny the blood lust. Some of the infected, with time and effort, may come to control the parasite as vampires, but ultimately the infected need blood to survive. The parasite consumes its host's own red blood cells from the inside, devouring them and excreting powerful hormones that speed up the metabolism to provide accelerated healing. It's a vicious circle of hunger pains and the dopamine reward that follows a feeding. The host *must* feed on fresh blood. Without it, both parasite and host will die."

I slung the rifle over my shoulder and followed Celwyn toward the door of his apartment. "So how many vampires have you killed?"

Celwyn stopped. "None. Never had to fight one before today, just shades. I was trained to run from a vampire unless we had the numbers. If you can't run, cheat. Don't fight one straight up. It's suicide."

"What? But I thought that's what you do? You're a vampire killer."

"There hasn't been a new vampire made in my lifetime, Mel. At least not one that was officially known to the Knights. The ones already alive are protected by the Accords so long as they remain hidden and follow the rules. They're allowed to feed, and sometimes things get … messy. If a shade gets created through a vampire's indiscretion, then the Knights put it down. And we stay busy."

Celwyn's face darkened. "But the most important rule—the one that is punishable by death—is making new vampires."

"But why would you let the vampires live at all? Why not destroy the parasite completely? I don't understand."

"The Accords ended the last war with vampires. You probably know of it as the Black Plague, but the truth was buried. One hundred million people died, and most of the vampires, too. The Catholic Church brokered a truce to stop the killing, creating a delicate balance, and it's held up for seven hundred years...until broken by Idrissia." Celwyn shook his head and his eyes narrowed. "I can't imagine what the world would look like if hundreds of new vampires were unleashed. Do you now understand why it's so important for me to share what we saw in that lab?"

I nodded slowly and Celwyn began moving. Truthfully, I didn't understand it at all. Every time I observed proof of something said by Celwyn, and thought I might actually begin to understand what was happening, a new more fantastic revelation slapped me back into the realm of uncertainty. I didn't want to believe that I would have to fight my way through vampires to escape the Silver Castle, but I had accepted that reality. Now, Celwyn expected me to believe in a war I had never heard of. The stakes were even higher, and a disaster of biblical proportions could occur if he didn't do his part to stop it.

How did I get myself into this mess?

I thought briefly about Emma and Alex then willed my feet into movement. If I had to save the world, so be it. But I would start with those two little girls.

CHAPTER SEVENTEEN

I FOLLOWED Celwyn out the door of the apartment, returning again to the darkness of the Maze. We turned on the night vision in our helmets and crouched down low, scanning the stairways and scaffolding in every direction for signs of movement.

Nothing stirred.

"Follow me," Celwyn commanded. "We've got a long way up."

I generally consider myself to be in good shape, but nothing can prepare you for climbing forty stories of stairs, in the dark, all the while constantly wondering if that sound you just heard was the building settling or the approach of a deadly monster. Both my knees and my brain were frazzled by the time I made it halfway to the top. Pure adrenaline and a fear of being left behind somehow kept me moving steadily upwards.

Celwyn, of course, never complained. He kept moving ahead, waiting for me at each new level while he stared out into the Maze. Luckily, in the vastness of the Castle, two people moving in one of the hundreds of dark stairwells would be easy to miss. We were counting on it. But the same wouldn't be true on the roof. There, we would be much more exposed.

"I assume you have a plan once we reach the roof? I asked.

"I do."

"Care to share it?" I looked up at the number on the wall as I marched past a doorway marking a new level. Forty three. We had passed the upper Tube level, and were only three away from the roof.

"I clear the door. Send an encoded message on my sat phone. You wait here. I'll be back in five minutes tops."

"What? You want me to wait here? By myself?" I wheezed to keep up with Celwyn as his pace increased.

He stopped at the next level and turned to face me. "I'll be right back, and you and I will both get out of here. Trust me. I *won't* leave you." He took a few steps forward and slowly poked his head around the staircase, looking upwards. "But I can move quicker if I'm by myself. And I don't know what's on the other side of that door to the roof."

Part of me was happy to wait in the stairwell, but the other part of me wondered what I would do if Celwyn didn't return. "Look, I...I want to come with you. An extra gun might help. And let's be honest —if you don't make it, I'm not going to make it, either."

Celwyn shook his head. "I appreciate the offer. I really do. But this is going to need to be quick. If I'm not back in five minutes, you have my permission to come save me." He smiled. "But I promise I won't need saving."

Before I could react, he dashed up the stairs, taking them two at a time. Within a few seconds, he disappeared through the door at the top of the stairwell leading outside to the roof. I sat down on the concrete floor, took a deep breath, and made a mental note of the time on my watch.

I sat in the dark, listening for the sound of the door opening, signaling Celwyn's return from the roof.

The minutes ticked off.

I stared at the small screen on my wrist and listened. I heard nothing except my own breathing, still hurried from the rapid vertical ascent of the Castle's full height.

Five minutes came and went, then six.

At seven, I stood and began pacing. Celwyn was in trouble, otherwise he would have returned. If I followed him, I would likely suffer the same fate. *Should I wait in the relative safety of the stairwell, or risk my life out in the open on top of the roof where I would be a sitting duck?*

At this point, dying seemed to be the most likely result no matter which decision I made. Maybe I could make a difference if I went to find Celwyn. Doing nothing would undoubtedly doom us both.

I summoned enough courage to begin moving up the stairs. I reached the top landing and reached for the door handle. Before I could open the door, it flew open and Celwyn rushed inside, panting for breath.

"You said five minutes!" I hissed. "You're late. I was about to go looking for you."

"I know," he whispered. "But we have a problem." He showed me his satellite phone. The screen said 'no signal' in small letters at the top. "I can't send a message."

"I don't understand. Is the phone not working?"

"That's the thing. The phone is fine. It's being jammed. I checked a couple of different spots, and it was the same. I can't pick up a satellite even though there isn't a cloud in the sky." Celwyn seemed deep in thought. "I don't understand why Paloma would choke off his own communications. He has to be using satellite to communicate with whoever is sending those helicopters." He stroked the stubble on his chin and placed the phone back into a pocket on the side of his pants.

"So what now?"

He grabbed my hand. "Mel, my people *have* to know what happened here. We need to find somewhere on the roof that isn't jammed so I can send that message. I can't leave you here, so that means you have to come with me."

"Lead the way. I didn't like sitting here, anyway."

Celwyn nodded and placed a finger in front of his lips to signal that I needed to be quiet. He opened the door and stepped out into the night air.

I followed.

———

WE EMERGED onto the roof in the middle of Idrissia's elaborate rooftop garden. I breathed a sigh of relief once I realized I knew this place. I had run through this garden on the night of my attack.

Trees and shrubs of every size and type surrounded us, arranged in symmetrical patterns simulating an English garden. A vast white gazebo loomed in front of us, a large hollow structure casting shadows from the light of the moon.

To our left, the garden eventually turned into orchards and fields of corn. I knew this path. To our right, bright lights from the industrial half of the roof twinkled in the distance, and I heard the sounds of equipment and voices.

Celwyn pointed away from the lights. "That way." He carefully made his way between hedge rows and waist-high stone walls, periodically stopping to check for a signal on his phone. We made our way through groves of fruit trees, eventually reaching the acres of corn that would forever be a part of my nightmares.

"You sure about this?" I asked.

"We need to stay hidden," he replied. "Come on." He disappeared into the corn field.

I followed Celwyn for half of the length of the building and then back again, keeping ourselves hidden from the occasional patrol of Idrissia soldiers. It quickly became apparent that Celwyn was moving in a grid pattern, systematically testing every inch of the rooftop for satellite reception.

Eventually, we made it back to the gazebo in Grid Six. There, as I crouched in the shadows, a look of frustration crossed Celwyn's face.

"Where to now?" I asked.

"I have to try the other side of the roof," he replied. He didn't seem happy with the idea.

"But it's covered with soldiers over there. Someone will see you."

"I know, I know. I'm thinking." Celwyn sat beside me in the gazebo, staring up at the stars through the open sides of the circular structure.

We just sat there silently for several minutes, staring at the sky. It felt good to just relax. For a brief moment, I forgot about the danger and death surrounding us. I moved closer to Celwyn.

The deep blues and purples of the Milky Way cut a jagged line across the starry night sky. "You know," I said. "It's amazing how much more you can see in the sky out here in the desert versus the city. I had forgotten about the colors. They're beautiful."

Celwyn sighed. "You should see the stars at the Kogaion Keep. It's in the mountains of Carpathia and it's a sight to see. If you choose to be a Knight, you could go there with me some day."

"Nothing is ever going to be the same is it? I mean, even if I somehow make it out of here alive, I can't just go back to being a nurse, can I?"

"Nope," Celwyn said softly. "You can't."

"Yeah. I figured you would say that." I paused. "I wish we could sit here and pretend that I was still just a nurse, and you were really a lawyer."

Celwyn finally broke a smile to match the one on my face.

In my mind I added one more unsaid wish. I wished we could pretend there were no vampires, but I left that thought unsaid. I feared that speaking the name of the horror roaming the Castle might bring them upon our hidden paradise and ruin my brief moment of peace.

I sat quietly with Celwyn and felt the warmth from his body next to mine. We drank in the beauty of the lights from the thousands of galaxies encircling our planet. Then, one of those lights moved. Then another, and another.

"Helicopters," Celwyn said. "Paloma's reinforcements. That might be the distraction I need to get closer and see if I can get a satellite. They have to have comms over there."

"Reinforcements are good, right? Maybe Paloma can get things under control."

"We can't trust Paloma," Celwyn said flatly.

"Why?"

Celwyn rose to a crouched position and watched the lights approach the roof of the Castle. "Can't explain now. Wait here. I won't go far. Just need to get out from underneath whatever is jamming my signal."

The noise from the three helicopters increased exponentially as they approached. The *thwup thwup thwup* sound of the rotors seemed to be coming from right on top of us, and I could make out the silhouette of the helicopters against the stars as they approached the far side of the Castle. The rooftop was now lit up like a mall parking lot from the lights pointed downward from the helicopters, and I could see crowds of soldiers in the distance waiting to greet the landing air craft.

Before Celwyn could move from beside me, a loud whistling noise added to the whirring of rotor blades, and something rushed overhead through the sky. The nearest helicopter exploded into a fiery mid-air inferno before it reached the Castle. Robbed of its momentum, the ball of fire and mangled steel plummeted downward to the desert floor, landing with a thunderous boom.

The remaining two helicopters jerked away from their trajectory towards the Castle and began to gain altitude.

Celwyn turned and stared past me into the dark sky. "Someone else is up there."

"Who?"

"That's a very good question. And I don't have that answer, but I do have my distraction." He turned and bolted into the darkness towards the soldiers.

CHAPTER EIGHTEEN

I BRIEFLY TRIED to track Celwyn's progress as he dashed between the shadows on the far side of the roof, carefully inching towards the war zone opposite my safe hiding place in the garden. Machine gun fire overhead quickly changed my mind, forcing me to duck down out of sight inside the security of the gazebo. After a moment, I peeked over the edge of the railing to look for Celwyn, but he had already disappeared into the chaos.

Above me in the skies surrounding the Castle, two helicopters lit up like fireflies darted and weaved to evade gunfire coming from an unknown combatant. Without the lights from the landing aircraft, the rooftop again plunged into darkness, with the only illumination coming from rifle flashes from Paloma's soldiers, shooting randomly into the sky, hoping to hit whatever attacked the reinforcements attempting to land.

A *whoosh* sound behind me signaled the release of another missile. It whistled over the Castle towards the helicopters attempting to land, but this time they were prepared. One executed a steep dive beneath the roof line of the Castle, quickly taking the helicopter out of my sight. The other turned sharply and climbed into the sky. The target-locked missile attempted to follow the diving helicopter, but it wasn't as nimble. Before the projectile could clear the building and turn toward its target lurking below, it smashed into a communications tower jutting upward from the roof of the Castle .

The tower broke from its mooring in a fiery explosion and careened over with a thundering crash. In the orange glow, I could see soldiers running across the roof, desperately trying to avoid being crushed. Those lucky enough to get clear of the falling tower's path took cover behind anything they could find—rooftop refrigeration units, crates of equipment, and raised maintenance doorways—and all vainly searched the skies for the source of the attack.

Blinding lights appeared at the far edge of the building. The diving helicopter rose from its hiding place, its pilot no longer using the Castle as a shield from the hidden attacker. It made a quick jerking movement forward until it hovered squarely over the rooftop, then it dropped like a stone, landing so roughly that it bounced twice and skidded before slowing down. The rotors never stopped turning, and at least fifty soldiers poured out of open doors on each side. Within seconds of it being emptied, machine gun fire from the sky riddled the rooftop and the helicopter abruptly resumed flight, retreating from the Castle.

The other helicopter sought to copy the successful tactic employed by its landing partner and spiraled downward from above the Castle, descending in a corkscrew pattern.

It didn't make it.

Another aircraft materialized out of the darkness above the Castle, this one much larger than the two helicopters. It resembled an airplane in that it had wings, but each side extension contained two rotors. The rotors made almost no noise, and only the outline of the plane could be seen against the stars. At point-blank range, a missile hissed from below one of the plane's wings, then, as abruptly as it had appeared, the aircraft disappeared again into the night.

The missile found its mark and the descending helicopter disintegrated into red hot pieces of metal that rained down on the rooftop. Smoke and streaking meteors of falling debris filled the sky. Most of the shrapnel fell on the soldiers, but the tail of the helicopter separated cleanly and screamed directly towards the gazebo where I hid.

I ran.

I sprinted out the open side of the gazebo, aiming for a large concrete fountain with a life-size statue of Poseidon holding a trident. I dove for cover behind the holding pool encircling the statue as the tail rotor of the helicopter, still spinning, sliced through the wooden gazebo. The entire structure collapsed in a cloud of smoke and dust that covered the flying tailpiece.

With the gazebo destroyed, I now had a direct line of sight towards the other half of the roof. Small fires burned everywhere, marking impact strikes from the downed helicopter. Pockets of smoke slowly filtered across my line of vision. The gunshots stopped, and I heard something extraordinary, a sound so foreign that I almost didn't know how to react.

Silence descended on the roof.

It was not a peaceful kind of silence. It was that nervous, uncertain kind of quiet that precedes the arrival of something calamitous.

I waited behind the concrete fountain, listening to the flowing water, but the sound did nothing to ease my growing fear. Celwyn was out there somewhere. He had left me again, and this time he might be dead, killed by a bullet or the barrage of deadly debris that had rained down only moments earlier. With the gazebo destroyed, he wouldn't even know where to find me in the dark.

I started weighing scenarios in my mind, and none of them ended up with the two of us escaping together from the roof.

In front of me on the rooftop, rifles began flashing again, and the steady sound of machine gun fire broke the silence. My stomach filled with butterflies, and a shiver of cold air hit me so hard it nearly knocked me on my backside. It was the same sense I felt when attacked in the hospice, but this time the feeling was stronger. Much stronger.

Above me, the airship appeared again, and a swirling crosswind swept through the garden along with the noise of powerful engines. Its monstrous shape blotted out the stars as the ship passed overhead so closely that it seemed I could reach above my head and touch its belly.

Without any lights, it navigated straight towards the soldiers' positions and began strafing the rooftop with machine gun fire. The soldiers returned fire in my direction, and I heard the thumps of bullets impacting the concrete barrier protecting me from the melee.

The airship turned its wings to face the far side of the roof and released another missile with a loud hissing sound. It streaked towards a cluster of rifle flashes and, within seconds, another fiery explosion rocked the night, this one accompanied by the screams of the dying. A soldier, bathed in flames, ran from the impact site and dived off the rooftop.

Ropes descended from the airship while it continued to strafe the positions held by Paloma's soldiers. Caped figures dressed in black effortlessly slid down the ropes and dropped silently onto the top of the roof. Their backs were turned to me, but I could see them clearly in the airship lights. Each wore a flowing black cape over body armor, with a winged helmet and a curved sword hanging by their side. None of them carried a rifle or gun that I could see.

The feeling of cold returned, stronger than ever, and I knew at that moment that Paloma's army would lose this fight. These were vampires. Powerful vampires like Celwyn had described.

The initial wave of armored vampires fanned out across the width of the roof and found cover. Each remained in place, staring forward, studying the battlefield while the airship above them continued to exchange gunfire with Paloma's soldiers.

They were waiting for something. But what?

After a few long moments, another figure dropped from the airship, this time without using the ropes. All I saw was a blur of motion, then I felt the ground beneath me shake when the vampire's feet hit the rooftop. This one, taller than the others, wore the same black cloak with body armor underneath.

I turned away and hid in fear behind the fountain. Expecting Celwyn to avoid being captured or killed by Paloma's forces seemed impossible, but avoiding an army of vampires on top of it? I had to be realistic. Celwyn wasn't coming back. I was on my own.

Loud sounds of cheering erupted from Paloma's soldiers in the distance. I peeked up over the side of the cement holding pool just in time to see a rocket streak across the rooftop and hit one of the wings of the dark airship. The two rotor encasements exploded, and the ship instantly lurched into a counterclockwise spin caused by the imbalance of propulsion. The bulky plane rolled over on its damaged side until the other wing pointed nearly straight into the sky. The airship tried to rise away from the building, but the damage was too severe. The airship continued its death spiral, corkscrewing under its own weight into the rooftop until nothing remained but a crumpled, smoking mass of metal.

The cheers from the other side of the roof intensified, then finally subsided.

The vampires remained quiet and a silent standoff ensued, each waiting on the other side to make a move.

The leader of the vampires arose from behind a mound of debris left by the crashed airship. He loosed his sword, pointed it into the air and yelled a hideous sounding war cry in the same guttural language I had last heard from Saul while he lay in his hospital bed after the attack from the female vampire.

The words boomed out into the night and seemed to electrify the air around me. The feeling of dread returned, this time accompanied by a dull buzzing feeling on my neck that slowly intensified.

The leader shouted the words again, this time even louder, rising and falling in tone, then rising again into a shrieking crescendo that sounded as if it was part of an unholy mass.

The buzzing grew even stronger, and I felt an overpowering sense of dread. Something bad was about to happen, and I instinctively knew that I needed to run away. Now.

With the vampires focused in the opposite direction on Paloma's soldiers, I slinked back towards the maintenance entrance Celwyn and I had used to access the roof. I opened the door and listened. Below me, I heard the pounding of feet on the metal stairs. I peeked over the railing and saw movement in the stairwell several stories below me.

Shades.

Quickly, I ducked through the door, back onto the roof, and exhaled sharply.

My heart sank. My way out was blocked, and there was no time to find another exit.

Dammit, where is Celwyn?

I scanned the half of the roof that wasn't a fiery war zone, looking for an adequate hiding place. I groaned as I realized my best option was the last place I wanted to be trapped alone in the dark—the cornfield.

By the time I made my way into the maze of six-foot-tall stalks of corn, I heard the maintenance door open and slam against the frame. The sounds of shoes hitting the pavement could be heard on either side of the field. A crowd of shades rushed by me towards the vampire leader and the buzzing feeling intensified to the point it almost knocked me down.

I knelt down in the dark and did my best to keep my body from sticking out into the neat, orderly rows plotted throughout the field. Luckily, in the dark, the floppy green leaves from the corn stalks offered a substantial amount of cover.

The staccato sounds of machine gun fire erupted in earnest. The battle had started and I had no idea what was happening, or how I would ever get off the roof. Even if I could somehow escape, without Celwyn I had no plan. And no hope.

Another explosion rocked the rooftop, and I felt the vibration of the building through the dirt. That was a big one.

In the distance, I saw flames shoot up from the rooftop into the sky. The gunfire briefly paused, then started again. Part of me wondered if Paloma actually stood a chance against the overwhelming numbers controlled by the vampire leader.

Although I was probably dead either way, I decided my best chance was to root for Paloma. Human beings could be reasoned with—they at least felt compassion. Vampires were nothing but killers.

As I tried my best to interpret the sounds of warfare around me and extrapolate them into clues as to the odds of Paloma defeating the vampires, I heard a rustling noise. Instinctively, I made myself small, melting into the surrounding corn stalks.

To my left, I heard a crunching sound, the distinct sound of feet trampling the dead leaves littering the ground within the field. I remained still, and heard the crunching noise again, this time moving closer.

Something or someone had found me.

I hoped it was Celwyn, but I had to face reality. I pulled the pocket knife out from its sheath on my belt. Firing a rifle would give away my position, but the knife would be quiet. A shade had ambushed me once before from this cornfield, and I wasn't going to let that happen again.

I moved.

At first slowly, then quickly, I made my way deeper into the middle of the cornfield. I crunched my way across the ground, then stopped and listened. The crunching noises followed me. I changed direction and circled around the source of the noise. I paused and waited until I heard the noises again, then smiled. The noises now came from beside me, not behind me.

I remained in place and waited, knowing my pursuer had lost my direction. When I heard the crunching noises moving away from me, I began to rapidly move in the same direction. Now, I was the pursuer.

Please be Celwyn. Please be Celwyn. I held out hope he had found me, but I didn't believe it. My grip on the knife tightened.

I jogged through the cornfield, zeroing in on my adversary, but the noise no longer moved away from me. The crunching noise grew louder and was headed straight towards me. Any element of surprise was gone. I slowed and raised my knife, ready to confront whatever stalked me.

A figure emerged from the corn stalks, walking calmly into the open row in my path.

It had weathered gray skin and moved with a speed and agility beyond any human being. It was undoubtedly a shade.

But I knew this one. It had a tuft of curly white hair on each side of its head.

Saul.

CHAPTER NINETEEN

I RAISED my knife and dug my boots into the soft ground, bracing for an attack. Saul stared at me quietly from ten yards away, then slowly walked towards my position. I began wrapping my mind around the fact that this time I might have to actually kill my friend. And that perhaps I should not have ignored Celwyn's warning.

Saul's hospital gown was gone, replaced with loose fitting jeans and a black t-shirt sporting the Idrissia logo on its sleeve. He appeared taller than I remembered, and muscles bulged against the fabric of his shirt. As he inched closer, I could see that the wrinkles in his face had smoothed and the liver spots were gone. Other than the pallid gray color of his skin, Saul looked healthy and strong, like a much younger version of the dying man I knew.

He stopped before reaching me and I finally saw his eyes. Instead of the clear blue I remembered, they were now a flat black. But in the center of the lifeless black orbs, a small patch of light sparkled in the darkness. He winced and forcibly began to enunciate words as if the sound of each one caused great pain to produce.

At first, the words were garbled. Saul shook his head then tried again. "Melanie…unsafe." He looked around and waved his hands. "Father has called…Everyone will come."

I shook my head in confusion. Saul was talking. He wasn't trying to kill me. He wanted to help me.

But his words didn't make sense.

"The *father* is here—on the roof?" I asked. Father? What did that mean?

Saul nodded affirmatively, preferring to communicate without the burden of speaking.

My mind slowly began to piece together the meaning of Saul's message. The vampire leader who landed on the roof somehow had the ability to call others of his kind to help in his fight against Paloma's forces. The shades in the stairwell and on the rooftop surrounding the corn field were responding to his call.

Every shade in the Castle was coming. All of them. Right on top of me.

My mind raced. Against those numbers, I didn't stand a chance, even with help from Celwyn. Hiding seemed like the only smart option, but what if one spotted me? Once any of them knew I was here, they would surround and kill me easily.

I looked at Saul. He had somehow found me in the chaos and understood what was happening. But could I trust him? Was this still Saul?

I took a deep breath. "Saul—what do I do?"

He struggled to spit out words, determined to communicate. "You. Cannot. Stay. Here." Each time he spoke, he gained confidence, and the words became less pained. "Follow me now."

I paused, unsure whether to follow. "Are you...still Saul?" I asked.

The old man nodded. "Yes. One more midnight."

That was good enough for me.

He set out through the rows of the cornfield, leading me towards the far end of the rooftop, away from the raging battle between the vampires and Paloma's forces. My heart pounded and my chest heaved as I struggled to match Saul's pace. Only days ago the old man couldn't make it across his hospital room without a walker. Now he sprinted across the ground like a deer.

Eventually, after covering at least a mile in the dark, we reached the end of the field, and Saul paused to stick his head out from between the stalks of corn. I stopped behind him and placed my hand upon his shoulder. His skin felt hot to the touch, even through the fabric of the black t-shirt, but there was none of the dampness indicating sweat.

Saul jerked away his shoulder and turned towards me. "Please keep your distance, Melanie. I am...in control...of the hunger, but it still...it burns inside me. I fear what it might make me do."

I nodded my head in agreement and took a step backwards. Saul disappeared as he left the protection of the corn field, stepping out into the open air of the rooftop. I pushed the floppy leaves in front of me to the side and joined him.

Rows of small bushy plants stretched the remainder of the way to the northernmost edge of the Castle's rooftop, taking the place of the tall stalks of corn behind us. The sounds of gunfire continued unabated, muffled by the distance we had traveled. To my right, near the perimeter trail, a doorway marked one of the many maintenance passages into the Maze below us that were spread across the roof.

The door hung open and a mass of gray-fleshed shades surged forward to join the crowd already formed on the perimeter trail. The shades streaked alongside our position back towards the call of their master, oblivious to Saul and myself standing still in the field.

Suddenly, my head snapped back and my feet flew forward. I screamed in terror and surprise. I knew it would give away our position, but I couldn't help it.

A powerful force pulled on my ponytail and I struggled to gain my footing as the night sky spun in circles and my body flopped around in the dirt. As quickly as it started, I felt the hold on my hair loosen and I found myself lying on my stomach, face down in the dirt. A powerful hand lifted me up by my shoulder, helping me to my knees before loosening its grip.

"Get up," Saul hissed. Behind him, the dead body of a shade lay on the ground, its neck broken and missing an arm. "They're coming."

I spit dirt out of my mouth and stood up, angry at myself for letting down my guard. The anger turned into determination and I chambered a round in my rifle. If I died tonight, at least some of these monsters would die with me.

The horde of shades streaking towards the vampire's call for aid had stopped, distracted by my scream. To my left, another handful of shades had also appeared, apparently the source of the one who grabbed me from behind.

We were now surrounded.

Saul divided his attention amongst both groups, turning his head from side to side. Without breaking his focus on the shades, he whispered instructions. "Prepare to use your rifle and move towards the open door."

A tall male shade missing a shirt stepped forward from the crowd on our right and let loose a guttural shout. Saul barked back a menacing response in the same language. The two stared coldly at each other, like two starving predators circling a dead carcass.

Behind us, the other group of shades surged forward, jumping over plants and kicking up fresh black dirt. I turned, raised my rifle, and squeezed the trigger in short bursts as Celwyn had taught me, aiming for the torsos. The shades weren't very smart and did little to avoid the barrage of metal projectiles hurled in their direction. I dropped all six of them before they could get close enough to be a threat.

A wave of confidence built inside me. I was actually getting good at this.

While I cleared the shades to my left, Saul engaged the alpha shade on the right. The two locked arms, wrestling for dominance. The alpha snapped his jaws towards Saul, but the old man deftly turned and swept the alpha's back leg, allowing the shade's momentum to carry him forward. Saul pivoted and cranked one of the shade's arms, twisting it behind his back then pushing him down into the dirt. The maneuver happened so quickly that Saul seemed to blink in and out of existence. One moment he stood in front of the alpha. The next moment, he appeared behind the shade, driving it to the ground.

Saul leaped on top of the alpha and curled around him like a snake. One arm locked beneath its neck while his legs intertwined its torso to keep it from standing. Saul screamed at the onlooking shades, consumed by a primal rage. He paused briefly, allowing them all to see the power he wielded over the alpha, then sank his teeth into the shade's neck, tearing the flesh from its throat. And he fed.

Saul consumed the shade's blood, right in front of me, then threw the bloody, lifeless carcass aside.

I had never really feared Saul until that moment. In my mind, he still remained the old man I knew from the hospice, joking about movies and fighting with doctors. I couldn't wrap my mind around him being one of *them*. After all, he came back to save me. He could reason and communicate. He wasn't like the others. He wasn't really a killer.

I was wrong.

Saul looked up at me, blood dripping from his mouth, his eyes fully clouded in black. I raised my rifle, wary of him turning his attention to me as his prey. Slowly, the speck of light returned to his eyes.

He turned away and wiped his mouth on his sleeve. He rose to his feet and bellowed a howl of triumph towards the remaining shades, still watching from the perimeter path lining the field.

I wondered if the shades would dare attack after Saul's demonstration, but they all mysteriously turned away, focused on a new threat. Down the perimeter path, in the direction of the cornfield behind me, I heard gunshots. The pop sounds seemed to be right on top of me, each one louder than the last.

More shades arrived, running towards me along the path, away from the battle between Paloma and the vampires. At first, I thought they ran towards me and Saul, perhaps attracted by my scream. But then I realized they were running away from something.

Behind the newly arrived shades, a blur of light followed. At the rear of the fleeing crowd, gunshots ripped the monsters into pieces, thinning their ranks as they approached my position. On the edge of the field, the distinct shape of a sword emerged from the shimmering light and the head of a female shade separated from its body, each falling in the opposite direction.

I knew that sword.

The shimmering light left the path full of shades and moved into the field, approaching Saul and me. The light died out and Celwyn materialized, covered in blood, holding his sword with his right hand while his left hung awkwardly by his side.

"Celwyn!" I ran towards him, disregarding Saul's grunts of protest.

"Careful with the arm," he said, breathing heavily. "I thought I lost you. I heard the scream and the gunshots. Figured it had to be you." He looked at Saul with distrust and then at me. "I thought you killed him back in the hospice."

"Well, it's a good thing I didn't. If it wasn't for him, I wouldn't have made it this far."

Celwyn raised his rifle at Saul. "He's one of them. Get out of the way."

I stepped forward and put my hand on the rifle. "No."

Celwyn glowered at me. "I don't approve." Then he studied Saul's controlled demeanor. "And I don't understand." He turned to look over his shoulder. "But none of that matters. There are more shades behind me, and one of the vampires followed me. If your new friend wants to cover our exit, that's fine by me, but he can't come with us."

I looked at Saul. He had undoubtedly heard every word, but showed no emotion, his attention fixed on the growing crowd of shades and occasionally emitting a threatening growl. I exhaled sharply as I made up my mind.

"He's coming with us," I said firmly.

"No," Celwyn said. "*It's* a shade. The person you knew is gone."

Anger surged inside me. Saul had saved my life, and I wouldn't leave him behind. I wasn't going to listen to Celwyn again. Not like I had with the girls.

I exploded. "We all stay and die on this roof, or we all leave together."

Celwyn took a step back, surprised at my outburst. After a few seconds, he shook his head and turned to Saul. "Bloody hell, what do I even call it?"

"Why don't you ask him his name?"

"A shade can't talk. It was barely turned last night."

"My name is Saul," he replied calmly.

Celwyn nearly fell over with surprise, then raised his rifle, aiming it at Saul's head. "Okay, Saul, let's be clear. I don't trust you. If you make a move I don't like, I will kill you. But right now, Mel and I are going to head for that maintenance door. You watch our backs. Got it?"

Saul nodded.

Celwyn sprinted for the maintenance door leading down into the Castle, and I followed. Saul walked slowly backwards in our footsteps, keeping himself between the door and the crowd of attackers.

Before Celwyn even left the field, more shades poured out of the stairwell and joined the others on the perimeter path. I felt a chill and turned to see one of the cloaked vampires from the aircraft approaching with a host of shades following closely behind him.

"Blast," Celwyn said. "I don't like these odds." He spun around wildly. "We need another exit." He finally stopped running, staring towards the far northern edge of the building. "I have an idea. We're going to jump."

"What? It's too high."

Celwyn grabbed my hand. "Trust me." He looped a small wire around my belt and fastened it with a carabiner. "There isn't much slack. Stay close, and when we go over the edge, hold on tight."

The vampire stopped about fifty feet away, and the shades closed ranks beside him. It wore a black helmet with tall soaring wings over the ears. His face radiated a soft pink glow, his gaunt features pale but still strikingly handsome. A symbol stood out on the black breastplate of his armor, an intricate series of lines and squiggles emblazoned in gold. A black cape flapped behind him, seeking to take flight with the aid of the blustery winds on the rooftop.

Saul's courage left him, and he cowered in the presence of the vampire. He looked like an old man again and stepped awkwardly backwards, retreating from the fight before it even started.

The vampire smiled and I saw his teeth, stained in blood. He pulled a curved sword from a scabbard at his side and shouted at the shades surrounding him. At his command, they all rushed towards us across the field of crops.

We ran in the only direction we could, straight towards the edge of the Castle's rooftop.

Celwyn pulled a small gun from his belt and aimed it at the concrete base of the metal railing that lined the edge of the rooftop. He pulled the trigger and a cable fired into the concrete, lodging in place with a thump sound. The other end of the cable remained in Celwyn's hand, and he looped it into a device on his belt.

He grabbed my hand and pulled me close as we neared the edge. "Do you remember if the northern garden terrace is on thirty-five or forty?"

"How should I know?" I shouted.

He leaped onto the railing and peered downwards. I struggled to climb the rails before joining him on the next to last rung.

"It's our lucky day. It's forty." He grabbed me by my waist and yanked my body over the edge, sending us both into a free fall from the roof of the Castle.

CHAPTER TWENTY

I WISH I could say that I flew through the air like a bird, spreading my wings in flight as I fell from the rooftop of the Castle. That would be a lie.

The truth is I fell like a stone.

I closed my eyes and squeezed Celwyn so hard that I nearly lost consciousness. In less than a second, my body jerked to a stop and Celwyn released the cable on his belt, dropping us both like rag dolls onto a manicured lawn jutting out from the north face of the Castle facade. I looked up from my landing spot on my back and saw Saul descending hand over hand from the rooftop using Celwyn's cable. Before reaching the bottom, he leaped down and landed on his feet beside me in the grass like a cat.

Once Saul had landed safely, Celwyn lowered his night vision visor, raised his rifle and aimed towards the roof top. A few seconds passed, then he squeezed off a round. I heard the ping as the bullet hit the railing supporting the cable. He muttered to himself and pulled the trigger again. This time, the cable fell to the ground, ripped apart by the bullet from Celwyn's rifle.

In the dark, I saw the outline of figures peering downward at us over the railing, including the helmeted vampire, standing on the top railing with his cloak billowing behind him in the wind. "That's too far for him to jump right?" I asked.

Celwyn kept his rifle mounted at his shoulder and ignored my question. "There are several stainless steel cylinders on the back of my belt. Grab one for me please."

I located the pouch and removed a two-inch-by-four-inch cylinder that felt cold to the touch. "What do you want me to do with it?"

"Push the button on the end. When the needle comes out, plunge it into my thigh, then push the button again."

"What's in here?"

"It's a steroid to help me fix my arm. Our proprietary blend."

I followed his instructions, jabbing the needle into the back of Celwyn's leg then pushing the button. A hissing noise erupted from the cylinder and it immediately felt lighter in my hand.

"Bloody hell. He's going to jump." Celwyn moved away from me and began firing the rifle into the sky.

I looked up in time to see the vampire leap from the railing. Unlike my awkward descent, the vampire fell in slow motion, holding the sides of his cloak like wings as he seemed to glide from the rooftop. Before he reached our garden veranda, he straightened and bent his knees to absorb the impact. He landed on the lawn, no more than twenty feet away from our position, flattening the grass and throwing up chunks of dirt. The platform shook as if an earthquake had struck, and for a moment I worried the entire veranda would sheer off from the face of the Castle, sending us all to our deaths below.

The vampire stood up straight and drew from a scabbard on his hip a short curved sword with etched symbols that shimmered in the moonlight. "Tell me Knight, why are you interfering with the affairs of Idrissia?" He stopped talking and inhaled deeply, breathing in the night air, then he stared directly at me. "Ah another one—how exciting. Are you a Knight, too, or just tainted meat?"

"Ignore him," Celwyn hissed in my direction, then looked at Saul. "Mel, stay behind me, and if Saul lifts a finger to help this thing, you put a bullet in his head."

Celwyn drew the long sword from his back and stepped forward towards the vampire, holding it with both hands. "You tell me, vampire. Why is Idrissia breaking the Accords? You know the penalty is death."

"The Accords are a relic of the past." The vampire stalked Celwyn, circling towards his flank on the lawn. "We will not voluntarily subjugate ourselves any longer, and Idrissia will lead by example. Once Tarek demonstrates the weakness of the Knights, the other Bloodlines will follow."

"You're wrong. That will mean war, not just with humans, but between the Bloodlines. They'll never unite behind Tarek. Millions will die."

Millions. The thought sent shivers of dread down my spine and I tightened my grip on my rifle. I thought of Alex and Emma and their grandmother. This would not just be soldiers, but the innocent. Women...*children*.

The vampire smiled. "So be it."

He rushed forward and slashed at Celwyn's head with his blade, seeking to decapitate him with his first blow. He hit nothing but air.

A flicker of light appeared beside the vampire and Celwyn's sword materialized, already in motion. The blade sliced across the back of the vampire's knee, one of the few areas not protected by armor, lodging itself deep in the flesh like an axe wedged in a tree. The sparkle of light beside the vampire disappeared and in its place stood Celwyn. With a tug, he pulled the sword from the vampire's calf, then placed a vicious kick in the same spot with his boot. The vampire fell.

The vampire tried to stand, but his injured leg wobbled and he dug his sword into the ground for support. Celwyn swung his much heavier longsword into the vampire's blade and smacked it out of his hand, sending it tumbling away. The vampire dropped down onto his knees and Saul surged from behind to tackle him, sending them both rolling across the ground.

Saul screamed wildly as he attacked, but the much larger vampire easily ended up on top. He rained vicious blows down onto Saul's face with his elbow and opened up a deep cut over one of Saul's eyes.

While the vampire focused on Saul, Celwyn rushed forward and swung his sword at the monster's neck. The vampire ducked at the last second and the blade struck his steel helmet, making a loud clanking sound. Saul lunged forward and reversed his position, now pinning the dazed vampire on his back. He ripped the helmet off the vampire's head and threw it into the rose bushes lining the lawn.

"Move!" Celwyn shouted at Saul. He wasted no time and the sword came down in a fatal arc, severing the vampire's head from his body.

Saul remained on top of the vampire's body, savoring his victory. Its limbs continued to thrash for a few seconds until finally collapsing into a heap. Saul stared at the blood oozing from the neck and appeared to be in a daze.

Celwyn cleaned his sword on the grass then returned it to the scabbard on his back. "Go ahead, Saul. Feed before the blood cools down. It'll help you heal. Just don't do it here. I don't want to watch."

Saul turned to me as if to ask for permission. The thought made me nauseated, but I nodded as well.

He quickly grabbed the vampire's body by the leg and within seconds relocated it to a small shaded area underneath a tree, surrounded by rose bushes loaded with red blooms. I turned away, wanting nothing to do with the sight of my friend satisfying the thirst caused by his curse.

"Might as well take a look, Mel. That's what he is now. He's not your friend, and he isn't some kind of hero. The parasite will make him feed one way or another or else he'll die."

"You're wrong. The man I know is still there. He's fighting to control it."

"Well, I'll give him that—he's a fighter. To master the parasite in a day is unheard of. Most shades take months, and lots of help, to regain some semblance of their former humanity. Many never do."

I smiled. "He's been fighting cancer longer than the parasite. He's had some practice."

Celwyn looked up at the sky and stroked the stubble on his chin. "It's going to be dawn soon. We need to make a plan."

"Before we talk about any plans, I want to know what happened on the roof. How did you do the 'disappear' thing? Did you get the signal out?"

Celwyn touched the disruptor clipped to his shirt and suddenly he disappeared, replaced by a flickering light that moved counter clockwise to my left. I followed the light and Celwyn reappeared, now standing on the opposite side of me from where he started.

"The disruptor can also camouflage. It generates an electronic field that bends light. At night, you can see the light, but during the day it makes you almost invisible."

I looked down at my own disruptor. "Why didn't you tell me I could do that?" I pushed the small switch on the side of the clip and a sparkling blanket of light fell over me. Everything in my field of vision outside the blanket appeared distorted and in constant motion. Suddenly, my head hurt and the world spun around me.

"You had enough yet?" Celwyn asked.

I couldn't see him because I had closed my eyes. I moved my hand back down to the disruptor and flicked the switch back to its prior position. My eyes opened, and the world finally stopped spinning.

Celwyn stood in front of me, looking down in pity as I struggled to peel myself off the lawn. "That's why I didn't show you," he said. "It takes a little getting used to."

"Yeah," I coughed. "Clearly."

Saul walked towards us from the alcove underneath the tree. The bruises on his face had healed, and the gray complexion had lightened, replaced by a soft rosy white hue. His stride was now powerful and agile, and he wore the black cloak from the vampire that only moments earlier had stood on the same lawn attempting to kill him.

"I need to get inside before dawn," Saul said firmly.

I studied Saul, amazed at the transformation. His white hair seemed thicker and he stood straight, no longer slumped by age. Back in the hospice, he always appeared to be shorter than me, but now I realized his height actually exceeded mine, standing toe to toe with Celwyn's six-foot frame.

"What happens if you're exposed to the sun?" I asked.

"I...I don't really know," Saul replied. "I just feel a powerful urge to avoid it, like a fear, really."

"Instincts are kicking in." Celwyn began walking towards the door leading back inside the castle. "Like I said, he's a vampire now. Can't change that." He pulled on the door handle and held the door for myself and Saul. "And if you want to know what happens if he gets touched by sunlight, I'll tell you. The sun's radiation will cook him like a microwave. The parasite can't survive in the ultraviolet light—that's why it evolved to infect humans. The host acts as a protective shell, but it's still infected by the parasite. After a few seconds in the sun, his skin will burn. A few seconds after that, he will be driven mad by the parasite seeking to find a dark place to hide. I've seen a shade tear his fingers down to nubs trying to dig a hole through concrete."

Saul stepped inside the darkened Castle, then turned back to watch the first rays of dawn rise over the horizon. I recognized the look on his face. I had seen it on my mother's face at my father's funeral. That same look stared back at me in the mirror after my husband Alex died. And now I saw the look on Saul's face as he watched the sun rise, knowing he could never set foot in the light again.

I followed my friend through the doorway and put my hand on his shoulder. "C'mon Saul. Don't listen to Celwyn. He's an asshole."

"I'm just telling you the truth, Mel. It is what it is." Celwyn closed the door behind him, plunging us all into near-darkness. He raised his rifle and turned on the flashlight, illuminating our immediate surroundings. I turned on my light, too, for good measure. I was done with surprises.

The garden veranda on the north side of the Castle was apparently part of a recreation facility. Inside, a lounge filled with sofas and chairs greeted us, arranged in small living room formations around the room. To my left, a glass wall revealed a room filled with exercise machines. On the other side of the lounge, pictures of animals and flowers lined the walls of a children's play area filled with toys and a miniature two-story castle with a slide jutting out of one end.

"Look," Celwyn said. "They have food." He sprinted ahead to a snack machine and smashed the glass on the front with the hilt of his sword. "You want something?" he asked.

My stomach grumbled and I realized that I couldn't remember the last time I had actually eaten food. "Yeah. I'll take some peanut butter crackers if they got 'em."

Celwyn walked over to a small dining room and dumped out a mountain of snacks onto the table. He raised a small rectangular item wrapped in plastic and motioned for me to join him. "Found one."

He separated my prize out from the rest of his stash, and began dividing his haul into separate 'eat now' and 'save for later' piles. I pulled out a chair and joined Celwyn at the table. Saul did the same.

I turned to Saul. "Can you eat?"

He shook his head firmly. "No. I'm not hungry. Not in that way."

I looked at Celwyn and he froze, a pack of Oreos in his hand. "What? I didn't say anything."

I rolled my eyes and turned my focus to satisfying my own hunger. The wrapper in my hand didn't stand a chance. I tore into the crackers and rolled the peanut butter over my tongue, savoring every sticky bite. As I sat in the dark smacking my lips, a realization hit me—this could very well be my last meal. Peanut butter and crackers. A hell of a way to end it all.

A bottle of coke sat on the table in front of Celwyn, next to a bag of chips. "Mind if I take this one?"

"Not at all," he replied. He pointed behind him at the machine. "There's more where that one came from."

I opened the lid and raised the bottle. "Thank you both," I said. "I don't know if we're going to make it out of here, but I know I would be dead if it weren't for the two of you. Thanks for keeping me alive."

Saul nodded his head in acknowledgment then watched me eat.

"I have a question," I said to both Saul and Celwyn. "I thought vampires fed on people, not other vampires. I'm confused."

"The hunger is for all blood," Saul replied. "Shades and vampires have blood, so I can feed on them."

"But they prefer humans," Celwyn added. "They only turn on their own kind if they get real hungry."

"Those monsters are not my kind," Saul stated firmly. "And I choose not to feed on the innocent as they do."

Celwyn snorted. "For now, maybe."

"What's your problem?" I asked Celwyn.

"My problem is that we are about as far away as you can get from a way out of here. We are on the fortieth floor of Grid Ten." He rose to his feet and started throwing food from the remaining stack into his backpack. "And our only chance is to get out of the Castle before night falls."

"What happens then?" I asked.

Celwyn stopped packing and looked at me grimly. "I don't know, but with that many vampires running around, it won't be good."

CHAPTER TWENTY-ONE

I SLUMPED down in my chair. Celwyn had filled me in on what happened on the roof while we were separated. He had successfully transmitted evidence from the roof showing the Accords had been breached by Idrissia. The jamming stopped when the airship exploded.

The Knights were coming. The vampires would never be allowed to escape. It was out of his hands.

I pushed for a decision on our next move. "So, you think the Knights will destroy the Castle. Are you sure?"

"They'll try to wait for me, but if I'm not out, they won't hesitate. I can't communicate, so they won't even know I'm alive."

"And the people still inside—they'll all die with the vampires?"

Celwyn nodded. "I'm afraid so. Mel, I've never lied to you. You've seen these things. You know we can't let them get out."

"And the girls," I said quietly. "They'll die, too."

"It'll be better than whatever the vampires will do to them."

"How long until they get here?' I asked.

"I don't know," Celwyn replied. "Maybe a day. Could be less."

"So we have to get everyone out of here before the Knights destroy the Castle. How do we do that?"

"You can't," Celwyn replied. "And I'm not going anywhere."

"What are you talking about?"

A cloud passed over Celwyn's eyes, and his voice changed. "Tarek is here—the one mentioned by the vampire outside." He paused. "And I'm going to kill him."

Celwyn's words dripped with anguish. It felt almost wrong to argue, but I couldn't leave it alone. I wasn't going to get out of the Castle without his help. I was desperate.

"But you said it yourself—it's suicide to fight a vampire alone. Why not let the Knights kill him when they take out the Castle? You can do both. Just help us get out first."

Celwyn shook his head. Anger replaced the anguish in his voice. "He took someone from me and I will make him pay. I did my duty and sent the transmission. I'm done." He pointed to Saul. "Take your friend and go. I hope you find the girls and some way out of here before nightfall. I truly do."

I stood up and walked around the table. "No, no, no! You don't get to do this to me. When I wanted to save the girls, you told me duty came first. Fine! I listened! I went along with you to the roof, and you did the transmission thing so you could save the world." I kept shouting. "And now you want to just forget about your duty so you can get revenge? No! We made a deal! The world still needs saving, starting with the people still alive in this city."

Celwyn jumped to his feet and his face turned red. I thought he might actually explode. The anger passed, and the grief returned. He just looked at me.

"So who did he take from you?" Saul asked. His tone reflected genuine concern, like a father comforting a child.

"My wife," Celwyn said softly. The tears finally flowed, but quickly stopped once Celwyn regained control.

"I know that pain," he said. Then he turned to me. "As does Melanie." He turned back to Celwyn. "Yet here we still are, doing our best to live. To survive." He waited for a moment, then straightened his back proudly. "I had the privilege of loving my wife for fifty-five years. For a long time after my wife died, I was lost. I didn't see the point of living anymore. But then I realized that I carried a piece of her in me. She rubbed off on me along the way, you know. Not just memories, but the way I talked, the things I liked to eat. Part of her is now a part of me."

Saul was the last to rise from the table. "The people we loved are gone, Celwyn. But some parts of them remain. And as long as we are alive, a piece of them will live, too. You honor them by living, not by throwing your life away."

Celwyn sat in silence weighing Saul's words, then he turned to me. "Fine. I'll help you get out of here."

"And what about me?"

Celwyn turned to face Saul. An awkward silence descended on the room. "You can come, for now. I've never met anyone like you, but it's not just about me. Paloma won't see it the same way. The Knights won't spare your life. I give you my word that I won't be the Knight who hunts you. But others *will* hunt you."

Saul's face remained expressionless. "You know I will fight to survive. I'll kill if I must."

Celwyn extended his hand over the table. "I believe you. That's why I won't be the one coming after you. Do we have a deal?"

Saul grabbed Celwyn's hand. "We do."

I threw my hand on top. "Good. Now that we've got that out of the way, we need to figure out how to save the rest of the people in the Castle."

Celwyn looked at me sternly. "Impossible. We would never even make it to them in time, and Paloma wouldn't just let them walk out the door. It's suicide."

"I'm not leaving those girls to die here in this hellhole. You better figure out a way." I mustered every bit of confidence I had into my words, knowing Celwyn would try to talk me out of it. I didn't care. My mind was made up.

Something inside me refused to accept that Alex and Emma would die. It was the same piece of me that fought in vain to avoid the deaths of my hospice patients. Maybe I was fooling myself. Maybe I just liked picking losing battles. But this time I believed I could win. This time it would be different.

"You with me, Saul?" I asked.

He nodded.

"So what's it going to be, Celwyn?"

The Knight paced the floor of the lounge, muttering to himself. He walked over to the glass doors leading out into the streets of the Castle and stared outside. After a few minutes, he returned to the table and placed the helmet on his head.

"Something is going on here that I don't understand. Paloma isn't really working for Idrissia, that's clear now. Tarek is taking back his city and Paloma is in trouble. He will need whatever help he can find."

He tapped the side panel and spoke into the radio. "Hector, it's me. I know you're listening. We need to talk."

After a long pause, Paloma's voice answered. *"This line is not secure."*

"They already know I'm here," Celwyn hissed. "I've got nothing to hide."

Another long moment of static. *"What do you want? I have a lot on my plate."*

"I saw what happened on the roof. You need every hand you can get. I can help you fight Tarek."

"If I were you, I would get the hell out of here. But if you want to help kill these bastards, I won't turn down the help."

Celwyn nodded approvingly in my direction. "We're coming to you. Just make sure you let the welcome wagon know to be on the lookout."

"One more thing," Paloma said. *"This is my show. The Knights don't give me orders any more."*

"Understood. I expected no less." Celwyn tapped the button on his helmet. "There, we have our plan. Make it back to Grid One and somehow convince that madman to evacuate whoever is left alive."

"Do you think he'll listen?" I asked.

"Paloma? No way. He's only worried about himself. He was a Knight once, now he works for whoever pays him the most money. He'll probably kill us all, but we have a more immediate problem."

"What?"

"We have to get all the way back to Grid One. That's nearly ten miles of dark Castle filled with shades and who knows how many vampires."

"Maybe we can turn the power back on so we can take the train?" Saul added.

Celwyn removed his helmet and extended it in his hand. "Would you like to politely ask Paloma to turn the power back on? While you're at it, tell him you're now a vampire. That'll surely work."

"You don't have to be so mean to him. He's trying to help. He was a mechanic, you know."

Saul nodded. "Twenty years in the IDF. I can fix anything."

Celwyn got excited. "Come with me. Both of you."

We all walked out the doors of the recreation center onto a landing for the Tube. Saul backed into a corner to avoid the few rays of morning sunlight already filtering through the Atrium skylight that ran the length of the Castle.

In front of us, at the end of the landing, the train car for the Upper Tube sat lifeless. To our right, the machinery for operating the train loomed from the landing up towards the roof of the Castle, several stories worth of complex motors and hydraulics idled by the lack of electricity. Here and there, orange emergency lights flashed on the giant marvel of engineering, still running off emergency power.

Celwyn pointed ahead. "Alright Saul, you said you can fix anything. Can you fix that train? We need to get it moving in the next hour."

Saul pulled the hood over his head and bounded up onto a system of ladders and catwalks that climbed alongside the equipment powering the Tube. Due to its position at the far end of the Castle's Atrium, the machinery enjoyed almost complete shade from the sun entering through the skylight, and would likely remain that way until midday.

Not convinced of the low risk of getting burned, Saul looked up at the skylight and turned to Celwyn. "Get me some gloves to protect my hands from the sun. And tools. Whatever you can find."

"I'll help." I joined Celwyn and we left Saul alone to work, looking for any place where tools might be stored. Celwyn quickly located the maintenance office strategically placed on the landing behind the soaring tower of machinery. He shot the lock off with his rifle and kicked open the door.

We both entered a small office attached to a locker room on our right. Ahead of us, behind another door, a small kitchen lined with windows marked the end of the hallway. To our left was a workshop.

"Find some gloves," Celwyn instructed. "I'll take the workshop and see what I can do about tools."

I entered the locker room and slid the handle up on the first one. Inside, a few blue shirts hung on a rod in the middle. A small bag of tools sat on a shelf at the bottom, next to a pair of tennis shoes. On the back of the locker, a child's colored picture of a spaceship hung precariously by a piece of tape.

At the top of the picture, a child had written 'To Dad' in red crayon. As I admired the artwork, it occurred to me that the owner of this locker was likely dead, along with the child who made it. My commitment to getting the train moving intensified. I had to know if Emma and Alex remained alive.

The next locker contained nothing but an old detective novel and two pairs of socks. I quickly moved down the line.

On the third one, I hit paydirt. A set of black work gloves hung over a hook on the inside of the locker door. Another bag of tools, this one larger than the first one, sat on the shelf inside. I grabbed it.

I picked up my haul and looked for Celwyn. I met him coming out of the workshop beaming from ear to ear. "They've got everything in there."

"Will this help?" I showed him the two bags and the gloves.

"You did good. Let's go see Saul."

We walked outside and Saul bounded down two flights of stairs to meet us on the landing.

"I found some gloves," I said, handing him the black pair from the locker. "And plenty of tools." I held up both bags.

Saul took both bags from me and placed them down on the stairs behind him. "Thanks."

"Idrissia has a full workshop back behind there. You tell me what you need, and I'll probably be able to find it for you. I saw a full welding setup and a stack of extra battery packs if you need them." Celwyn looked up at the still blinking lights. "You figured out a way to get the train moving yet?"

Saul nodded. "I can get it moving. The problem will be getting it to stop on the other end. The train moves on magnets, like the train outside, but only smaller. The magnets inside the Tube are passive, so they don't need electricity. They're still working fine best I can tell, but when the power went out, the safety protocols kicked in. Computers locked down the train and restored air pressure inside the Tube."

"How can I help?" Celwyn asked.

"Look for a diagnostic computer inside that workshop. It should be the size of a laptop. I need to override the safety protocols and de-pressurize the Tube. If I can't recreate the vacuum, this thing will barely get above a crawl."

Celwyn sprinted back towards the workshop to look for the computer, leaving me alone with Saul. I looked around at the dark and quiet husk of Idrissia's state-of-the-art train system.

"Do you really think you can get this thing moving without power?" I asked quietly.

"Yes, Melanie. I believe I can," Saul replied.

"Good. There are two girls back in Grid One who are waking up alone, with their parents probably dead. Shades attacked them during the evacuation of the Castle, and Celwyn and I saved them. I let them go once, but I'm not going to leave them again. I'm not going to leave them here to die."

I looked up at Saul, leaning over the railing on the landing above me. "I have to do this, but you don't. If you want to go a different direction—if you don't want to fight against the others like you—I'll understand."

The light in Saul's blue eyes flashed, and he smiled. "When I was in the hospice, bitten in my bed, you could have ended my life. But you chose to spare it. You called me a friend once, and even though I'm not the same man, I remain a friend. Rest assured, I know what side I'm on. I am not like those monsters out there, and I will stay by your side until we are all out of this place."

I touched his hand. "Thanks, Saul."

He studied my left hand. "Where's the wedding ring?"

I blushed. "It has a new home on my necklace."

"Hmm." Saul replied. "It's because of the Knight, isn't it?" He shook his head. "I don't like him."

Celwyn ran up behind us carrying a laptop computer. "Found it."

Saul took the computer in one hand and picked up the tool bags with the other, then made his way back up to a giant control panel behind the train car.

"Give me twenty minutes," he said. "I'll get this train moving."

CHAPTER TWENTY-TWO

THE GIANT TURBINES behind the Tube roared to life, filling the Atrium with the loud hum of air compressors. Moments later, Saul climbed down to meet Celwyn and me on the landing, clearly pleased with his success.

"The generators are working and the Tube is de-pressurizing," Saul said triumphantly. "I told you I could fix it."

"I'm not going to lie. I'm impressed." Celwyn stepped closer to the Tube which remained dark. "What about the lights?"

"No lights. The onboard controls for the train are not on the backup generator. We're going to unlock the safety controls here at the station and give it a little push so to speak."

"What do you mean give it a little push?" I asked.

"Once I've sucked enough air out of the front of the Tube, I'm going to reverse the compressors and insert air into the Tube behind the train. We will be moving in a partial vacuum, so theoretically if we get enough of a push, it should keep moving."

Celwyn looked nervous. "How do we stop the train once we get to the other end at Grid One?"

"We can't. We crash. Hopefully, my estimates are correct and there will be enough air left in the Tube to create plenty of friction. That will keep our speed under control."

"That's your plan? We crash?" Celwyn looked at me. "You okay with this plan?"

"Yes," I replied matter of factly. "It's all we've got." I turned to make my way back to the locker room. "We need to make seat belts. It's going to be a bumpy ride."

———

I SAT INSIDE THE TRAIN, tying rope to one of the poles. With the aid of a couple of carabiners from Celwyn, I had crafted a homemade seat belt system on one of the rows. I'm not particularly crafty, but I was impressed with my handiwork.

Saul had insisted he would be fine without a seat belt, worrying more about the sun that would filter through the glass ceiling of the train once we left our protected little corner of the Castle. Behind me, two giant blankets found by Saul lay on the floor, ready to serve as a protective layer on top of his cloak. It was mid-morning, and looking southward through the Atrium, the sun already poured through the skylight.

The train's other two passengers walked through the open doors together. Saul pulled both doors shut by the handles, then turned a red lever in a control panel he had opened on the floor. The doors made the same familiar hissing noise signaling the pod's sealing from the outside vacuum of the Tube.

Celwyn sat down beside me and clicked in the carabiner of his makeshift seat belt across his lap. "You did good," he said.

I smiled back. "I may not be the best in a gun fight, but I can make a mean craft project."

Saul draped one of the blankets over his head and tucked it into the other one he had wrapped around his body, creating a puffy, layered cocoon. He sat cross-legged on the floor in the middle of the train and grabbed a pole with each hand.

"I manually programmed the turbines to release air into the Tube behind us when the PSI level reaches thirty percent. That should be a strong enough push to get us to the other side, but soft enough to avoid a high speed train crash."

"You really think this is going to work?" Celwyn asked.

Saul sat perfectly still, his voice seeming to float out of the open space in the blanket wrapped around his head. "I once had to fix a damaged helicopter engine in Syria. Two of my friends had already been shot. Just me and the pilot left. I had no tools, nothing but elbow grease and whatever I could use from the stuff in my team's kits." Saul paused and I noticed that Celwyn hung on his every word. "I got the helicopter running again in seventeen minutes—about two minutes before the crash site was overrun. So the answer to your question is yes, I think this is going to work."

I listened to him tell his story, and realized I had never really known Saul. The old man I knew in the hospice was only a pale reflection of what he had been earlier in his life. That old man I knew wasn't the real Saul.

The real Saul was not just a fighter, he was a fierce friend. That thought brought me comfort as we waited for the train to move.

The wait didn't last long. Normally, the train left each station slowly, then gradually picked up speed as it moved through the Tube, carefully controlled by onboard computers designed to maximize human comfort. Without those computer controls, the sudden increase in air pressure behind the train propelled it abruptly forward through the Tube like a bullet shot from a gun.

I dug my heels into the floor and steadied myself, fighting the g-forces pushing me back into the seat. The dark industrial surroundings of Grid Ten whizzed by us as the train flew through the Tube at a speed faster than anything I had ever experienced in the Castle's transportation system.

"You sure that was just a little push?" Celwyn asked.

"The train has to go ten miles," Saul replied. "I didn't fully de-pressurize the Tube, so theoretically the friction from the partial vacuum will gradually slow us down. You're used to the train operating in a full vacuum with automatic speed controls and braking. We're doing it the old-fashioned way."

The visual surroundings along the Upper Tube lacked the aesthetic architectural beauty of the main transportation artery along Broadway, more than thirty stories below. The Upper Tube served as a more utilitarian option to move through the city, a lesser-used backup option to avoid crowds, and the preferred mode of transportation for the ultra wealthy who inhabited the few penthouses on the top floors of the Castle.

The Upper Tube was also something else—scorching hot. Even on a good day when the climate controls were at peak efficiency, the Upper Tube could be warm when its translucent shell baked in the desert sun. Hot air rises, and without power to cool it down, the Castle acted like a giant steel oven, warmed by the sunlight shining through the glass panes lining the top of the Atrium.

We had barely passed Grid Nine and already beads of sweat ran down my face. I could only imagine how Saul felt, wrapped inside thick blankets. "You doing okay, Saul?"

"Yes, Melanie. I am adequately protected from the sun."

"That's...good, I guess." I watched the empty ghost town of Grid Eight fly by us at high speed. Smashed windows and an occasional dead body lining the pedestrian landings along the Tube served as a reminder that the daylight was only a brief respite from what would come when the darkness returned.

Make no mistake, we were traveling through a war zone.

Celwyn sat quietly beside me, staring out the window on the opposite end of the train car. The speed had finally subsided enough to allow comfortable movement, and he had his arms crossed on top of his chest.

"You're not much of a talker, are you?" I asked.

"Hmm?" Celwyn broke his concentration on the window, and turned in my direction.

"What were you thinking about?" I studied Celwyn's face. "You're worried, aren't you? What are you not telling me?"

Celwyn looked away again. "Paloma was a Knight. He found me and helped train me at the Keep a long time ago. He was like a father to me."

"So what happened?"

"I don't know. One day he just up and left. He started doing his own thing, working for whoever paid him the most. Usually that meant working for one of the vampire Bloodlines."

"So how do you go from fighting vampires to working for them?"

Celwyn shook his head and exhaled. "He never approved of the Accords, or thought much of the Knights. In his mind, we were hypocrites, allowing rich monsters to run the world as long as they followed a bunch of silly old rules. They're basically royalty and they all hate each other, constantly trying to wipe one another out. I guess there aren't any rules against killing vampires if you work for them." He paused. "And it pays better."

The train continued to gradually decrease its speed and we passed Grid Seven, entering into Grid Six. Yesterday, somewhere below us on a landing next to the Broadway line, I had met Emma and Alex. I wondered if they were still alive and part of whatever group awaited us in Grid One.

"So you know Paloma? He'll listen to you, right?"

"No, I *knew* Hector. He's changed. The only chance we have of getting these people out of here alive is to convince him that it somehow accomplishes what he was paid to do. Their lives are meaningless to him."

I looked straight into Celwyn's eyes. "If those girls are still alive, I'm going to get them out. I'll do whatever I have to do."

Celwyn looked past me at the Upper Tube landing platform at the entrance into Grid Five. "Turn around. You need to see this."

The bodies of dead soldiers littered the landing. A makeshift barrier, crafted from desks, couches and other large furniture, had been ripped into pieces. At least ten shades, easily identified by their gray skin, lay dead on top of and around the barrier. But the other shades had obviously made it through, and killed everyone guarding their position on Grid Five.

My mind instantly turned to Gloria and her promise that she could take the girls to the safety of Grid Five before the soldiers waiting there on Broadway retreated. *What if she was wrong? What if she found a scene like the one I just saw on the Upper Tube?*

"We don't know that the same thing happened down below,"

Celwyn said softly. "Even if it did, they could have made it through before the shades attacked."

"I know."

The train suddenly jerked and I reached for the stability of the pole. The train jerked again violently and slowed.

The mass of blankets on the floor of the train formed into a human figure and Saul stood to his feet. "Something's wrong."

The jerking motion had finally stopped, and we now coasted comfortably again, but the train had definitely slowed down. We entered Grid Four, where the most luxurious accommodations in the Castle lined both sides of the Tube. Many of the penthouses enjoyed their own private Tube landings, so the spacing on either side of the Tube narrowed, creating a tunnel effect. And within that tunnel, shadows cloaked the Upper Tube in darkness.

The sunlight from the Atrium faded, blocked by abutting garden verandas and fancy penthouse facades, imitating every type of gaudy architecture. It got darker. And we were still slowing down.

I saw Celwyn tense on high alert, then it hit me. That feeling of dread in my stomach returned, followed by a cool blast of air on the back of my neck.

We weren't alone.

CHAPTER TWENTY-THREE

SAUL ROSE from his cross-legged seat on the floor of the train and threw off the blankets he had wrapped around his body. Within the shadows now covering the Tube, the cloak offered more than enough protection from the sun. He peered out the front windows of the train, with a faraway look in his eyes.

"They're here, in this place," he said.

We entered the Heights, home of the wealthiest and most important residents of the Castle. It looked untouched by the chaos inflicting every other part of the city, still opulent and beautiful.

I wondered how many of the rich people and celebrities living in Grid Four had been entombed in pods in the lab next to my hospice only days ago and now roamed the Heights as shades, or perhaps full-fledged vampires.

We passed underneath La Scala, the bridge of multi-level gardens capped by Greek columns. Only residents of the Heights could access La Scala, and needless to say, I didn't know anyone who ran in those circles. I had passed through the Heights many times on my way to and from work, wondering what it would be like to live in one of the giant mansions. Now, in the shadows of the dimly lit Atrium, without the benefit of their fancy lighting, the homes seemed garish.

Celwyn pointed to a veranda to the right of the train. "There."

A small crowd of shades watched the train pass their hiding spot, their position given away only by movement from one of them who stood on a stone wall to get a better view of the unexpected visitors. The gray complexion and dead eyes left no doubt as to its condition, although his clothing suggested wealth in his prior life as a resident of the Castle.

As the train swept through the Heights, I periodically caught movement in the gardens surrounding the Tube. Every nook and cranny seemed alive. No doubt, hundreds or even thousands of enemies hid around us in the dark, camouflaged from sight. I knew they were there.

I felt it.

"What are they doing?" I asked. "Sleeping?"

"More like resting, conserving energy until the sun goes down," Celwyn responded. "As long as the parasite is kept fed, it will rejuvenate the host. They don't need sleep."

Saul remained still as we swept through Grid Four, stoically monitoring the surrounding landscape for threats from his observation point inside the train, but something caught his attention. He raised his finger, pointing to a large home up ahead to the left of the Tube. On the private platform, a tall figure in black armor and a cloak that matched the one taken by Saul stood motionless, watching us approach. He also wore the same winged helmet as the other vampires who had descended from the airship.

"The Father," Saul said.

"Yes," Celwyn replied softly. "That's him. Tarek. The Successor to the Idrissia Bloodline, and the creator of every shade and vampire crawling around in this place."

The platform extended outward from the largest residence in the Castle, that of the Governor, and marked the end of the Heights. Before we passed him, Tarek removed his winged helmet, allowing a clear glimpse of his face through the train window. Long black hair spilled out, falling around his shoulders. He had a firm jaw, high cheekbones, and the rugged good looks of a fairy tale prince—except something wasn't quite right.

It was the eyes. They weren't pitch black and lifeless like a shade. Instead, they burned with a red flame threatening to engulf everything in sight. Our eyes locked for only a micro-second as the train passed, but it was enough to fill me with both a deep primal fear and a sense of awe.

We finally put the Heights behind us, and I relaxed as sunlight from the Atrium again filtered into the train through the glass roof. Saul recreated his cocoon of blankets and sat back down on the floor.

Celwyn stared out the window, still lost in thought. He hadn't said a word after seeing Tarek.

I leaned into Celwyn, hoping to break him out of suicidal thoughts of revenge. "So who is Tarek? Who is he really?"

"He's a rich and powerful vampire, and the Successor of the Idrissia Bloodline."

He'd already said that. I tried harder. "So Idrissia is owned by vampires?"

Celwyn grunted. "Yeah. Anywhere you find old money, you usually find vampires."

"How many Bloodlines are there?"

Celwyn leaned back and placed his boots on the railing in front of us. "Damned good question. The number fluctuates over time, politics you know. Under the Accords, we leave them alone unless they step out of line, but the vampires still fight amongst themselves. There are currently sixteen Bloodlines recognized by the Accords, that's down from eighteen a year ago. Paloma's been busy."

"What is a Successor?'

"Under the Accords, the Head of each Bloodline is allowed to make a Successor. There can be no more than two. The compromise in the Accords ended the great war, but the Bloodlines could survive only if they accepted limits on breeding."

The train entered Grid Three. The shadows cast by the elaborate surroundings of the Heights gave way again to the airy open Atrium filled with sunlight, but my gut told me we were still not alone. The train entered the beginning of Broadway, where restaurants, bars, and shops lined the middle artery of the Castle, from top to bottom.

Although at first glance, all of Broadway seemed alike—one big column of flashy signs and colorful facades. The businesses surrounding the Upper Tube differed greatly from those at the bottom. Lower Broadway had a distinct Las Vegas vibe, family friendly by day but naughty at night, while Upper Broadway would have made Amsterdam blush. If there was a color beyond a red light district, Grid Three should have been painted that color.

Every vice was well-represented in Upper Broadway, although drug use and prostitution stood out as its specialties. The swankiest clubs offered every variation imaginable, both traditional and perverse. At first, I thought it strange that such a place would be housed so close to the lavish residences of the Heights, but the stories I heard from Deirdre made it clear that this place, more than anywhere else, served as a playground for the wealthy inside the Castle.

Now, Broadway's bright signs and street lights remained dark, and beyond the illumination of the Atrium, the connecting streets and alleyways filled with darkness. The alleys of Upper Broadway offered a hearty dose of danger even under the best of conditions. I could only imagine what horrors now lurked in those shadows.

My thoughts returned to Deirdre. She frequented the clubs in Upper Broadway and could have been right here when the shades attacked and the Castle shut down. I imagined what it must have been like to be plunged into darkness without warning, surrounded by desperate, confused people trying to escape the chaos. I wondered how long it took for the soldiers to reach Grid Three, and whether the shades reached this place first.

I shuddered as I soon got my answer. Dead bodies littered the streets on both sides of the Tube. None of them wore a uniform, although it was hard to tell in the bloody mess left by the shades. The people never stood a chance.

"Take a good look," Celwyn said. "That's what these monsters do. That's what will happen everywhere if we let them get out of here."

"It doesn't have to be this way," Saul said. His muffled voice dripped with remorse. "What you call monsters were once people—mothers and fathers, sons and daughters. They are sick and need to be helped. I have control of the parasite and have regained my humanity. They can do it, too."

Celwyn shook his head. "With all due respect, you haven't regained your humanity, Saul. You can never go back. Do you really think a lion's choice to lay among the sheep for a day means it's now a lamb? You can resist the hunger to feed, and for a while you may be able to overcome the parasite's influence, but you'll eventually give in. It's biology. You think you're the first person to try to fight off the parasite? You're not. I admire your determination and welcome your help. I really do. But you are what you are. And that's a monster."

Saul scoffed audibly. "Many so-called normal humans have committed monstrous acts of violence. Was that simply biology? You and I aren't as different as you would like to believe. We both have free will, and I choose to not be a monster. My soul is unchanged, even in this new shell."

"Vampires don't have souls, Saul."

Saul perked up. "Ah, I stand corrected. Clearly, since you are Roman Catholic, you are an expert on the great theological mysteries of the soul." He shook his head in disgust.

"I'm not Catholic. It's just my job."

Saul looked confused. "Then what *do* you believe?"

"I—I don't know," Celwyn stuttered. "I just know that vampires are different from us, and something that evil just can't have a soul."

"Clearly, sir, you are uneducated." With that last retort, Saul returned to his position under the blankets on the floor.

Celwyn shook his head and returned to staring out the window.

I desperately wanted to believe Saul. I wanted to believe that my friend wasn't going to become a cold-hearted murderer, feeding on innocent people. And more importantly, I hated the way Celwyn spoke to him, so callous and uncaring. But, somewhere in my mind, I doubted Saul and feared Celwyn's words might be true.

The train suddenly jerked again, this one more severe than the last. The halting motion caught me off guard and threw me back into my seat. The train immediately resumed its forward movement, but now its speed barely reached a crawl.

"Saul," I shouted. "What was that?"

He stood up and walked to the edge of the windows on the front of the train, his blanket trailing on the ground behind him. "There must be a break in the Tube up ahead. The vacuum is failing, so our speed is decreasing."

"What happens to us if there is a break in the Tube?" Celwyn asked.

"It's a problem. We could get stuck. And just because the vacuum is too weak for the train to move through it doesn't mean it's not there. If we break the seal between this train and the Tube, the resulting difference in pressure could crush us like a soda can. It would be like stepping foot into outer space."

"We have another problem," I said.

A figure waited on a landing platform ahead. He wore gloves and a black cloak from Tarek's guard. A balaclava enclosed his face, with only a small slit for his eyes. Completely covered and protected from the sun that had Saul hiding in blankets. He waited for the train to slowly approach the platform then jumped atop the Tube, landing in a crouched position.

The vampire looked down through the roof, straight into our train car, his expression masked by the face covering. He rose to his feet and ran along the top of the Tube, easily keeping pace with the train moving slowly inside it. He stopped, barked out a series of commands impossible to hear inside the train, then resumed his pursuit, remaining above our car.

"Saul, could you make it out? What did he say?" Celwyn asked.

"He's calling for the others," Saul replied.

Alongside the train, deep in the dark alleyways of Upper Broadway, I spotted movement, shades responding to the vampire's call.

"And they're coming," Saul said.

"How could Saul hear anything outside the car?" I asked.

"He's one of them," Celwyn replied. "He can hear a heartbeat through a wall."

From the floor, underneath a blanket wrapped around his head, Saul nodded. "And I hear something else. Up ahead, I can hear the sound of air entering the Tube. The seal is damaged. We aren't going to make it to Grid One."

CHAPTER TWENTY-FOUR

THE VAMPIRE KEPT pace with our train car on top of the Tube. Shades now openly joined him, chasing the train car in the shadows alongside Broadway. They followed us, waiting for the right moment to attack.

I worried they knew something we didn't know, something about what lay ahead.

Above the Tube, a sign announced our entry into Grid Two. Only a mile separated us from the safe zone at the south end of the Castle. Under normal conditions, the short trip through the remaining parts of Broadway would have taken less than a minute on the Tube, but our train car barely moved forward, sliding painfully slow along magnets through whatever vacuum remained in the cylinder outside our train car.

Saul was the first to identify the reason for the slowing of the Tube. He rose to his feet and threw off the protective blankets.

Something terrible had happened in Grid Two. Fire charred the buildings on both sides along Broadway, their windows all blown out by an apparent explosion.

"Paloma did this," Celwyn said. "He must have covered his retreat by blowing up everything behind him." Ahead of us, two of the giant steel beams supporting the Upper Tube's structure lay collapsed on top of the protective cylinder, along with a mangled mess of what remained from an upper-level platform. Unlike the Tube below, built upon support beams rising from the foundation of the Castle, the Upper Tube's construction relied on tying the hyperloop train line into the roof of the Atrium structure itself.

The Upper Tube actually hung suspended in mid-air, held in place by steel beams hanging down from the top of the Castle, and a network of platforms along the Line which connected the Tube into the skeletal structure of the city. In the absence of a platform to safely step onto, exiting the Upper Tube meant a free fall of hundreds of feet.

Now one of those platforms lay shredded on top of the Tube, along with two of the supporting beams that had been torn from the roof of the Atrium by the earlier explosion. I wondered how many other support beams had been weakened—and how many more would have to give way before the whole structure broke apart, plunging us to our deaths. I guessed these were the types of thoughts that ran through your mind when you were moving in slow motion towards your potential doom, completely helpless, unable to do anything about it.

The train slowed as it approached the wreckage. We sat in silence while the seconds ticked off, waiting for the inevitable point when the train would completely cease its forward movement, leaving us trapped. The vampire on top of the Tube ran ahead, disappearing into the steel jungle left by the fallen support beams. The shades stalking us alongside Broadway did the same, finding plenty of hiding spots in the shadows underneath the twisted mass of steel.

Celwyn unbuckled his seat belt and exploded out of his seat. "Bloody hell."

The train finally came to a dead stop. Above us, a mountain of debris blocked out all but a few rays of sunshine that somehow managed to break through the tangled wreckage. Where one of the beams fell on top of the hyperloop, a jagged crack ran down the side of the outer shell. The Tube bent downward in front of us, strained by the weight pressing down from above. The train came to rest in the middle of the dip, leaving us stranded at a slight downward angle.

Figures moved all around us in the dark, and my stomach churned.

I unbuckled my seat belt and stood next to Celwyn, never moving my focus away from the windows. "Any ideas?"

A female shade leaped out of the maze of metal and landed on the side of the Tube. She dug her unnaturally long fingernails into the plastic shell and pressed her face against the side of the cylinder. Her dead black eyes tracked from me to Celwyn and eventually to Saul, then stopped. She cocked her head to the side in what I interpreted as surprise, then she leaped away, disappearing into the darkness.

Celwyn turned on the radio in his helmet. "Hector, we're trapped in the rubble of what's left of the Upper Tube in Grid Two. Surrounded by shades. Could use some help."

Static poured out of the radio.

"Do you think he can hear you? Is there reception in here?"

"He heard me." Celwyn tried again. "Dammit, Captain. You owe me one." He waited as nothing but static answered his calls. After a few seconds, Celwyn tapped the radio button again and looked at me before taking a deep breath. "I've found another one in the Castle who's immune and she's with me. You know what that means. Whatever you need to do, it's worth it."

Celwyn continued to look at me as we waited for Paloma to answer. The sides of his lips curled in a nervous smile. "He'll answer," he said confidently.

Finally, Paloma's smooth voice piped through the radio. "*I'm sending a team. You better not be lying.*"

Celwyn placed the radio back on his belt. "We need to find a way out of here."

"Wait," I said. "What was that about? I mean, why am I 'worth it'?"

"It's become harder to find those who are immune, Mel. We don't know why. Something in the gene pool maybe. Who knows? I was the last one Paloma found. He gave up looking right before he left the Knights."

I felt a rush of adrenaline. What did this even mean? I had never thought of myself as special. Far from it. To say my life was boring would be kind. Pathetic would be more accurate, especially after Alex died.

"I hate to interrupt," Saul said from the front of the train. "Look."

The cloaked vampire had returned. He crouched on a piece of metal jutting out from the beam that lay on the cracked shell of the Tube. Behind him, a small army of shades moved around within the steel jungle lying on top of us, careful to avoid any penetrating ray of sunlight.

He lifted his arms above his head. In them, he held a two-foot-long chunk of steel he had pulled from the debris. The vampire slammed the steel chunk down, hitting it against the cracked section of the hyperloop shell. The entire Tube shook from the blow.

"How do we get out of here, Saul?" Celwyn asked.

"I...I don't know."

"What do you mean, you don't know? You had to have a plan for us to get out if we made it?

"Yes, but that would have been at a landing platform. Here, if I open the side doors with the emergency lever, there will just be the outside shell of the Tube."

"Saul, there must be another way out," I said.

"Mel, even if we could get out of this car, I don't know if the pressure of the Tube is safe. We could asphyxiate the moment we break out of this protective bubble."

"I think we're about to find out the answer to that question," Celwyn said.

Another impact from the vampire's makeshift battering ram shattered the already cracked shell casing of the Tube. Inside our soundproof train car, we watched as pieces of clear molded plastic fell into the Tube without making a noise, leaving a gaping hole facing outside. The vampire dropped through the hole and lowered the covering on his face.

"Looks safe to me," I said.

Saul ran to the back of the train car and ran his fingers along the edges of one of the windows. "Here, this is glass. It will break if you shoot it."

Celwyn joined Saul at the rear of the train and studied the window.

The vampire glared at me through the front of the train. He wore the shiny black Idrissia armor without the winged helm on his head. White teeth sparkled against dark skin as he smiled at his success in breaking into the Tube. A rabid mob of shades flowed through the hole to join him in the tight confines of the Tube.

"They're coming!" I shouted.

A series of loud pops rang out inside the train car. The sound of Celwyn kicking through glass signaled his success in creating an exit out the back of the car into the Tube. I took one last look at the vampire closing in on the train car, then turned and sprinted down the aisle.

Saul and Celwyn were already through the open window, standing behind the train car in the Tube. I quickly joined them.

"Those cracks in the Tube must have been all the way through," Saul said. "It had already pressurized, or else the whole thing would have exploded when the vampire broke the shell."

I followed the two of them, running through the Tube away from the train car. We quickly reached a landing platform where two sliding doors built into the frame of the Tube barred our exit. Saul raised the crowbar he had removed from the train and pried it between the doors.

Behind us, I heard more breaking glass. The vampire was in the train. In seconds, he would be out the back window and sprinting after us through the Tube.

"Hurry up!" Celwyn shouted.

Saul pried the doors open. He threw down the tool, grabbed one door in each hand, and pulled them apart. Slowly, they creaked open wide enough for me to squeeze through, out onto the platform. I wasn't claustrophobic, but it felt good to be out of the Tube with solid ground under my feet, even if I was standing on a platform forty stories above the ground.

Celwyn followed behind me, then Saul.

Once outside of the Tube, Celwyn immediately removed his backpack and began digging inside.

"What are you doing?"

He ignored me, removing two small discs from the backpack. I watched as he calmly stuck one of the metal discs on the bottom of the Tube and the other one on the top.

The vampire had made it through the train car and closed quickly. The shades flowed out the back window of the train, not far behind.

Celwyn pushed a button on each metal disc and a red light began to flash. "Go, go, go!" he shouted.

The three of us jumped down from the platform, landed on the street, and ran for the nearest alley.

I didn't make it.

The explosion set off a concussive blast that knocked me down. I flew forward and landed roughly on the stained concrete. The only thing that saved me from flying head first into the side of a strip club was Saul's quick reflexes, catching me mid-flight and yanking me toward the opening of the alley.

I turned and looked for the vampire, but he was gone, along with an entire section of the Tube.

The charges set by Celwyn had created another break in the Tube. With the Tube already broken up ahead, and a heavy train sitting in the middle, the damaged section collapsed, crashing down through the Atrium, taking the vampire and the shades inside with it. A cloud of dust and smoke billowed up through the center of the Atrium, clouding the view of the other side.

Celwyn helped me get up. "Let's go. We're running out of time. It's already midday."

I tested my legs and followed Celwyn and Saul down Broadway toward Grid One. We quickly made it back to the site of Paloma's explosion, and noticed that much of the large debris had been dragged down with the Tube when it fell, including the two steel columns that had previously sat on top of the hyperloop.

But it still looked like a battlefield. The bombed-out remains of buildings loomed on my left, gaping holes in the fronts of the structures where elaborate entries and bright signs once stood. On my right, the tangled remains of steel hyperloop platforms and elevator shafts separated us from the central abyss of the Atrium. Up ahead, I could see the jagged end of what was left standing of the Tube's cylinder after being torn apart.

Acrid smoke filled my nostrils. The fiery smell lingered in place with no air circulation to clear the residue of the explosion. Without power, the temperature controls had long since stopped working, rendering the Castle nothing more than a hot and stuffy metal box sitting in the middle of the Mojave desert.

Celwyn slowed and lifted his rifle to his shoulder. "Be careful," he hissed. "Not all of the shades went down with the Tube." He looked at me. "Try to stay in the sunlight."

Saul flitted silently from one shadow to the next, making his own way through the devastated remains of Broadway. I walked carefully through the maze of rubble, with my own rifle in hand, occasionally spotting the remains of a dead shade. Apparently, Paloma had taken out quite a few of them with his fiery retreat.

Celwyn brought up the rear, his head on a swivel, searching the ruins on both sides of the street for movement.

Ahead of us, a building along Broadway had fallen over, partially blocking the street. Saul stood frozen in a shadowy doorway and motioned for me to stop. Celwyn reached my side, and we both sensed it at the same time. Shades were nearby.

"I'll go first," Celwyn said. "Stay close." He made his way around the pile of rubble towards the edge of the street, close to the central opening in the Atrium protected by a small metal railing. There, away from the buildings lining Broadway, the sunlight shined the brightest.

Saul didn't follow. Instead, he remained in the shadows and began shouting in the language of the vampires.

"How can he do that?" I asked Celwyn.

"Once they turn, they all have the ability to communicate with each other. The language is Thracian. It's a dead language today, but it was the language spoken in the geography where the first infections occurred thousands of years ago. From that original bloodline, the parasite evolved to use the common language to link the infected, allowing them to immediately communicate and work together. They come right out of the box speaking it."

In response to Saul's shouts, shades filtered out of the alley next to the destroyed building. Another small group of shades emerged from the base of the tangled ruin, blocking the street where they had been hiding, led by a young man. The leader of the shades first looked at Saul, then turned his attention to Celwyn and me. He took a step in our direction and the shades behind him followed.

Saul shouted and the shades froze. I guess some words are universal. Saul stepped out of the shadows and shouted again, "No!" He calmly walked into the middle of Broadway and stepped in front of the young leader. He shouted one more time in a voice that rang with an authority that one can only acquire with age and experience. "No!"

I wasn't sure what to make of Saul's effort to communicate with the shades. At first, I thought he was trying to simply stave off their attack, but I quickly realized that he was *talking* to them. He barked out words in the language of the shades, and the young leader responded. Saul placed his hand on the man's shoulder, then said a few more words. Under Saul's spell, the shades almost seemed human again, restored to the young men and women who no doubt were working in the clubs of Upper Broadway when the attack occurred. Left for dead, they somehow survived, only to wake up as shades themselves, consumed by the parasite and without the benefit of their former humanity.

Saul left the shades and walked towards me, stopping before he exited the protection of the shadows. "I'm staying here," he said firmly. "Go save your girls, Melanie." He looked over his shoulder. "But there are others here in the Castle who need to be saved as well."

I had seen that look on Saul's face many times and knew full well what it meant. I had seen it the first time he told me he wanted to walk the hospice at night. I had seen it when he argued with his doctor over how long he had left to live. And I had seen it on his face the night he was bitten.

Saul was a man of determination, and once his mind was set, he would not be swayed.

CHAPTER TWENTY-FIVE

AT THAT MOMENT, the Atrium erupted with the sound of gunfire. Bullets pinged off the metal debris lying in the street and the young leader of the shades dropped to the ground, his head ripped apart by a barrage of bullets.

Saul bellowed out a horrible cry, then bolted towards the shades. Some ran towards the gunfire while two remained with Saul, furiously yelling and motioning with his arms.

"Paloma's rescue team," Celwyn said. "They're here."

"I can see that!" I shouted. "Tell them to stop shooting. They're going to kill Saul."

Celwyn shook his head. "I don't think we're going to convince them to stop shooting at shades, Mel. Hell, I don't think I'm convinced." He looked over at Saul, crouched behind a twisted piece of plastic that once made up a sign for one of the clubs, then back to me. "I'll step out into the open so they know we're back here. That will take away the line of fire. And when I do that, tell Saul to leave quickly before they see him."

He nodded at Saul. Celwyn didn't speak, but the simple gesture conveyed both a measure of respect and a not-so-friendly reminder that if he saw the old man again, he may have to end his life.

Celwyn charged around the rubble blockade and began shouting at Paloma's team. Within a few seconds, the pinging sounds of bullets impacting metal stopped, and the shooting moved away from our position.

Behind the downed building blocking the road, the remaining shades huddled next to Saul like a flock of sheep with their shepherd. Many of the young men and women's clothes were tattered. Most were missing shoes. In barely more than a day, they had been reduced to dirty savages roaming the streets of the Castle, looking for blood. I wondered whether Saul could truly help them follow his path, or if his faith in his ability to help restore their humanity was a misguided and grave mistake.

"Go!" I shouted at Saul. "You don't have much time before they get here. They'll kill you."

He rose to his feet and pushed the shades towards the dark alley leading away from Broadway. I followed at a safe distance, rifle in hand, still not entirely convinced of Saul's ability to control his newfound wards.

Before he disappeared, Saul turned and spoke. "I should be dead. You allowed me a chance to live, Melanie. I thank you for that."

"Please don't make me regret that decision. Whatever happens, know that you're not a monster. You can find a way to survive without becoming like the others." I nodded to the shades standing behind Saul. "Save as many as you can, but get out of here tonight and run away. Find a small town somewhere and hide from the Knights."

"That's good advice," Saul said. "You should take it as well. Don't listen to Celwyn. You're not like him. Now go! Time is running short for us both." He shouted something in Thracian and two shades ran behind him into the alley. Within seconds, they turned a corner and Saul disappeared from sight.

For a moment I felt the sting of loss. The loss of a friend. The loss of a protector. But I also felt something else—pride. After escaping death's door only days ago, Saul had gained not only an extension of his life, but a newfound purpose. And I had played a part in that.

It was ironic that in all of my years as a hospice nurse, and my tireless fight to save my patients from the inevitable end of life, I had never actually succeeded until I arrived in this god forsaken place. Saul—one of my patients—had actually cheated death. But to what end?

I prayed I hadn't created a monster, and that my friend would somehow do some good. That seemed like more than enough to ask of anyone.

Then I walked away, content in my decision to save Saul's life, knowing I would likely never see him again.

———

CELWYN WAVED me forward as I ducked and weaved my way past the tangled mess of plastic and steel sprawled across Broadway. Beside him stood twelve Idrissia soldiers armed to the teeth wearing combat helmets with raised visors. They looked surprisingly relaxed under the circumstances. One smoked a cigarette. Another one stood near the front window of a club, focused intently on the graphic pictures lining the walls.

I quickly made my way down the middle of the street, no longer worried about avoiding shadows. I stepped around the dead bodies of several shades who had made the mistake of ignoring Saul and charging off in search of a meal at the earlier sounds of gunfire. Within a few seconds, I made it to Celwyn.

"This is Dax," Celwyn said. "He's in charge."

"Hey, I'm Mel."

Dax towered over me and held a big gun in both hands, so I figured he wasn't exactly expecting a handshake. I tried to get a close look at him, but it was impossible to see much of anything past the jet black mustache and thick beard that covered his face.

"Just picking up the two of you?" Dax asked. "No one else right?"

I paused then looked at Celwyn. "Yeah. Just the two of us."

"Alright then, let's get you back to Grid One. Paloma's waiting."

Dax whistled like a professional referee, and the soldiers immediately formed up without speaking into a tight circle formation with Celwyn and me in the middle. Dax led the way through the bombed-out remains of Grid Two, and we never saw a soul, not even a shade. Celwyn didn't say a word the entire trip, so I followed his lead. Dax's team moved like professionals, always scanning the dark alleys lining the brightly lit protection of the Atrium, always looking for threats.

Eventually we made it to a check point at the start of Grid One. A makeshift barricade blocked Upper Broadway on both sides of the Atrium. Soldiers patrolled the Tube landing platforms perched immediately above the barricade, and a long-barreled gun that looked more like a cannon pointed downward towards Upper Broadway on my side of the Atrium. To go beyond this point required a traverse up several flights of stairs, a short walk past the heavy weaponry mounted to the steel landing, and down more stairs to return to Upper Broadway.

Once we made it into Grid One, everything changed.

I finally saw people. Lots of people. Something I hadn't seen in days. Most of them were soldiers, but I spotted a few who didn't wear the black military uniform.

"This way," Dax said. He turned on the flashlight mounted to his rifle and led us into a stairwell next to an inoperable glass elevator mounted to the side of the Atrium. Prior to the shutdown, the elevator would have been the scenic way down, allowing a view of the Atrium spanning the length of the Castle, descending from Upper to Lower Broadway. Now, like everything else, it sat idle.

Celwyn and I entered the stairwell behind Dax. Three of his team followed us, flicking on their flashlights as well. The rest of Dax's team stayed behind at the check point.

As we spiraled downward, all I could think about was the prospect of making the trip in reverse. If there was an attack up top, those men and women manning the checkpoint wouldn't have help for a long time, if ever. The climb up would be like ascending nearly half of the Empire State Building.

About halfway down the thirty-five story descent, Dax paused and turned. "You need a break?"

Celwyn never even bothered to look in my direction before answering. "No. We don't have a lot of time."

Dax laughed. "Ain't that the truth."

We kept moving, and I finally mustered enough courage to attempt small talk with Dax. "So how many people from the Castle made it into Grid One? Must be a lot of people down below, right?"

"Couple of thousand made it here, mostly from the nearby Grids," he replied. "There are some still holed up inside the Castle, but it's too dangerous for us to go looking for them. A few have trickled in over the last few days, but those who venture out don't last long. Too many shades."

"So what's the end game here, Dax?" Celwyn asked. "Seems like Paloma has just backed you all into a corner. Nightfall is coming and you know what hell is coming with it."

Dax grunted. "I know what's coming. I've been fighting with the Captain for a while now."

Before Celwyn and Dax's banter could devolve further, we made it to the bottom of the stairwell and the familiar sounds of the city returned. The natural sunlight in the Atrium revealed a bustling Broadway filled with people coming and going. Even without power, the restaurants were open and serving food.

Some things never change. People have to eat.

The ratio of soldiers to civilians was almost even down here, and no one seemed panicked. Many of them busily worked on a construction project at the edge of Grid One. The defensive barrier erected by Paloma was much taller than the one on Upper Broadway, and wide enough for soldiers to walk across the top.

Like above, the landing platforms on each side of the Tube had teams of soldiers posted next to large mounted guns bolted to the steel floors, pointed down to deal with any approaching threats. But they had something else. Next to each of the big guns, a wheeled trailer held a rectangular lamp ten feet across with violet-tinted cylindrical bulbs lining it from top to bottom.

I pointed at the closest lamp and nudged Celwyn. "What's the deal with the giant light bulbs?"

"UV lights," he said. "Smart. Paloma's not playing around."

"You think they can actually hold back the shades?"

Celwyn stroked his chin and looked around. He nodded affirmatively. "Maybe. Maybe."

Broadway narrowed as we left the open-aired Atrium and neared Silver Castle Station. Up ahead, sunlight filtered though the familiar wall of glass doors marking the south entrance to the city. Only a few weeks ago, I had entered those doors, excited to embrace a new chapter in my life. Little did I know that chapter was straight out of a horror story.

I just hoped it wasn't my last chapter.

Dax led the way outside, and I took a deep breath of the fresh desert air. A gentle breeze hit my face, a reminder that the concrete platform where I stood rose five stories off the ground.

I finally got my answer as to where all the people had gone. Silver Castle Station had been turned into an encampment, filled mostly with the older and infirmed, along with women and children. One corner functioned as a makeshift triage area, with cots lining the wall and the familiar sight of Idrissia nurses wearing blue scrubs.

My heart skipped a beat at the sight of children. Somewhere out there in the mass of humanity, I knew Emma and Alex huddled together, missing their mother, scared of what would come at nightfall.

Dax pointed with his rifle barrel at the shiny mag lev train parked at the edge of the station. "There. Captain is waiting for you inside."

"Thanks," Celwyn replied.

Two female train attendants exited the closest car and motioned for us to follow them. Once inside, we walked through cars filled with rows of empty seats until we reached the back of the train. There the cars housed large suites, lavishly decorated for VIPs traveling by train to Idrissia's city.

We walked through several of the cars housing suites, each one of them nothing more than a narrow hallway with two doors opening up to a suite on either side. The last car in the train contained only a single private entrance.

The attendants stopped. The closest attendant pointed to a bronze lever on the wood-grained door. "You can go inside. The Captain is waiting for you."

Celwyn wasted no time, flinging the door open and barging into the suite. I followed more cautiously behind him, not sure what to expect based on my last meeting with Paloma.

167

Inside the door, a marble entryway turned into a living area lined with floor-to-ceiling windows larger than the small portholes I recalled from my train car. Beside a cluster of chairs and a couch, Paloma sat at a desk intently studying a map.

He rose from the desk when we entered, and a flash of recognition crossed his face when he saw me standing next to Celwyn. "Ms. Sanger. So good to see you again." Paloma looked at Celwyn. "So she is the one you mentioned on the radio? She's immune like you and me?"

"Yes," Celwyn replied.

"Well, that explains a lot. I imagine you are tired and hungry after making your way through the Castle." He pointed to a dining room table next to the living area which contained place settings for three. Behind me, the door to the suite opened and the attendants returned, this time holding stainless steel trays with platters piled with food.

The smell of freshly cooked food overwhelmed the small confines of the train car. And coffee. They brought coffee.

It was glorious.

Paloma pointed with his hand at the dining room table and the edge of his cheek curled upward. "Sit down. We have much to discuss."

CHAPTER TWENTY-SIX

I SAT down at the dining room table and promptly poured myself a cup of coffee. If I was going to die tonight, I was going to make damn sure I was sufficiently caffeinated. Celwyn hesitated at first, then slowly pulled out the chair next to me and slid into the seat.

"Go ahead," Paloma said. "Eat whatever you want. They're cooking everything in the Castle. Without refrigeration, it's going to spoil anyway." He sat down at the head of the table, plucked a chicken breast off a platter with his fork, and transferred it to his own plate. Before cutting into it, he turned to face Celwyn. "It's good to see you again, Celwyn. It's been too long."

"We don't have time for Thanksgiving dinner, Hector," Celwyn said. "We saw what happened on the roof last night. Tarek is here and he'll be coming for you tonight. We must get these people out of here and destroy this place."

Paloma poured himself a glass of wine then held up the bottle. "Anyone else?"

Celwyn rejected the offer, then I did the same. In the resulting awkward silence, I grabbed a piece of bread. I knew better than to jump into this conversation but figured I might as well chew on something while listening.

Paloma set down the bottle of wine and continued. "And how exactly do you propose that we safely remove thousands of people from a powerless city isolated in the middle of the desert?"

"Turn the power back on and let them call for help. It will come."

"Is that Celwyn talking? Or the Knights? I can't turn the power back on. I didn't turn it off. And even if I could, what good would it do? Yes, help would come, and those who are rescued would tell stories of what happened here. Is that what the Knights want? And how do you propose we fight Tarek and a city full of shades with rescue operations under way? No, we would be leading more to the slaughter and creating a very messy public embarrassment for your employer and mine."

"And who is your employer exactly?" asked Celwyn quietly.

Paloma shook his head. "It's complicated. Suffice it to say, all is not well within the Idrissa Bloodline. You're in the middle of a vampire family squabble."

Celwyn shook his head. "I don't believe you."

"How do you think I took over the city so easily? I had the full backing and resources of the Head of the Idrissia Corporation. My orders were simple—enter the Castle and eliminate the breeding facility, then get the hell out. Everything went well initially. We took control of the laboratory, but then Tarek found out Idrissa was pulling the plug on his science experiment. So he let loose a horde of shades. The power went out, everything went to hell, and you know the rest."

"So who's side are you on?" I asked.

"I'm not on anyone's side," Paloma replied sharply. He heaped a pile of roasted carrots onto his plate and began cutting the chicken. "Tell me, Ms. Sanger, how do you know you are immune?"

"She was bit," Celwyn answered. "I was there."

"Is this true?" Paloma asked.

I nodded. "On my shoulder. Hurts like hell."

"Yes, I know. It does." His hand instinctively moved to his collar. "Has Celwyn tried to recruit you to his cause, since you apparently are one of the few left in the world who are qualified?"

I offered a shy smile. "He may have mentioned it. Right now, I just want to get out of here. Not really the time to discuss career opportunities."

"Fair enough," Paloma replied. "One question—did Celwyn tell you who pays the bills for the Knights? It obviously costs a lot of money to be the worldwide enforcer of the Accords."

"Don't! This is not the time and place," Celwyn said.

"Why not? She should know what she is getting into." Paloma took a bite of chicken, chewed slowly for a few seconds, and then looked at me. "The Accords required the surviving Bloodlines to pay reparations in perpetuity to the Catholic Church, a tithe if you will." He then turned back to Celwyn. "The Knights are compromised. The Church will never give up such a huge source of revenue. You know I'm right."

Celwyn remained quiet and refused to look at Paloma.

"You are being uncharacteristically quiet, Celwyn. If you keep this up, I might have to recruit Ms. Sanger myself." He smiled again in my direction. "You're quite special you know. Always room for someone who can't be turned."

Celwyn seethed and he could barely control the anger in his voice. "You and I both know what we have to do. The difference is I care about the people sitting out there. I would save as many as I could."

Paloma slammed his fork down into his plate. "What do you think I am doing here exactly? I'm feeding and sheltering thousands. I'm preparing to fight Tarek and his army. I ask you again—where are the Knights? Why haven't *you* mounted a rescue mission? Surely with such vast resources at your organization's disposal you could handle the task yourself? Unless…unless you have no interest in actually saving these people and would sacrifice them *all* to prevent the parasite from escaping this city. Heavens man, get off your fancy Carpathian high horse. I know what the Knights do. The *only* one doing any saving around here is me. If it was up to you, this place would be a smoldering ruin and everyone inside of it dead."

Celwyn sat still, trying hard to muster a poker face. Whatever little control he thought he had over his situation was rapidly dissolving. "You're a liar," he said flatly.

"Am I? I don't think so."

"Paloma, you've bought us time. The Knights are coming. We can work together again to save everyone."

"No doubt the Knights are coming," Paloma said. "But in the meantime, I have to deal with Tarek's army. Two fighters who can't be turned would be invaluable." He paused and his demeanor softened. "And I imagine you would like to settle the score. This is your chance, Celwyn. Tarek is here. He's somewhere in the City. This is your chance."

I looked at Celwyn. Paloma wasn't lying about his anger towards Tarek. It bubbled below the surface, ready to explode. Clearly, Celwyn had his reasons to stay and fight. And if the girls were here, I had my reasons, too. My look said it all, and Celwyn knew my opinion without me speaking a word.

Celwyn shook his head in resignation. "Fine, we'll fight with you." He started filling his plate with food and settled into a more comfortable position.

Apparently, Celwyn decided that fighting on an empty stomach wasn't a good idea, and I tended to agree. I started picking at the contents of the platters on the table, starting with the chocolate cake on the far side. As far as last meals go, I didn't see the point of eating healthy.

Paloma's expression changed, and he visibly relaxed. "Good. Eat up. We'll all need our strength tonight."

We sat in silence for a few minutes as the three of us ravenously attacked the contents of the table. I finally slowed down after my second piece of cake and became brave enough to talk.

I looked at Paloma. "We saw Tarek. He was in the Heights."

Paloma suddenly straightened in his chair and quickly finished chewing his food. "You saw him?"

Celwyn nodded. "We passed him in the Upper Tube on the way here. It looks like they're massing in the Heights, waiting for sundown."

Paloma bit his lip. "Of course they would hide in the most luxurious part of the Castle. It's in their privileged nature." He picked up a glass of wine and took another sip. "I'm going to kill him, you know." He looked at Celwyn. "Not because of my employer, and not because of the Accords or some punishment for what he has done. Revenge is your department. I'm going to kill Tarek because he is a vampire. And for that simple fact he deserves to die."

I looked nervously at Celwyn. He remained quiet, and resumed work on finishing his plate.

"So what did he look like?" Paloma asked me quietly.

"I really didn't get a good look," I said. "The train moved through there so quickly." Paloma hung on every word, and stared at me with a plea in his eyes. "But I did see that he was tall and wore some sort of armor. Tarek had his helmet off, and I saw long black hair. And his eyes—they were red. I've never seen anything like that before."

"I have," Paloma replied. "The day he did this to me." He pulled down the high collar on his black uniform and revealed a scar that started on the left side of his neck and continued down toward his collar bone. The top of the scar, the only portion visible, consisted of a pink mass of burned flesh. "I cauterized it myself," he said, then he changed the subject. "Celwyn, have you heard the story of how the Head of the Idrissia Bloodline picked Tarek as his Successor?"

Celwyn shook his head.

I perked up. This sounded interesting.

Paloma stood from the table and began his story. "Tarek Malik is the youngest vampire of all the Bloodlines, only a little over three hundred years old. Zeidan Malik, the Head of the Idrissia Bloodline is not his father. In fact, they share no blood relation at all, which is rare. Most of the Heads choose a Successor who is family, but not Zeidan. It's widely believed Zeidan killed his own father to assume control of the Idrissia Bloodline in the 1400s, not long after the end of the Great War, but he never married or had any children. Having no family, he waited to appoint a Successor. In fact, he waited almost four centuries."

"I always thought Tarek was his son," Celwyn said.

"He claims him as a son," Paloma interrupted. "But he isn't. He is a thief and a murderer. One night Tarek and his gang broke into the wrong home. The gang killed all of Zeidan's human guards, but as you would expect, Zeidan made quick work of them. Tarek was the last to die, and he cursed Zeidan as he lay there bleeding on the floor of

Zeidan's mansion. In that moment, sitting together at the edge of death, Zeidan saw something in Tarek. Hate. He knew that if he turned him, this man would be his weapon. A weapon he could use to restart the Great War."

"Where did you hear this story?" Celwyn asked.

"Zeidan told me the story himself. Right before he sent me here to stop Tarek," Paloma replied.

"But why would Zeidan be trying to stop Tarek?" I asked.

"Good question. Allow me to finish. At first, Zeidan's plan worked. The Mothers nursed Tarek to maturity as a vampire in record time, using the old ways to help him master the parasite. Tarek relished being a vampire and embraced Zeidan's plan to start a war. He traveled the world to recruit others to Idrissia's cause and left a trail of death behind him. He was perfect—brash and direct, unlike the other vampires. Over the years, Tarek gained a following among many young Successors in other Bloodlines. He bought off politicians and governments all over the world. But Tarek went too far. He threw out the old ways. The old vampires, like Zeidan, are steeped in tradition— beholden to the Mothers, the ones who gave them back their humanity. Tarek's been making vampires without the Mothers, and his technology would allow him to make vampires by the thousands."

Paloma took a deep breath, then slowly exhaled. "No way those witches were going to let Tarek make them obsolete. So they got Zeidan to pull the plug, and he hired me to do it."

"There's never been vampires created at that kind of scale," Celwyn exclaimed. "With an army that large, humans wouldn't stand a chance."

"*No one* would stand a chance," Paloma corrected. "If Tarek was allowed to breed an army of rich and powerful vampires, he could get rid of the Mothers and rule over all of the other Bloodlines, including Zeidan. Zeidan was fine with a war, but wasn't good with...bending the knee. He has a vested interest in the status quo. It's quite lucrative, I assure you."

"Wow. Some things never change. Even for vampires it's all about the money," I said.

"Yeah, and for Paloma, too," Celwyn muttered.

Paloma stepped forward and rested his hand on Celwyn's chair. "I'm telling you this so you understand what I've been doing. The Knights aren't in the business of killing vampires any more, but I am. I've taken out more of them since I left than I ever did as a Knight, even though I was being paid to do it by their own kind. One way or another, we have to eradicate every one of the Bloodlines, root and branch. The Accords won't last. The Knights have become weak while the Bloodlines have grown in wealth and power. The only thing keeping the Heads of the Bloodlines from openly declaring war is distrust of the younger ones like Tarek—and each other. They have had the whole world to themselves for nearly a thousand years, just the few of them, spread out across the world ruling their individual fiefdoms. They have become accustomed to it. They prefer to scheme and manipulate against us from the shadows, but the idea of open war is growing more acceptable every day. If it's not Tarek leading the way with this new technology, it will be someone else."

"The Knights will never throw out the Accords," Celwyn replied flatly.

"And that's why I left," said Paloma. "Because war is upon you. You just don't see it yet."

We all sat in silence for a few moments, then Paloma turned to me. "There is one more story you should hear about Tarek, the one about the day I received this scar—the day Celwyn and I first met."

"No," Celwyn roared. "Don't."

"She should know why you hate him, don't you think."

"She knows. I told her."

"Ah, but did you tell her everything? Somehow I doubt that, Celwyn."

The two men stared at each other in a silent battle of wills. Celwyn finally relented and picked up a glass to fill it with wine. "Tell her if you want. It doesn't matter any more."

Paloma looked at me longingly. "You truly are special, Ms. Sanger. A long time ago, it was my job to search for people like you. It was my life's work really. I searched every inch of this planet looking for needles in a haystack—people immune to the parasite. And with every year that passed, my job became harder and harder until I couldn't find them any more. I thought about giving up…I almost did. Then one day, I discovered a boy, a descendant from one of our most accomplished Knights who had been hidden from his family. His mother had placed the boy with an orphanage and his name had changed, but the boy's lineage was true. He was immune.

"Through great effort, I made the discovery. The identity of this boy, now a married man, was known *only* to me and a few others inside the Order. But when I arrived at his home to talk to him, to reveal to him his duty, and thus fulfill my own, we were attacked by Tarek. Five Knights, and Celwyn here, fought off the vampire. Two Knights died that day. I almost killed the monster…and he left me with this scar." Paloma pointed to his neck.

"Paloma's too mean to die," Celwyn said softly.

"Yes, that's what they say behind my back, don't they? I suppose it's true in a way. But I've never had to shoot my own pregnant wife in the head after she turned into a shade, now have I?" He looked at Celwyn, and his voice dropped to a whisper. "Don't sell yourself short. You, my friend, have ice in your veins."

Paloma sipped from his glass and turned to me. "And that was the day Celwyn joined the Knights. And it was also the day I lost faith. I was betrayed by a spy within the Order." He shook his head firmly. "No one else knew about Celwyn. I had searched for so long to find someone to add to our ranks—someone to provide a future for the Order—and when I finally found one, I lost two in the process. So I gave it up. I stuck around for a bit, but my heart wasn't in it anymore. I left the Knights within a year."

I looked at Celwyn. "I didn't know. I'm…sorry."

Paloma took another long drink, working hard to finish his wine. After turning it upside down, he put the empty glass down on the table and stared at me. His gaze lingered far too long, but not in a disrespectful or lecherous way. Paloma looked at me like a man who had seen a ghost, like a man who didn't believe his own eyes.

After a moment of awkward silence, he turned to Celwyn and shook his head. "Dammit, Celwyn, I can't believe you found a new Knight in all this mess." He then looked away and mumbled something unintelligible about his duty.

For a moment, I thought Paloma was drunk, but I was quickly proved wrong.

A whirring noise slowly rose in volume then quickly receded. Machine gun fire followed.

He jumped out of his chair, springing to his feet like a cat, then sprinted toward the door. "They're back," he shouted.

CHAPTER TWENTY-SEVEN

I RAN through the empty train cars, following Paloma and Celwyn until we stepped out onto the concrete floor of the Silver Castle Station. Shouts and cries erupted from the men and women sheltering underneath the giant alcove cut into the South side of the building. On the edge of the Station, soldiers with automatic rifles pointed them out towards the desert sky.

Somewhere above us, the whirring sound grew louder.

"It's Tarek's ship," Paloma yelled. He ran to the railing at the edge of the Station and leaned out, twisting his body to look upwards.

A silver airship like the one I saw on the roof dove from above our sight line. Sunlight flashed from the stainless steel wings as it flew across the distant train tracks, completing its circle around the end of the Castle. Paloma grabbed a rifle from a nearby soldier and fired it in short steady bursts, but the bullets never hit home. The craft remained just out of range, as if it intended to tease Paloma.

"What's it doing?" I asked.

Paloma handed the rifle back to the soldier. "Tarek is poking and prodding at us—trying to keep us confused, not knowing when and where he will attack. He's been doing it all day, sending shades at us up front, and doing flybys in the back." He smiled. "But he won't dare get too close. We took out his other toy last night. This is his last one, and he needs it to jam our satellite communications."

He turned towards us, a steely look of determination crossing his face. "Celwyn, we have work to do." He buttoned his collar closed as he walked, forging his way through the mass of people blocking his way to the entrance of the Castle.

I looked at Celwyn. "It's okay. Go ahead. I have something I need to do, too."

"I know," he said. "Find those girls." He followed Paloma, quickly disappearing into the crowd of people still buzzing with activity from the threat of the airship.

I approached the railing and stared out into the desert. The air had already begun to cool, and the afternoon sun cast the surroundings of the tall steel monolith in shadows. The world seemed so peaceful, but in a few hours, the sun would set and the Castle would again become a war zone.

Both Paloma and Celwyn left me frustrated. We needed a way to escape, not a fancy battle plan. But what do I know, I'm just a nurse.

My mind kept returning to the girls. They were alive and somewhere in Grid One, waiting for me to get them out of this place. Whatever danger lurked in the desert paled in comparison to the horrors waiting for them inside the Castle. Out there, they might have a chance.

I took a deep breath of fresh air, then turned to start my search around the Station. The gateway to the city now served as a refugee camp. Hordes of former Castle residents congregated in small groups, and I began systematically examining each one, looking for a specific combination—two little girls with an older woman.

The concrete floor spanned more than a football field and must have sheltered at least a thousand people. I walked up and down the length of the Station multiple times, making my way through the makeshift aisles used by the soldiers. Each time I saw a child with blonde hair, my heart soared and then sank again when I didn't recognize the face.

Nearly a half hour passed with no luck, and I grew more desperate. In my heart, I knew Emma and Alex had survived, but I had underestimated the difficulty of finding them amongst the hordes of survivors crowded into such a small space. I needed help from someone who knew the Grid.

Someone like a cop.

THE POLICE STATION on Broadway looked nothing like the last time I saw it. Now the space served as a makeshift hospital, the cabinets and desks pushed to the side and replaced with chairs and cots filled with injured people. Weary eyes from blood-stained soldiers and Castle residents of all ages tracked me as I entered.

Two uniformed officers positioned by the door stepped into my path. The large male to my right spoke. "You don't look hurt. You here to help?"

I thought for a second. "Yes. I'm looking for Detective Serrano. Is she around?"

"Back there." The man pointed towards a familiar hallway leading to jail cells and a detention room that I hoped to never be locked inside again.

I stepped gingerly around a young woman with a bandage on her arm and entered the hallway. The thick metal security door with bars lining a small center window hung open, and once I crossed its threshold, I entered familiar territory. The smell hit me first, the pungent odor of fresh disinfectant laced with the metallic stench of blood. I knew what came next.

Bodies filled the beds in the jail cells on either side of the hallway. Some of the bodies showed signs of movement. Some did not.

Doctors and nurses, many in street clothes, darted in every direction, in and out of the open cell doors, speaking and moving in a rhythm I knew too well. For a moment, I wondered if I should drop my rifle and join them, but I ignored that thought and kept pushing forward. That wasn't me. Not any more.

At the end of the hallway, in one of the cells, Detective Serrano stood next to an IV pole with a tube entering the arm of a soldier lying still in the bottom of a bunk bed bolted against the wall. She fumbled with a replacement bag, trying to remove the tab on the bottom port while holding the empty bag in her other hand.

"Hey, Detective. Need some help?" I asked.

Serrano turned around and flashed a weak smile once she registered my identity. "I don't know where you came from, but I'll take the help. Glad you're still alive." Sweat rolled down her face, and her long curly brown hair was trapped in a loose fitting pony tail that seemed as if it would explode at any moment. The dark bags under her eyes suggested she hadn't slept in days.

I leaned my rifle against the wall and took the replacement bag from Serrano. "I got it," I said. My training kicked in and, without thinking, I hooked the bag on the pole, removed the tab from the tubing spike on the bottom, and carefully inserted the tube leading to the unconscious man on the bed. "Gravity infusion. It's been a while since I've done it the old fashioned way."

"Power's out, so it's all we have," said Serrano. "We've raided every clinic and doctor's office in the Grid for supplies and brought everything we could find here to the jail."

I looked down at the fresh bandages wrapped around the chest of the man lying in the bed. "What happened to him?"

"He came in last night and had surgery this morning. Bunch of soldiers were injured up on the roof. It's been chaos all day, and everyone with medical training is pitching in." She looked around. "And there aren't nearly enough of us. We could use help from someone like you who knows what she's doing."

I closed the clamp on the tubing and made sure the drip started before answering Serrano. "I wish I could help, Detecti—"

She interrupted. "I think we can do away with the 'detective' title at this point."

"Right, and you can call me Mel, too, but the reason I came here was to get your help. I'm looking for two girls, blonde hair, around six and ten, who may have came in with their grandmother. I ran into them out in the Castle after all this started and, you know, I wanted to make sure they were still alive."

"I haven't seen two little girls, but I haven't really been looking." Serrano walked over to a sink in the corner of the cell and began washing her hands with a bar of soap. "Luckily, the water still works, but it won't last. The pipeline is stopped and we're running off the storage tanks." Serrano dried her hands and turned around. She studied my face, and an unspoken communication occurred, as if she herself felt the concern I was trying hard to control. "I am due for a break and have an idea of where they might be. Wash up and I'll take you there."

All I could muster was a polite "Thank you," and I fought back the mix of excitement and dread building inside me as the soapy water flowed across my hands. I was so close to seeing the girls again. They had to be here. And if they weren't? I couldn't let my mind wander down that path. I couldn't allow myself to believe that I had left them to die. Once I finished, Serrano led me out of the jail-turned-military-hospital and back out onto Broadway.

"I don't have any kids myself," she said. "Never even been married. It's tough with this job. But I have a niece. She's twelve now and lives back in Texas. If anything ever happened to her, I would… well, I'm not sure what I would do."

Serrano led me out into the Atrium, now partially bathed in shadows. "When I have cases involving children, I think of my niece and how I would want someone to protect her if I wasn't around to do it. So yeah, I get it. I understand the need to protect a child, even if she's not your own. God knows they all need protecting in this craziness."

The Atrium bustled with activity. Spread out along Broadway, near the restaurants and clubs idled by the lack of power, people milled about nervously, watching the preparations for the attack everyone knew would accompany the arrival of nightfall. Up ahead, along the streets lining the Tube, hundreds of Idrissia soldiers massed behind barricades, busily positioning weapons and material.

"It's not enough," I said softly. "I was up on the roof last night. There's too many of those monsters—and if they break through, everyone will die."

"Maybe. But we have to try."

I grabbed Serrano's arm. "You could run. We could get out of this place."

"How? Paloma welded shut every access door into Grid One. The only way in or out of the rest of the Castle is through the Atrium. We tried to send a truck outside this morning through the garage, and the airship took it out in less than five minutes. Face it, the good news is you made it to Grid One. The bad news is we're all trapped."

Serrano began moving again, and after a few minutes pointed toward a familiar-looking bar with a giant neon tree in the front. "We're here. Hurry up. We don't have long until everything goes on lockdown."

CHAPTER TWENTY-EIGHT

"THE JOSHUA TREE SALOON?" I asked.

"It's a daycare now. I always thought the place looked like something out of a cartoon, and I guess they figured the kids would like the colorful signs on the walls." Serrano opened the door, and I followed her inside. "Last night they moved everyone into the warehouse underneath the Station. It's the only secure location big enough for everyone to fit—but it's pitch dark. As soon as the sun rose, and they figured it was safe, everyone came up top and spread out. This is where they brought the kids who were unclaimed."

I looked around the bar, and the dimly lit space sat empty with the exception of a few children sitting in booths and a cluster lying on their stomachs on the dance floor, surrounded by white paper and colored markers.

Serrano turned and whispered. "As you can see, there haven't been many."

Once inside, a well-dressed woman with gray hair rose from a seat behind a table in the front, where she sat next to an older man. Colorful artwork of animals, flowers, and landscapes were haphazardly strewn across the top of the table. She slowly made her way around the table and approached the door.

"Can I help you?" she asked. "Are you looking for one of the children?"

Serrano stepped forward. "This is Mel. She just arrived to the Grid and is looking for two girls. They may have come in together, around six and ten years old."

The woman turned around to speak to the old man behind her sitting at the table. "Frank, I don't think we have any sisters, do we?"

He looked up from the book sitting in front of him on the table. "No, don't think so," he replied. "We have those boys from Grid Three. They're brothers."

The old woman shook her head with frustration. "I don't think that's who they're looking for." She smiled at me. "Hi, Mel. Are you family? Do you know their names?"

I carefully avoided the family question. "Alex is ten. The younger one, Emma, is six."

The woman frowned and looked back nervously at Frank. He placed down his book and stood up from his chair.

"You've seen them?" I asked. My heart raced. The old couple clearly knew something. *What did they know?*

The old man now stood by his wife's side, a grim look on his face. "We have a girl named Alex. She's about the right age and has blonde hair." He paused and looked away to avoid eye contact. "She hasn't said much since the soldiers brought her in yesterday. I think she had a tough time out there before being found."

"Take me to her," I said. "Please." I could barely spit out the words.

Serrano stepped forward. "Go ahead. I'm right behind you."

I didn't object to Serrano's company, and we both followed the old couple to a booth where a blonde girl sat next to a dirty torn yellow bumblebee backpack. Alex sat with her feet up on the cushion, wearing the same clothes as a day earlier, her hands wrapped around bare knees that were scratched and bruised. She stared at the other children coloring on the floor and didn't notice our approach.

"Alex, someone is here to see you," the old woman said.

The girl didn't move.

"Hey, Alex." I approached and sat down on the other side of the table in the booth. "I'm glad to see you again."

She looked up, and I saw a flash of recognition in Alex's eyes. Then she turned away again.

"You're safe now. There are a lot of soldiers here and they're going to keep the monsters away."

Alex sat in silence, lost in some unknown trauma. Somehow, I had convinced myself that I would find Emma and Alex, safe and sound, and that I would rescue them from the Castle. Perhaps they would love me for it. Perhaps out of all this horror, I would find something special that I had never been able to find my entire life.

I had failed.

With every second I spent watching Alex, I became angrier at myself. *How could I have been so naive?* There would be no happy endings. Emma was dead, and Alex wouldn't survive the night. Neither would I.

Celwyn had been right all along. Staying and fighting meant dying —the only question was how many shades and vampires we took with us. In my moment of clarity, I marveled at his commitment. I admired his willingness to kill every human life in the Castle to prevent the spread of the parasite. He knew we were dead already, but he kept fighting anyway.

I had no such commitment.

Instead, the thought of dying filled me with fear, and the thought of the little girl in front of me joining her sister in death filled me with profound anger. Alex deserved a shot at life. She deserved a chance to fight.

So I pulled out the Leatherman from the compartment on my belt and placed it on the table. "Alex, I have something for you."

The girl turned and looked at me, and then at the knife on the table.

"Remember I told you that I knew someone else named Alex? He gave me this knife, and it was special. It has kept me safe, and now I want you to have it."

Alex looked up at the old woman as if asking permission to touch the knife. I glared at the woman, daring her or her husband to object.

Serrano smiled at Alex. "Go ahead. You can have it." She looked at the old woman. "Right?"

Frank spoke up before his wife could speak. "She can have the knife if she wants it. Just show her how to use it. That's no toy."

Alex paused for another moment before grabbing the knife and cupping it against her chest. She waited to see if anyone would stop her, then opened each and every one of the blades and tools on the knife, multiple times.

I watched Alex intently, hoping she would speak. Part of me wanted to ask about Emma, holding out some slim hope that her sister hadn't died on the way to Grid One. But I saw Alex's face. I saw her pain. Deep down, I knew the answer, so I never asked.

Shouting from outside the Joshua Tree Saloon disturbed my descent into self pity. In the distance, someone blew an old-fashioned referee whistle.

I turned to Serrano. "What's going on?"

"They're locking down for the night."

I nodded and looked back at Alex. "I have to leave now."

Without looking up from the knife, she finally spoke. "The monsters are coming for us tonight, aren't they?" Her quiet words were matter-of-fact, without a hint of emotion.

"Yes, they are. I'm sorry, Alex."

"Am I going to see you again?"

I felt a twinge in the back of my throat. "I don't know, honey. I don't know." I paused and thought about what to say next. "You know, I'm not really a soldier."

Alex looked confused.

"Before this happened, only a few days ago, I was a nurse. I took care of sick people who were dying. And I worked at night. At first, the night shift seemed scary, being alone in the quiet and the dark, but then I discovered something."

The girl looked up with curiosity in her eyes. She listened intently.

"No matter how much I was afraid, or I worried that someone I knew would die, the morning always came. You just have to be strong and believe that the darkness will end—because it will. It always does." I looked down at the knife still clutched in Alex's hands and smiled. "And if that doesn't work, you stab the bad guys with the knife. Deal?"

187

The edges of Alex's mouth moved, and I thought I saw the beginnings of a smile. She nodded.

"That's one hell of a pep talk," Serrano said.

The old couple began moving around the saloon. "Time to go!" the old man shouted to the children. "Gather your stuff. We're going back downstairs."

Alex quickly stuffed the Leatherman into a pocket on the side of her shorts. She rose from her seat and held out her hand. I grabbed it, and walked with her to the front of the bar where the old couple now had nearly everyone standing in a straight line, ready to march to what they hoped would be a safe location—a dark warehouse in the bowels of the Castle where they would be locked in for the night.

One of the younger boys remained in a booth, refusing to move. He began screaming at the top of his lungs, "No! I'm not going back! I'm staying here!"

The old man scooped him up from the booth and carried him to the front of the line, holding him tightly with one arm. The boy buried his head in the man's shoulder and continued to wail.

The old man led the line of children out to the street and joined the crowds making their way back to the Station. I walked next to Alex. Serrano and the woman took up a position at the end of the line right behind me.

People now filled Broadway, moving to stairwells that led downward to the vast warehouse network that lay beneath the train station. Surprisingly, the whole process seemed remarkably orderly. I saw no fighting or pushing. I couldn't help but wonder how many of these people really knew the horror that awaited them, and if they did, how they could be so calm.

I walked with Alex as far as the Lower Tube station at the Atrium where I saw Celwyn standing next to Paloma.

I leaned over to whisper to Alex. "I have to go now." I looked back at Serrano. "You going down, too?"

"All of the cops are going down with the people, so that's what I'm going to do. We're sort of a last line of defense in case it all goes to hell up here."

"I'm going to stay," I said. "With my friend Celwyn. You know, the guy who saved me on the roof."

Serrano smiled. "I get it. He seems like your good luck charm, so let's see if he can get you out of this one, too."

"Let's hope so." I bent down and gave Alex a hug and then kissed her on the top of her head. "I'll see you in the morning." I gave Serrano a quick nod, then watched as the line of children merged with the rest of the crowd moving towards the Station.

I retreated in the opposite direction, moving against the flow of people until the crowds subsided. The vast, open Atrium loomed in front of me, the empty Tube bisected by a now-abandoned Broadway, empty street fronts stretching as far as the eye could see. The evening shadows nearly covered the Castle's central chamber, and I knew that soon the entire building would be plunged into darkness.

And that's when Tarek and his army of shades would come.

CHAPTER TWENTY-NINE

CELWYN WAITED for me on a catwalk near the Tube, staring along its length into the empty depths of the city. Paloma was nowhere to be found.

"Hey," I said. "You Knights come up with a plan to keep us alive until morning?"

He nodded, then looked around at the soldiers filling the Atrium. "Yeah. I think we are ready. Did you find the girls?"

The question stung and it showed. I took a deep breath. "Alex made it here. I talked to her for a few minutes before everyone went downstairs to be locked up for the night."

Celwyn studied my face for a minute before answering. "I'm sorry."

I wanted to lash out at Celwyn, to blame him for what had happened. My expression betrayed my anger momentarily, but I fought it back without saying a word. I walked up next to him and leaned forward on on the catwalk railing, pushing my rifle around to the back of my shoulder. "I need a new knife."

"What happened to the Leatherman?"

"Someone needed it more than me. Do you have an extra one or not?"

Celwyn reached down and pulled a long leather pouch out of his boot. "You can have this one."

He handed me a sheath filled with a fixed-blade Bowie knife that had to be at least six inches long. I fastened it to my belt so it hung on the side of my waist. It felt heavy.

"Can I tell you something?"

He nodded. "Sure."

"I lost my husband. To cancer. He died in my own hospice." I looked straight into Celwyn's eyes. "It hurt … and it still hurts." I turned away, then instinctively fumbled for the absent ring on my left hand. "His name was Alex, too, so when I met the girls, you know, it hit home."

"I didn't know," Celwyn replied, shaking his head. "I'm sorry. And I think I understand now." He squeezed my hand. "My wife's name was Jessica. And my son. His name was going to be—" Celwyn's voice broke when he tried to speak his unborn son's name.

"It's okay. You don't have to talk about it. Trust me, I know how hard it is to remember. That's why I came here, actually. I wanted to forget." I let out a nervous half-giggle and did a little shrug. "And see where that got me?" I felt the tears beginning to flow, but I fought them back, took a deep breath, then changed the subject. "How do you do it? I mean, aren't you afraid of dying?"

Celwyn quickly regained his normal stoic demeanor, but now I knew it was a mask, like mine, that hid a deep pain. "Of course." He pointed to the soldiers around us. "Everyone out here is bloody-well terrified, but we have a job to do. And if we do that job, we might stay alive. That's how we honor the dead."

"So what's my job?"

"Your job is to stick next to me and do what I tell you. Dax is holding the top of the Atrium by the Upper Tube. We have to hold the Atrium down here. If Tarek's army breaks through, we fall back to the Station."

"What about the Knights? Did you mean what you said about them showing up?"

He shrugged. "The truth is I don't know. They didn't know I was here. I came here because I wanted to prove Tarek was violating the

Accords—it was the only way the Knights would kill him. I didn't trust anyone else to come with me." He shook his head. "Paloma's right. The vampires have spies in our Order. Everyone knows it."

Celwyn looked into my eyes. "But I got an encrypted transmission out from the roof when the first ship went down and the jamming stopped. I have to believe the Knights know what is happening now and will send help. They won't allow the parasite to spread beyond this city."

"There is another way this ends," I said.

"What's that?"

"Maybe we stop Tarek here, tonight, and walk out of here tomorrow. Maybe no one has to destroy the Castle. I don't trust Paloma, but I don't think he's a fool. He thinks he has a chance. Do you...do you think we have a chance?"

Celwyn leaned over the railing and a necklace spilled out of his shirt. He stroked the medallion on the end of the chain before tucking it back underneath his shirt. "I think we're all going to die in this place." He chuckled. "But that's what makes the job interesting."

"What's that necklace?" I asked.

"Standard issue for Knights. Our Captain assigns a patron saint when we complete training."

"So who is your saint?

Celwyn winced. "Saint Jude, patron saint of lost causes."

"Yeah, that fits you," I said.

The radio inside our helmets crackled, then Dax's deep voice flowed through clearly. "We're seeing movement up top. They're hanging in the shadows so we can't tell the numbers, but it's a lot. Stay on your toes."

Celwyn looked at me, and his tone became serious. "It's time."

The last few rays of sunlight disappeared from the Atrium. An eerie quiet descended on Broadway, the normal sounds of crowds and whizzing trains replaced with nothing but the occasional cough or click of a soldier checking their magazine. I thought about Alex, huddled in the darkness below me with thousands of others, hoping she would make it to the morning.

Deep down in my core, a fluttering feeling of fear solidified into cold determination. I would do whatever I needed so that Alex could see another day, even if it meant giving up my own life. I looked at Celwyn and felt the same calm courage. I grasped his hand in mine and gave it a quick squeeze.

"Remember when we first met on the train, and you asked me out?"

Celwyn coughed awkwardly. "Sorry about that. I'm normally not so forward. You know I just wanted to get into the lab, right?"

"Obviously. But, well, I've thought about it some more. And I've decided that I would nonetheless be honored to have you call on me sometime."

He flashed a wide smile. "If we get out of here alive, you have a deal."

I smiled back. "I'm going to hold you to it." I released his hand and positioned mine back on the rifle.

A second later, Celwyn's expression darkened and I felt it, too—a feeling of dread building deep in my core.

He motioned out toward the darkening Atrium. "The light's dying. Turn on your helmet so you can see."

I tapped the control panel on the side of my helmet and the view of the Atrium returned, this time illuminated by a soft green hue.

And then the gun shots started.

———

THE FIRST SOLDIER fell over before I even heard the distant crack of a gunshot. The bullet entered through the face plate on the helmet, killing the man instantly. Three more shots rang out in succession from deep within the Castle, and three more soldiers fell, killed by a hidden assailant hiding somewhere within the network of ledges, catwalks and perches hanging above us in the cavernous Atrium.

"Move!" Celwyn shouted. "Over there!" He pushed me behind one of the giant batteries attached to the spotlight stationed on the Tube platform. The stainless steel box took up half of the living-room-sized platform and stretched at least ten feet in the air. You could hide a football team behind it.

I crouched down and peered around the side of the smooth metal box that served as my protection. Soldiers on Broadway scrambled to find cover from the continued assault from above, diving into alleys and stacking metal containers to eliminate the sniper's line of sight.

On the floor of the catwalk, next to me, a portly, middle-aged soldier calmly rested on his butt, leaning against the side of the battery. He lacked a helmet and the top of his tussled black uniform hung open, exposing a sweat-stained t-shirt.

Celwyn leaned over to talk to the soldier. "What's your name?"

"Amos," he replied.

"Alright, Amos, can you get this spotlight working?"

"Yep," he said matter of factly. "Where do you want it pointed?"

"Everywhere," Celwyn replied. "Paint the whole damned place with UV light. Blind the bastard. That vampire can see better than us in the dark, but let's see how well he can see with the sun in his face."

Amos stood up and began flipping switches and turning dials on the back panel positioned above our heads. A gentle humming noise began emanating from the battery. He sprinted around the giant box and climbed the metal stairs of the adjacent catwalk two at a time, displaying a remarkable agility for a man his size.

On the ledge above me sat a giant rectangular light fixture that looked like it belonged in a stadium. Behind the spotlight, a small angular seat jutted out, surrounded by a semicircle cockpit with two levers on the floor. Amos leaped into the chair and looked down at us through the gaps in the latticed metal floor of the catwalk.

"Light it up," Celwyn said.

Amos went to work and the rows of horizontal bulbs on the spotlight came to life with a popping sound. The flash almost blinded me, and I immediately tapped the side of my helmet to disable the night vision. After my eyes adjusted, I saw a soft blue beam bathing Broadway in light.

Across the gap in the Atrium housing the empty Tube, on a parallel landing, another spotlight's blue beam began making sweeps of the Castle's towering thoroughfare. The twin beams moved up and down, then side to side, sometimes crossing like swords, in a grid pattern illuminating every inch of the Atrium.

It worked. The shooting stopped.

Above me, Amos yanked on the floor levers of his cockpit which moved together with the spotlight as it jerked back and forth in every direction like a three-hundred-and-sixty-degree mechanical bull. Sweat poured out of his face and soaked the collar of his loose fitting shirt, now flapping behind him as the chair swiveled.

"You're doing great!" Celwyn shouted. "Keep that thing moving!"

Amos responded with a quick nod, but remained focused on his job, never slowing down the movement of the giant spotlight. Around us, soldiers peeked out from behind crates and stairwells where they had taken cover from the sniper's attack. A sense of confidence returned to their faces, but I knew something they didn't.

The uneasy feeling in my stomach hadn't subsided. It had only become stronger, and a cold breath touched the back of my neck, slicing the heat of the stuffy Castle like a knife.

I looked at Celwyn and he nodded.

"Be ready!" he shouted. "They're coming!"

I stepped out from behind the battery, and focused on the strip of Broadway in front of our position, a darkened three-lane highway leading into the depths of the Castle. A few blocks ahead of us, the soldiers had erected a makeshift wall constructed from abandoned street cleaners and ubiquitous electric golf carts. The barrier stretched from one side of the Atrium to the other, separated only by the gaping chasm in the middle for the Tubes.

As soon as Amos's spotlight left Broadway to make the sweep of the ledges above us, a horde of shades poured out of one of the side streets. With my helmet's night vision turned off, I couldn't make out much detail other than figures moving in the dark. They moved like a pack of animals, rushing toward the makeshift barricade.

Time sped up at that point. Celwyn shouted something at Amos and the cockpit spun around to focus its massive UV light on the scene unfolding in the street. The light acted like a laser beam, scorching a fiery path through the figures unlucky enough to be touched by the light. Crowds of what were once human beings, now shades possessed by the bloodthirst of the parasite, burst into flames, staining the streets with bloody trails left by the spotlight. Howls of pain echoed around the Atrium, and the stench of burning flesh stung my nose.

The twin UV lights were brutally effective, inflicting massive damage on the attacking shades. Both Amos and his counterpart criss-crossed Broadway, striking down shades by the dozens with their swords of light. Some shades made it to safety, avoiding death by hiding behind the blockade of vehicles, but most were reduced to ash. One shade, already on fire, leaped over the blockade and exploded upon impacting the street.

Somewhere in the middle of the burning and the screams, the gunshots resumed. This time, the sniper focused on the spotlights. Above me, bullets smacked into the rows of UV lights, each impact triggering a small explosion of popping noises that diminished the strength of the light. It didn't take long before the spotlight on the other side of the Atrium went dark, leaving only Amos taking bullets. He shouted curses at his unseen attacker and the cockpit groaned as it whirled around, along with its giant light, away from Broadway in a defensive move to again blind the shooter.

The shades hiding behind the barricade on Broadway surged forward as soon as the deadly beam of light moved upward. The mass of shades flowed over the barricade like ants, and Celwyn ordered the soldiers to open fire.

I stepped forward to the edge of the catwalk, raised my rifle, and began shooting into the approaching crowd of shades. Celwyn was already squeezing off shots, but I couldn't distinguish the sounds of his rifle from the hundreds of others filling the Atrium. It sounded like never-ending strikes of thunder as the rifle shots echoed through the Castle's interior.

In the chaos, I don't even know if I hit anything. I pointed into the crowd of moving targets and pulled the trigger. But they didn't stop. The shades kept rushing forward.

"Amos!" Celwyn shouted. "We need the light!"

I heard the levers grinding and the whir of the cockpit turning. The spotlight cut a trail of death through the mass of shades running up Broadway, but the diameter of its beam had grown smaller. The blazing supernova that could have illuminated an entire block now resembled a giant penlight only capable of surgical strikes that were becoming increasingly easy to avoid by the nimble shades.

To compensate for the lack of coverage, Amos increased the speed of movement. The spotlight scorched rapidly back and forth, and I could hear the cockpit straining above my head. Bullets from above us again rained down on Amos's weapon, accompanied by the pings of striking metal and the cracks of shattering bulbs.

But Amos never stopped working the levers, and every second he coaxed out of the flickering spotlight reduced the number of approaching shades.

Finally, the thin remaining beam of light jerked to the side and remained motionless. I looked up and saw Amos hanging lifelessly in his cockpit with one arm still clinging to a lever by his feet. The cockpit continued to whir and grind, driven by the dead weight from Amos's body which pushed the lever forward, aiming the spotlight at an increasingly steep downward angle.

Shots again peppered the spotlight and the handful of remaining bulbs shattered. The Atrium immediately plunged into a darkness so thick that it felt like being trapped in a cave. I tapped the side of my helmet and the soft green glow restored my sight.

I exhaled slowly. Only a few shades had made it past Amos's death ray, and they were easily mopped up by the soldiers. A string of bloody corpses lay in front of us along Broadway, but the defenses had held strong.

We had survived, for now.

Celwyn slowly retreated away from the railing, back towards the safety behind the giant battery. He motioned for me to join him. "Sniper's still out there."

Quiet again settled into the Atrium. Celwyn peered into the depths of the Castle, searching for signs of movement. At any moment, I expected bullets to rain down on our position, this time without our ability to blind the shooter. Or perhaps a new rush from an army of shades. But nothing happened.

We just sat still, alone in the dark. The seconds ticked off, and the minutes felt like hours. Then, as I crouched on the metal floor of the landing, I felt a vibration. The vibration quickly became an explosion, knocking me backward as the entire Castle shook with the impact from the blast. I closed my eyes and braced for death, expecting the roof to collapse on my head.

Celwyn grabbed my hand, jolting me back to my senses. "Are you alright?"

"Yeah…yeah, I'm fine. What was that noise? Did the Knights do that?"

"No." He looked around nervously. "I don't think so."

Both of our helmet radios sputtered to life. *"We need help in the basement. Under attack. Send help now. Repeat. Send help now to basement."*

"That's Serrano," I said. "They've got no one down there except a few police."

Celwyn stood up. "Bloody hell, this was all just a distraction. They found a way into the basement."

I listened to Serrano repeating her pleas for help on the radio and all I could think about was Alex, huddled in fear, wondering if she would share her sister's fate.

I would not abandon her again.

I leaped to my feet and began sprinting toward the stairs.

CHAPTER THIRTY

CELWYN CAUGHT up to me and grabbed my hand. "This is another trick. As soon as we leave our positions, they'll attack up here again. Once they make it into Grid One, we'll be overrun. There's nowhere to go."

"Didn't you hear? They've already made it *into* the Grid. Thousands of people down there are about to get slaughtered. And the ones who don't die will end up turning into shades. We have to help them."

Celwyn shook his head, frustrated with the impossible choice. He shouted into the radio on his helmet. "Paloma! Paloma!" He waited for a response but none came. He shouted again into the microphone. "Dax, you still holding down the fort up top?"

"Beat up but still hanging in there," Dax replied.

Celwyn looked at me and nodded, then he turned back to the soldier. "Dax, I'm taking half my team below. If things go to hell, fight your way down to the Station. We're going to get as many as we can out of the basement and I'll meet you there."

"Understood," he replied.

I patiently waited as Celwyn barked out orders and separated the teams on both sides of the Atrium into those who would stay and those who would follow him below. With the glass-enclosed elevators next to the Tube rendered useless due to the lack of power, the stairwells offered the fastest way down to the basement from Broadway. A crowd of soldiers massed near the doorway to the stairs on each side of the Atrium.

A soldier in front opened the door, and the steady popping sounds of gunfire echoed in the distance.

"Go!" Celwyn shouted. Celwyn pushed me forward, merging us into the line of soldiers rushing into the narrow stairwell. "I'm right behind you!"

I had never been into the lower levels of Grid One. Broadway started on the fifth floor, leaving the four lowest levels of the Castle effectively hidden to most of the residents who didn't work in one of the restricted areas near the South end of the Line. These restricted levels were reserved for the utilitarian industrial functions necessary to support a large condensed metropolis.

The space beneath Grid One served as the heart of the transportation and distribution hub of the Castle. Below the high speed train station were loading docks for trucks and an elaborate network of warehouses stretching all the way through the neighboring grid. The warehouses normally bustled with activity—receiving deliveries all hours of the day and night, moving food and other supplies necessary to keep the Castle functioning. Somehow, that connection to the outside world had been turned off by Idrissia, just like the power. Now, the lower levels of Grid One stood idle, just an empty space big enough to fit thousands of people.

A perfect hiding place.

Sweat ran down my forehead as I followed the line of black uniforms through the narrow stairwell. Without the helmet's night vision, I couldn't see six inches in front of my face. I knew that, but I still hated the damned thing. I desperately wanted to open the visor and relieve the constricting feeling of being trapped in a fish bowl. I would have given anything for a breath of fresh air, but I knew there was none to be had in the staircase, or in our final destination in the bowels of the Castle. So I kept moving.

The sounds of boots hitting metal steps clanged around me. I focused on my feet, making sure I made good contact with each step. The last thing I needed was to trip and fall and start a domino effect that would get a bunch of people killed, including myself. The first two levels went quickly. Then the noises got louder. Gunshots. Screaming.

The line of movement stopped. I looked over the railing and saw a crowd of soldiers clustered by the door to the ground floor, rifles raised, shooting at something or someone outside the open metal door.

Celwyn rushed past me, yelling at the soldiers to keep moving. "Get out that doorway and protect those coming behind you!"

Adrenaline pumped through my veins. An icy hand touched the back of my neck, and I knew what lurked for us in the dark on the other side of that door.

I followed Celwyn through a door marked 'Restricted Access' and entered a cavernous loading dock. To my left, rows of overhead doors for unloading trucks stretched as far as I could see. In front of us, a vast warehouse the size of multiple football fields spanned across the width of the Castle, divided into rows filled with the large machinery and equipment that couldn't fit into the individual warehouses. The Atrium ended at Lower Broadway, so there was not even a distant bit of moonlight. The ceiling above us must have been at least three stories tall, but it was hard to tell in the dark. Forklifts and cranes dotted the floor of the loading dock.

In front of me, the warehouse resembled a panicked escape from a burning building, but instead of people escaping for their lives, they were monsters trying to kill us. Hordes of shades sprinted through the center toward a dimly lit metal cage on my right where I saw gunfire and heard shouting. Right outside the stairwell, huddled along a warehouse wall, soldiers organized at a security station near the door began moving in groups toward the cage. Through the chaos, far away from me, I could see the muzzle flashes of soldiers arriving from the other side of the Atrium, also making their way toward the cage.

"There! The cage!" Celwyn shouted, pointing at our goal.

"I know!" I shouted. "I see it!"

But the shades had seen us, too.

A group broke off from the charging crowd and redirected their momentum toward our side of the dock. A barrage of gunfire from the soldiers in front of us kept them from getting close, but I knew it was only matter of time before they all discovered our presence. And there were hundreds of them. Maybe thousands. Too many to count.

Celwyn tapped my helmet with a magazine for my rifle. "Reload. Now. There won't be another chance once we get out there."

I released the magazine like I had been trained and inserted a new one from my belt. I gave Celwyn a meek thumbs up sign.

He crouched with me behind the partial wall offered by the security station, then we rose together and followed a trail of soldiers. I struggled to run while simultaneously shooting at any shade on my left who broke away from the horde and headed in our direction. My progress quickly turned into an awkward pattern of stumbling forward a few yards, then turning and shooting. I cleared everything else from my mind and focused on keeping up with Celwyn. I kept moving forward, scared to death that at any moment I would get left behind or run over by someone behind me.

I made it to an idle forklift the size of a pickup truck where I crouched down and loaded another magazine. Celwyn did the same. Behind us, more soldiers steadily made their way to our hiding spot. We had at least fifty soldiers on our side, waiting to attack, and I assumed the same on the other end of the dock. But the shades barely noticed. I watched as the warehouse filled with wave after wave of howling, murderous remnants of human beings, all massing near the cage, focused singularly on tearing through its metal bars, or crushing the cage underneath their weight.

Finally, the waves of former humanity ended. Behind them, a lone figure walked steadily forward, howling and shouting in the same language as the shades. Except his sounds demonstrated an intelligence lacking in the cries of those he drove forward. His words were instructions. Orders.

The vampire wore the winged helmet of Tarek's guard, and black-plated body armor bearing the mark of the Idrissia Bloodline. He was short and bulky, his armor resembling a perfect cube, with arms and legs attached. A long rifle with a scope hung from a strap on his shoulder. It definitely wasn't Tarek, but I knew he would be no less deadly.

The gunshots from inside the cage had stopped. Only the screams remained, echoing around the cavernous dock, barely audible over the sounds of the horde.

"If they break through that cage, they'll kill everyone inside," I said.

"I know, I know," Celwyn replied. "But there are too damn many. We don't have enough bullets." He loosed his backpack, sat it on the ground, and opened a side compartment. He quickly rummaged inside and located what he sought—a disc like the one used to blow up the Tube.

His last.

He pressed a button on the side and a red light began flashing.

"Everyone get down," he hissed. He stood and threw the disc like a frisbee, straight toward the middle of the horde of shades.

I ducked down behind the forklift. A few seconds later I felt the concussion blast. Even with the helmet, my ears rang from the loud explosion. I fought back the urge to remove my helmet, instead taking deep breaths until my ears popped back to normal. Once some semblance of hearing returned, I stood up to survey the damage.

In the middle of the dock, a charred circle marked the location on the concrete floor where Celwyn's disc had exploded. Nearly half of the shades had simply disappeared, their bodies torn to pieces and scattered, their blood painting the ground red like a dark tapestry. The remaining shades, covered in a dark sludge of flesh and fluid, resumed pushing forward, pushing and pulling on the walls of the cage.

I don't know if the cage gave out because of the onslaught of shades, or if it was weakened by Celwyn's blast. But it fell.

The anchors holding the twenty-foot-tall cage in place against the wall of the dock came loose and the entire structure fell forward, its three sides collapsing in upon itself with a loud clang of metal impacting metal. The shades swarmed over the rubble and tore open the double rolling doors that led into the adjoining secure warehouse.

Within seconds, the monsters would be loose on the people hiding inside, defenseless in the dark. I could only imagine Alex's terror as she waited in silence, listening to the explosions and screams of those in the cage who bravely fought outside. Then a sudden rush of movement, the eruption of panic, and the ever present sounds of death as the shades invaded what she had been told would be a safe haven for the night.

It was too much to bear.

My mind snapped back to reality. Celwyn was already on his feet, firing into the crowd of remaining shades who had not yet made their way through the rolling doors on the other side of the cage. Every soldier began emptying their rifles, hoping to distract as many shades as possible. I joined them, blindly firing my rifle at the approaching horde of monsters that we hoped to draw away from their designated prey. A sense of desperation filled the air. My adrenaline surged and my vision focused laser-like on the swarming hordes.

There were still too many of them, and too few of us.

In the chaos, I didn't notice that soldiers began dropping. I bent down behind the forklift to reload another magazine. It was my last one.

Before I could stand back up, I heard a *ping* sound, and Celwyn dropped lifelessly beside me. The soft green glow on the visor went dark, and a dent the size of a quarter appeared on the side of his helmet.

"Celwyn!" I shook him and he didn't move. "Celwyn! Don't die! Please don't die!" My heart raced.

I removed his helmet and ran my fingers through his hair. In the dark, I couldn't find any evidence of a bullet wound. "Celwyn. I need you to wake up right now or we are both going to die. I don't know what to do."

The gunshots subsided. I looked around and only a few soldiers remained on their feet. The others lay dead or bleeding on the ground. I peeked above the hood of the forklift and spotted the vampire, perched on top of a crane in the middle of the loading dock, aiming in my direction with his rifle.

I quickly ducked back down and cursed. The sniper from the Atrium had followed us. We were all sitting ducks.

I grabbed Celwyn's hand. "Please wake up. We don't have any time. They're coming." I shook his body as hard as I could, screaming his name. He didn't move.

The shades were now on top of us. I could hear the growls. The forklift shook with the force of the impact from the mass of bodies flinging themselves towards us.

But something inside me refused to give up. From an unknown place I found a surprising reservoir of courage. I had to keep fighting. I would not give up on Alex.

I knelt down and kissed Celwyn on the lips. "Goodbye."

Then I closed my eyes and clicked the button on the disruptor device attached to my collar.

CHAPTER THIRTY-ONE

I OPENED my eyes and the brightness nearly blinded me. Quickly, I tapped the side of my helmet to turn off the night vision and the light diminished, leaving only enough to see. I slowly scooted away from Celwyn and rose to my feet, leaving my empty rifle behind.

All around me, soldiers fought vainly, stabbing and punching against the overwhelming number of shades. One by one, the soldiers became surrounded, pushed to the ground, and covered by shades like a piece of bread being devoured by ants. For the fallen, I wished a quick death. The unlucky ones would be left alive, suffering, and eventually heal and turn into shades themselves.

I turned my back and ran.

Celwyn warned me about the disruptor and he was right. Boy was he right.

I tried to run toward the warehouse where Alex and the others were hiding, but my knees wobbled. The blanket of light spun around me while the reality inside the curtain stood still. My head erupted in a splitting pain, burdened by the sensory overload.

If Celwyn can do this, so can I.

I closed my eyes again, pausing to regain my sense of equilibrium. When I opened my eyes, I focused my vision on the ground in front of my feet, ignoring the spinning curtain of light around me. That was the trick—like a picture where you can see a hidden message if you look at it from the right angle.

But my confidence in discovering how to use the disruptor quickly evaporated with the realization that I still had to navigate a sea of shades between me and Alex. They couldn't see me, but I knew they could see a flickering light, just like the one I had seen when Celwyn used his disruptor at night to fight the vampire on the roof.

And I suspected they could smell me, too, or even hear my heart beat. I only hoped that I would be lost in the backdrop of noises and smells of the dead and dying that filled the dock. If not, I would be dead long before I reached the doors of the warehouse.

I slowed my pace after I reached the blast zone from Celwyn's explosive disc. My shoes slipped through the blood and ichor staining the ground, and I strained to remain on my feet as I stepped over body parts. Nearing the edge of the blood-stained concrete, I gained confidence and broke into a jog.

That was a mistake.

My foot slipped in a puddle of dark fluid and I lost my balance. My momentum propelled me forward until I ended up perpendicular with the floor, avoiding a nasty concussion only by my fortune in falling into a corpse that, best I could tell, used to be severely overweight.

Now covered in blood, I removed the knife given to me from Celwyn from its sheath and eyed the scene in front of me. On either side of the subterranean warehouse, all the soldiers who left Broadway lay dead, and the remaining shades had already filtered back to the entrance to the warehouse where they joined the rest of their kind. Above the closest of the two doorways, a jagged piece of wavy sheet metal hung from the top of the rolling door, its bottom half lying in pieces on the concrete floor.

Beyond the doorway, I saw murder on a scale I couldn't imagine. The shades bit and clawed their way through men, women, and children like a horde of locusts. The screams from their victims merged with the guttural howls of the shades into a horrible symphony of death as they killed without mercy or feeling of any kind, stopping only for the occasional opportunity to satisfy their blood lust before moving to another, fresher piece of meat in the crowded warehouse.

I turned to look for the vampire, but he no longer perched on top of the crane's cabin. *Crap. Where did he go?*

One step at a time I reminded myself. The odds were that I would be killed by shades long before I escaped the warehouse with Alex. I would cross that vampire bridge if and when I came to it.

Without hesitating, I sprinted around the mangled steel cage and through the doorway into the warehouse. A sign beside the door read, 'High Security Area — For Valuables Only.'

Pallets filled with boxes of expensive handbags, electronics, and jewelry littered the floor of the warehouse. In the aisles between them, people ran in every direction, chased by shades. Some fought back with whatever weapons they could find. Others hid in the dark corners of the warehouse, softly crying. Some prayed.

Something told me the children would be in the back of the warehouse, so I moved down the center aisle, hugging the pallets wrapped with plastic, dodging and weaving to avoid both shade and human. As I made my way deeper into the warehouse, the number of people diminished, along with the number of shades. I passed small groups of men and women huddled in silence, hoping they would avoid detection, but none of the groups included children.

I knew that somewhere in the warehouse, an old gray-haired woman sat by a husband named Frank, guarding the handful of children left in the Castle. Among them would be a girl with a Leatherman. By God, I would find her and do everything I could to get her away from this place.

Or die trying.

I reached a crossroads of sorts, where another aisle crossed the center one leading towards the back of the giant warehouse. A figure moved into view from my right, and a sense of familiarity hit me. Black jacket and long brown hair.

Serrano.

The figure turned and sniffed the air like an animal. The glasses were gone and part of Serrano's cheek had been bitten off, but it was her. It was definitely her.

I looked around and didn't see any other shades. I slowly approached Serrano, watching for any signs that she was alerted to my presence. Part of me wanted to kill her, to release her body from the parasite. But I didn't trust myself to be able to do the job. What if she saw me? What if I couldn't kill her with my knife?

She sniffed the air again and looked right in my direction. I froze.

Suddenly, a group of people darted around the corner with a small battery-powered light, and a woman began shouting in fear at the sight of Serrano. The shade of Serrano pounced on the closest human like a cat, and I pushed forward, leaving the screams behind.

I followed the center aisle until I reached the rear wall of the warehouse, hearing faint cries from what sounded like children. I inspected every pallet stacked against the rear wall before finally finding one with a large gap behind it. I walked around the pallet and there, behind boxes of flat screen televisions, I saw Frank holding a handgun. Behind him stood his wife, her hand on his shoulder.

Sitting on the floor behind them, in a perfect row, were the children. And Alex was among them.

My heart raced and I almost cried out. I tapped the disruptor and the shimmering curtain disappeared, along with my sight. I tapped the side of my helmet and the world became visible again, this time bathed in green.

The sudden appearance of green light startled Frank. "Who's there?" he asked, raising his pistol.

"It's me, Mel," I whispered. "I came to see Alex earlier today."

"How in the world did you get back here?" Frank's wife asked. "Are you here to save us?" She looked around. "Where are the rest of the soldiers?"

I looked back at the children sitting on the ground, all of whom stared directly at me. *Are you a soldier?* Alex's little sister, Emma, had asked me. She looked at me the same way those kids looked at me, and it broke my heart. I chose my words carefully, but I couldn't sugarcoat the truth. "There's no one else coming. The soldiers are gone." I thought about Celwyn and choked up. "They're all dead," I whispered.

Frank lowered his pistol and stroked his bald head with his other hand. "Then it's over." He looked at his wife. "They're getting closer. You know what we have to do."

The old woman looked defeated. "Dammit, Frank, give me a minute to think."

"We don't have a minute," he snapped. "Listen to the screams. Once they find us, it will be too late."

Frank turned from his wife, still holding the pistol, but with a newfound look of anguish on his face. "Well, if you ain't here to save us, then get out of here. We've made our peace with the Lord and know what we have to do."

At that moment, I realized the bullets in the pistol were not meant to be used on shades. Frank and his wife had a suicide pact, and they planned to take the children with them.

On the floor behind Frank, Alex looked up at me with eyes full of fear, but also hope. That little girl believed I was a soldier. That little girl believed I could save her. I had to try.

I pushed by Frank and grabbed his wife by the hands. "I can't save everyone, but I can save Alex. Please let me try. "

The old woman looked at me, her eyes filled with tears. "How can you save her? How can anyone fight such evil?" She looked at her husband. "He's right. We can't let these children suffer."

My frustration with the woman neared a breaking point. I hadn't made it this far only to give up. "You don't understand," I hissed. "I can get her out of here. They won't be able to see us." I pointed at the disruptor on my collar. "Look. Now you see me." I turned off my night vision and pushed the button on the side of the device. "And now you don't."

At that moment, a shade circled around the pallet of boxes and lunged into the narrow crevice. It happened so fast. Slashing and biting. Screaming. A gunshot.

Only I could see the shade lunge for Frank's throat. He managed to get off one shot, but it didn't slow down the shade.

The shade didn't stop until I had plunged my Bowie knife deep into its cranium, twisting it for good measure. Both it and Frank fell to the floor and lay motionless.

I waited to see if other shades would follow the sound of a gunshot. The seconds ticked off as I crouched against the wall, waiting silently.

To my right, Frank's wife repeatedly called his name. "Be quiet," I hissed angrily.

The old woman looked in my direction but saw nothing in the darkness.

After what seemed like an eternity, but couldn't have been more than a minute, I turned off the disruptor and reappeared. The old woman lay with her head on Frank's chest, sobbing as he labored to breathe.

Behind the woman, some of the children cried. Others had retreated to the back of the tight alley, obviously in shock. Alex stood in place, steely-eyed, with the Leatherman I had given her clutched tightly in her right hand.

I picked up the pistol from the floor and handed it to the woman. "Listen to me. He's going to turn into one of them. You have to help him die."

"I can't kill Frank," she said.

"Frank's already dead," I said. "You're not killing him. You're giving him the peace you so desperately want."

I stepped around the woman and approached Alex. "Do you want to go with me, Alex?"

The short blonde girl nodded her head affirmatively.

"Good." I grabbed her empty hand. "You hold onto my hand no matter what, do you understand?"

"Yes," she replied.

"You're going to see a light when I push this button." I pointed to the disruptor. "And it's going to make you feel sick. But you're going to stay quiet, do you understand?"

"Okay."

"Don't look at the light. Focus on something close. Like your feet. If you do that, it won't be so hard."

Alex nodded again.

I pulled on her hand and we wedged past Frank's body. For the first time I got a good look at the shade who had attacked moments earlier. The black jacket was gone, so I didn't recognize her at first in all of the chaos. There was no mistake.

Serrano's shade lay dead on the floor.

My mind immediately went to work. This was all my fault. I could have killed Serrano's shade when it passed me earlier in the warehouse. Instead I ran away, and now the thing had killed Frank. Maybe part of me thought Serrano still lived, and I didn't want to kill her.

I was no better than the old woman, unable to do what needed to be done.

"Close your eyes," I told Alex.

I released Alex's hand and knelt down by Frank. His skin had already darkened to a familiar gray tone. His body convulsed with every breath.

"It has to be now," I said gently to his wife. "I'll do it. Go sit with the children. They don't need to see this."

The old woman rose and gathered the children at the far end of the crevice behind the pallets. They knelt down and whispered a prayer together.

I plunged my knife into Frank's heart. His eyes opened suddenly, blackened by the parasite and filled with rage, then slowly closed. I stabbed him again for good measure and twisted the blade. He never moved again.

Behind me, I felt something move. I spun around and nearly knocked over Alex. "I thought I told you to close your eyes."

She shook her head defiantly. "No. I want to see. I want to fight them, too."

"You'll get your chance," I said. "But for now, we have to go." I paused and looked at Alex. "And it's good to hear you talking again."

Alex took my hand and I touched the disruptor. We hadn't made it fifty feet before I heard the gunshots from Frank's gun. Six quickly in a row, a long pause, then a final one.

After that, we heard only silence behind us. And screams ahead.

CHAPTER THIRTY-TWO

ALEX CLUNG to me tightly while we made our way to the front of the warehouse. Darting around and between pallets, we stepped over dead bodies and avoided the few live human beings who still remained hidden. Every time we saw a shade, we froze, pushing our bodies against a wall or a stack of boxes until we felt safe enough to move again.

The earlier chaos had subsided, replaced by an eerie silence punctuated by random screams as shades systematically eliminated the remaining souls hiding in the bowels of the Castle. The shades now hunted in packs, rushing to any sound, attracted by the promise of blood.

With each step towards the front of the vast warehouse, we gained confidence. We saw fewer shades, which meant fewer stops. By the time we made it to the front, the opening out into the dock sat empty, with all of the shades behind us. I looked down at Alex and wondered if she would be the only one to make it out of the warehouse alive.

Luckily, Alex had quickly mastered the physical discomfort caused by the disruptor. She was a much faster learner than me, and never faltered once as we quietly moved forward, nothing more than a barely visible twinkle of light moving through the dark space.

I squeezed Alex's hand tightly and flashed her a smile at the sight of the broken overhead doors. Together, we stepped out of the warehouse into the dock, climbing over the debris left over from the fallen cage that once guarded the hiding place.

Instinctively, I looked to my left towards the forklift where I left Celwyn, knowing full well that I couldn't see anything that far in the darkness. The black curtain around me overpowered the ambient light of the disruptor, obscuring everything in the cavernous dock except my surroundings a few feet in every direction. All I would have to do is walk closer and I would be able to see if Celwyn had died on the ground where I left him.

What if he was gone? Maybe he somehow survived?

But that would mean spending more time in the dark, putting Alex at risk. No. I had to get out of here, back up to the Station. There, we would find help. Down here, we would die. The icy feeling reappeared on the back of my neck. Shades still lurked nearby.

I moved out into the open, hastily steering Alex toward the closest stairway to Broadway. Alex's head kept turning, scanning the dock for shades. The girl had seen more than her share of danger, and she now gripped my arm with both hands, walking closely behind me. Alex increased her pace, pushing me forward as if she too felt the urgency.

The light from the disruptor flickered, then the curtain began to dim. The device was failing.

Behind us, I heard a noise in the dark. Someone was coming.

"I can see you, bouzen." The accent sounded like something you would hear in New Orleans.

I froze, then looked at Alex. One hand darted into her pocket to retrieve the Leatherman. I shook my head and mouthed *No*.

She glared back at me.

I began moving again, increasing my pace.

A bullet ricocheted off the concrete in front of our path. The voice called out again. "Knight, I said I can see you. Stop, or my next bullet will turn that child's golden hair red."

In front of us, a pack of at least ten shades materialized from the darkness, blocking our path to the stairway.

"Capturing one Knight is a prize for Tarek. But two? That's an absolute embarrassment of riches."

I turned back to the source of the voice, and a familiar-looking short vampire casually strode forward. It was the sniper.

His rifle lay cradled in his folded arms, leaning against one shoulder. He glared at me through the open face of the helm. A loop of solid gold hung off each ear lobe, and a scar ran from below his eye down to his chin, splitting his lip. His eyes glowed in the dark like a cat, illuminating the dark weathered skin on his face.

Another Knight? He must have meant Celwyn. I frantically tried to think of my next move. Celwyn was alive. I almost couldn't believe it. Celwyn was alive? But what if the vampire was lying? Why would he do that? He wouldn't. It must be true. Celwyn was alive.

I clicked the side of my disruptor. The last bit of light faded and the world went dark for a second before I turned on my helmet. Alex hugged my legs, unable to see without the blanket of light afforded by the device.

"It will be okay," I whispered, grabbing her head with one hand to pull the girl against my body.

With the night vision, I now saw Celwyn's body lying motionless behind the vampire. His helmet had been removed and dried blood covered his face.

"The Knights will never let you leave here alive." I decided to play along. At the moment, the vampire's belief I was a Knight was the only thing keeping Alex and me alive.

The vampire laughed and I noticed a missing tooth located conspicuously under the site of the scar on his upper lip. "I hope they all come. But I bet they won't. It's not your way. You Knights are just like us, hunting in the dark, slitting throats in the shadows." He looked at Alex and lunged forward. "I should kill this little one in the same way. You should feel the pain of losing family before Tarek cuts your heart out."

Alex heard the vampire approach and buried her face in my thigh, tightening her already python-like grip. She never made a sound. The girl was tough, and now I was angry.

"You're the ugliest vampire I've ever seen. And if you touch her, I'll kill you."

The vampire spit on Celwyn's body. "I'll do what I want, bouzen." He shouted a series of guttural commands in Thracian, and the shades rushed towards us, fighting amongst themselves to be the first to tear us apart.

Before the pack of monsters reached us, a booming voice rang out from across the dock, "Strigoi!" The voice spoke the language of those infected by the parasite. The voice's owner barked out new commands, halting the shades and drawing their attention away from us.

The sniper vampire shouted at the shades, but they ignored him, instead staring intently in the direction of the mysterious voice. Our would-be attackers stood motionless, suddenly calm, and for a moment, I almost thought of them as human beings. Almost.

The voice suddenly spoke again, increasing its cadence. It rose in pitch, then slowed, ending in a booming note that demanded attention. At that moment, I recognized the owner of the voice.

It was Saul.

Out of the darkness, he approached, flanked by three vampires on each side. Two I recognized from the group he saved on Upper Broadway, but I had never seen the others. Saul's ranks had grown since our separation.

"Who is it?" Alex whispered.

"A friend," I replied.

In the soft glow of the night vision, Saul resembled a vengeful angel sent by God to smite the forces of evil. His white hair now covered his head, and he wore a newfound scarlet red shirt, enclosed by the black cape he had removed from the vampire killed by Celwyn on the roof. In front of him, Saul grasped a thin piece of metal he used as a walking stick, except the top ended in a jagged point, fashioned into a homemade spear.

The men and women around him were all young. The two shades I recognized were clear-eyed and in control of the parasite, evolved into full-fledged vampires like Saul. Each of the pair, along with the others in Saul's entourage, wore an article of bright red clothing. Two of the men wore red shirts like Saul, while one woman had a red sash tied around an arm.

Satisfied the shades were under his control, Saul next spoke to the sniper vampire guarding Celwyn. "Brother, lay down your weapon."

"What is this magic?" the sniper vampire shouted. "How did you gain control of the parasite without the Mothers? It's not possible." He pulled the rifle up to his shoulder and aimed at Saul.

"Melanie, I suggest you remove yourself from here, along with this young girl."

"He's got Celwyn!" I shouted to Saul. "I'm not leaving without him."

The sniper vampire snorted. "You know this man? No Knight would fight beside a vampire." His voice rose an octave and became frantic. "This is madness. I'll kill you all!"

The sniper rifle in the vampire's arms twitched and bullets began flying towards Saul. The projectiles disappeared into the cavernous void of the loading dock, hitting nothing as Saul and his companions separated, moving in a zigzag pattern to surround the sniper.

The vampire attempted to follow Saul's movement, squeezing off rounds as fast as the rifle would allow, but the old man moved too quickly. The vampire paused, then howled in frustration.

"You're too fast, but your friends aren't." He turned the barrel of the rifle towards me, and I knew what would come next. I thought about running, but I had no time. Instead, I grabbed Alex and pushed her to the ground. I fell to my knees, turned my back to the vampire, and used my body as a shield to cover the child.

The first bullet whizzed by my cheek, sounding like a supercharged swarm of mosquitoes. The second bullet hit my back, right below my shoulder blade, on the same side where I had been bit. The momentum threw me forward on top of Alex.

She screamed. I cried out in pain.

I fought to stay conscious, immediately recognizing the familiar signs of shock—a pounding heartbeat, nausea, and an overriding desire to close my eyes and lie down. I expected another bullet to send me into oblivion. But it never came.

After a few seconds of staring at the ground, I heard Alex's voice, filled with urgency. "It's okay. You can wake up now, Mel. Please wake up."

A pair of powerful hands pulled me up from the ground, lifting me to a standing position on my wobbly feet. The woman with the red sash held me by my good arm, looping me over her shoulder. She had utterly transformed from the dirty monster who had attacked us in Upper Broadway. Her face had lightened from the beastly gray of a shade to a pale pink color, and her blonde pixie haircut made her seem barely old enough to buy a drink in the Joshua Tree Saloon.

I glanced back at the sniper vampire and saw him lying on the ground with a spear jutting from his chest. Saul stood over the body, twisting the metal rod for good measure, then yanked it upwards.

"Feed yourselves, then give him to the shades," he said to two male vampires by his side. They carried away the dead vampire into the darkness, and Saul waved us forward to join him by Celwyn. "Hurry."

I took a step and nearly collapsed. The bullet had cleanly exited above my breast, but I was a bloody mess. The blonde woman nearly dragged me to the wall where Saul waited, and allowed me to collapse by Celwyn. Alex followed silently, holding the hand of another one of Saul's female companions.

Saul worked on waking Celwyn but was having no luck. "You need medical attention, Melanie, and we cannot provide it. The sight of your blood is too much of a temptation. The only reason you are still sitting here is because the stench of your immunity counters the bloodlust. Those shades over there are not so disciplined as my friends, and even some of them are still struggling to accept this new life. We cannot stay with you in this condition."

"The back of Celwyn's belt," I sputtered. "Pouch. Find the cylinders. Give them to me."

Saul groped for a moment around Celwyn's back and handed me two metal cylinders. I pushed the button on one and handed it to Saul. "Stab his thigh. Push the button again."

I pushed the button on the other one and handed it to Saul. "Now do me."

Saul plunged the needle into my leg and I felt the rush of adrenaline. But with it came a surge of pain from the bullet wound. I thought I saw Celwyn move right before the world began to spin. I tried to speak, but my mouth didn't cooperate.

Everything slowed down, and then I fell into a deep dark hole that never seemed to end. The soft green glow of the world faded away, along with the pain.

I felt nothing, and it felt good.

CHAPTER THIRTY-THREE

I WOKE up back in the Castle's hospice wing, sitting at my desk surrounded by the beeping of computer monitors. Deirdre leaned over the counter, smiled, then handed me an electronic tablet.

"Saul's been waiting for you to get here. He wants to take a walk around the ward. It's all he's been talking about all day."

"I'll take care of him. You go enjoy yourself, but not too much. Don't get into any trouble on Broadway." I saw myself speak the words to Deirdre, but it wasn't me. It had to be a dream, but it felt so real, like I was floating above myself, watching a memory unfold.

I prepared my medicine cart and made the rounds through the ward. Each time I entered a room, I knocked, announced my name, then wrote it on the greaseboard. But I never received a response. Every time I entered, the figure in the bed remained still, hidden from my view as I carefully prepared medicine and left it on a bedside tray.

On the third room, I realized the reason I never received a response. The patients in my ward were dead.

All of them.

But I continued making my rounds, announcing my presence, writing my name, and leaving medicine that no one would ever take. I worked each hallway of my rectangular route, passing the barred door in the back of the hospice where I had fought the vampire. Its pristine condition made me doubt my sanity for a moment.

Had I really fought a vampire? Was I losing my mind?

Each room brought me closer to the final patient on my ward. Saul. My favorite patient. My friend.

I opened his door and was greeted by the unprecedented sight of a dark television screen hanging on the wall. I fought the fear in my belly and completed my routine. Like the other rooms, a figure lay in the bed, quiet and unmoving, but I refused to believe it could be Saul. He bore the record for cheating death before my arrival, and I had personally witnessed his transformation from human to shade, and eventually vampire.

No. Saul was most certainly alive. I didn't understand how, exactly, he lived, but he did.

I laid out the medicine on Saul's side table, but instead of turning and leaving, like I had in the other rooms, I stayed. Because I willed it.

The dream went away and I was no longer watching myself. I found myself standing in Saul's room, and everything seemed so bright. My shoulder didn't hurt and the stupid helmet was gone. I could actually touch my face. It felt so good.

"Saul," I whispered. "I'm here. It's time for your walk." I called out my friend's name, but he didn't move.

I moved closer and called his name again. "Saul."

The figure in the bed remained still. I became angry.

"Saul! Say something!"

I reached the edge of the bed and saw a man lying down on his back, covered in a white sheet. My hand slowly moved towards the linen, grabbed the edge, then paused. Did I really want to see? Why did it matter? This wasn't real. Whoever was under the sheet wasn't really there. This was only a dream.

But it felt real.

And I couldn't stop myself. My hand gently pulled down the sheet and curls of Saul's white hair sprung from their hiding place. My friend's face looked up at me with hollow eyes, devoid of the spark of life he fought so fiercely to extend. Sadness welled up inside my chest, and I felt an overwhelming urge to cry.

But I didn't cry. Saul wasn't dead. It wasn't him lying there.

I closed my eyes, assured myself of that fact, and when I opened them again, the bed was empty.

After a moment, my shoulder began to ache again. It started as a dull pain but quickly escalated to an agony so sharp it made me forget about everything. Only the pain remained.

Then I heard a noise behind me.

I turned. Saul stood at the edge of the room, his slender profile blending into the shadows. He lunged towards me, hands outstretched, howling in the guttural language of a shade. He crossed the small room in seconds, and I saw his face. His pitch-black eyes absorbed the light, reflecting no trace of my friend. His jaws opened, displaying bloodstained teeth.

The scream started in my core, built in my throat, and erupted from my vocal cords. But my mouth remained closed, trapping the sound, forcing it into my mind. I screamed again, this time louder and with more force, but it too reverberated only in my head, depriving me of the relief I craved.

Finally, my primal scream escaped its prison, a vocal expression of every emotion—fear, anguish, and anger—all mixed into one. The dream ended, but the scream continued, piercing my ears. The bright hospice room disappeared, replaced by a small flickering point of light surrounded by a sea of darkness.

From inside the light, I heard a familiar voice calling my name.

It was Celwyn.

———

IT DIDN'T TAKE LONG for my eyes to adjust again to the dark. My throat felt raw, and the fire in my shoulder from the gunshot throbbed with every breath.

I glanced up at Celwyn from my seated position against a wall. The dim glow of a broken light stick lying on the cement floor illuminated his face. A patch of deep purple encircled his left eye. Below the swelling, puncture wounds from a bite mark formed a semi-circle where the broken skin remained caked with dried blood.

"You had a nightmare," he said matter-of-factly. "The steroids make you have vivid dreams."

"I saw Saul. He was dead." I took a deep breath. "It seemed so real."

"Saul's very much alive," Celwyn said.

"But is he, though? I'm not sure of anything anymore."

"Do you feel guilty for not putting a bullet in his head when I asked you to?"

"No. Not when you put it like that. But, I just...I wonder if I did the right thing."

"I'll be honest, I don't know, either. I...don't understand Saul. He's able to do something I've never seen before, or even heard of for that matter. He gained control of the parasite by himself. And apparently he can help other shades do the same." He shook his head and grunted. "I didn't know him before, but from what I've seen, he's still Saul, and he is very much your friend." Celwyn paused as if deep in thought. "The enemy of my enemy is my friend, so I think the world right now is better off with Saul in it. And with you in it, too, but you need a hospital. Soon. I used everything I had in my kit and cleaned up the gunshot as much as I could, but you've lost a lot of blood."

"You don't look great either."

"I'll be fine." Celwyn rubbed the bite mark on his face then pointed to Alex, sitting cross-legged by my feet. "She's been waiting for you to wake up."

I forced a partial smile. "Hey, kid," I said. "You hanging in there?"

Alex nodded her head. "I saw you get shot. And then that old man killed the vampire, the ugly one with the gun." The girl paused. "Who was the old man? He helped wake Celwyn up, then he left with the other ones like him. "

"I see you are back to being a chatterbox. That's my friend, Saul."

"Celwyn said he is a vampire. Is that true? I thought vampires were bad?"

I gave Celwyn a dirty look. "Yes, he is a vampire, but he's not like the other ones. He's on our side."

Celwyn shook his head. "I hope so. He said he was going to get the power back on so you can get out of here on the mag lev train. You need a hospital, and that's the fastest way back to civilization." Celwyn leaned up on one knee, then pushed off with his other foot to slowly rise to his feet. "Saul and his crew backtracked to Grid Three. He took the shades and they're going for the power station."

"He can fix anything," I said confidently.

"We'll see," Celwyn replied. "He's going to have to get in there first. Tarek won't leave it unguarded." He positioned his backpack to evenly distribute the weight of his sword, then picked up the light stick on the ground. "I hate to leave you in the dark, but I need to get another rifle and a helmet with a radio. We have to find out what's going on above us, and what we're going to run into if we go back up to Broadway."

Alex looked at me nervously and grabbed the hand on my uninjured side.

"It's alright." I squeezed. "It will only be a minute, and we can watch him. He won't go far, right Celwyn?"

Celwyn looked out into the loading dock. "Yeah. I don't think I'll need to go far." He sighed. "There's a lot to choose from." He moved towards the nearby forklift where he had been shot in the helmet and lost consciousness. The bodies of soldiers lay nearby, and Celwyn clearly hoped one of them would have a full magazine in their rifle and a functioning radio in their helmet.

Alex scooted up beside me and leaned her back against the wall. "I miss my sister."

I heard sniffles and a few uneven breaths, but no crying. "I know. You might not remember, but when we met, I told you I knew someone else named Alex. It was my husband. He was sick for a long time, and he eventually died. I missed him very much, too, and I didn't think the pain would ever go away, but it did."

"Do you still miss him?"

I pulled Alex close with my good arm. "Of course. But it's different now. I came to the Castle because I knew that he would want for me to move on with my life." I managed a painful chuckle. "That didn't work out so well, but at least I found you."

"I wish I had never come here. I hate this place."

"*You're* going to get out of here. *We're* going to get out of here." I

224

squeezed Alex with the little strength I could muster. "But you have to believe we'll make it. You have to fight to make it happen, or else it won't. That's one thing this world has taught me. Do you understand, Alex?"

I felt the wispy hair moving through my fingers as her head nodded. "Yes. I want to fight—like you."

For a moment I felt the warmth of Alex's embrace and the pride of realizing that another human being wanted to be like me. I had never before experienced that feeling.

Many a night I had wondered what it would be like to raise a child, but I never appreciated the depth of the responsibility, the worry over future harm, and the fear and guilt in the inevitable failure to prevent it. The gravity of Alex's words hit me almost as hard as the pain in my shoulder.

Before I could respond, a speck of light approached, its field of illumination growing brighter by the second, eventually revealing Celwyn. A newfound helmet sat on his head, his face visible through the open visor. In one hand, he held a rifle and the light stick peeked out from the side of his belt where it had been shoved to hold it tight, lighting his path. Celwyn moved with a speed and agility I had not seen from him in a while.

The steroids helped.

"I talked to Dax and Paloma on the radio. Dax's team is making their way down from the Upper Tube and falling back to the Station. If we hurry, we can join up with them at the bottom before Broadway is overrun with shades."

I wrestled my good arm away from Alex and planted it firmly on the concrete floor, then pushed myself up onto my knees. A wave of pain shot through my body, knocking me back down on my butt. Suddenly, getting to my feet seemed a herculean task, and I worried what help I would be able to offer if we ran into more shades.

"Don't try to do too much. Take it slow." Celwyn approached and cradled his arm underneath my shoulder, lifting me gingerly to my feet. He held me until he was certain I could stand on my own, and wouldn't crumple again when the next wave of pain struck.

"I can walk on my own," I said.

Both Celwyn and Alex watched me anxiously as I took a few steps. "What's the matter? You've never seen someone get shot and walk it off?"

"Not funny," Celwyn replied.

A wave of pain radiated out from the gunshot wound in my shoulder. I stopped for a moment to take a deep breath and put a hand on my knee. "I need one of those scooters like they have at the grocery store."

"Apparently, Idrissia is out of those at the moment," Celwyn replied.

"I'm definitely going to give this place a poor rating. The customer service is severely lacking." I stood up straight, fought off another bout of pain, then began following Celwyn toward the stairwell. Earlier in the night, I had covered the length of the dock in less than a minute while simultaneously stumbling and shooting at a horde of shades. Now, I had barely moved at all and couldn't catch my breath due to exhaustion.

"We need to hurry," Celwyn said. I could feel the gentle urgency in his voice.

I thought about making another smart remark about crossing a football field with a bullet hole in my chest, but instead I only managed a quick glance intended to convey I was doing the best I could do under the circumstances.

As I struggled to put one foot in front of the other, something strange happened. Alex heard it first and grabbed my hand. A deep hum floated through the darkness, and my pulse quickened. The lights flicked on a second later, and this time they were real, not the product of some steroid-infused dream.

Saul had actually pulled it off.

The Castle rumbled back to life, and with the power restored, I allowed myself to enjoy the first small measure of hope we might actually escape this cursed place.

CHAPTER THIRTY-FOUR

EVERYTHING LOOKS different in the light. Nightfall shrinks the world and deprives it of color and contrast. Now, in the artificial illumination that flooded the loading dock, I saw the blood stains on the white concrete floor in great detail, the gray tones replaced by every possible shade of red imaginable. A panoramic view of dead bodies imparted the scale of what had occurred below Broadway, the combined death toll of shades and soldiers making the ground level of Grid One look more like a battlefield than a loading dock.

But through the horror, I saw something else that had been obscured by the shroud of darkness—a way up to the Silver Castle Station, an escape plan that would not have been possible until just this moment.

"Look," I said to Celwyn. "Those are the loading platforms for the Station. I remember seeing them when I arrived."

Near the back wall of the dock, three large metal platforms sat on the concrete floor, painted in bright yellow stripes. At the edge of each platform, a podium topped by an enclosed box containing flashing lights and electronic controls rose from the floor. Above each platform, a black sliding metal door in the roof of the dock marked our exit route from the basement of the Castle.

Celwyn grinned. "This just might work. Wait here." He sprinted over to the closest console and opened the box. After a few seconds of scrutinizing a small screen, he touched it multiple times then removed a handheld controller attached to the box by a tethered cord. He pressed some buttons on the handheld device, and a railing rose up around the perimeter of the platform. The metal doors above the platform creaked and slid open slowly, revealing a view of the Station. We got an enthusiastic thumbs up sign from Celwyn and a wave for us to approach while he talked into the microphone on his helmet.

The prospect of breathing fresh air again brought me renewed vigor, and Alex and I quickly made our way to the platform. I didn't know what awaited us in the world up above, but it had to be better than our chances down here in the dock, alone, waiting for the next horde of shades to stumble upon us.

"I told Paloma we're coming up," Celwyn said as Alex closed the small metal gate behind us, allowing our entry onto the platform

Once we made it to the center of the metal floor, Celwyn pushed a button on the controller. The floor jolted upward with a groaning sound and we began to rise. A trace of a smile curled up at the edge of Alex's mouth, a brief tease of an emotion I had never witnessed during our short time together. I responded with my own attempt.

The distant bodies on the bloodstained dock floor shrank in size as the platform rose higher into the air, lifted by two giant mechanical arms. Above us, I could see the helmets of soldiers peeking at us over the edge. A blinking orange light announced our arrival and it looked like we drew a crowd.

The platform kept rising until it lay even with the floor of the Station, blending in seamlessly. At least twenty soldiers and a handful of people without helmets stood outside the railing, waiting anxiously for the safety guards to drop.

One soldier closest to Celwyn shouted. "What happened to the people down there? Where is everyone else?" The rapid fire questions bombarded us from every direction, startling Alex. I pulled her close, fearing they would rush us, and flashed Celwyn an anxious look.

"Get back!" Celwyn said. "There's nobody left alive down there. Everyone's dead. And we will be, too, if we don't get the hell out of here right now." He looked around at the faces surrounding the loading platform. "Where's Paloma?"

The crowd parted and Paloma walked briskly forward. "I'm right here. And I couldn't agree with you more. It's time to get the hell out of here." He pointed over his shoulder toward the mag lev train. "We're prepping her now. As soon as Dax gets here, we're leaving. All of us."

———

I SAT on a bench near the train next to Alex. The girl rested her head on my good shoulder, eyes closed, ignoring the beehive of activity underway in the Station. Dawn would arrive in about three hours. I kept telling myself that all we had to do was survive the night, and everything would be over.

But a small part of me didn't want the night to end, to lose the girl clinging tightly to my side. Escaping the Castle would mean returning to the real world. And Alex surely had family somewhere who would be looking for her; family who rightfully deserved to have her returned to them.

I needed to stop pretending. I wasn't her mother. And she wasn't my daughter.

Paloma and a few other soldiers patrolled the edge of the Station facing the desert. In the distance, the sounds of Tarek's airship making a pass just out of firing range periodically filtered through the night.

Celwyn walked up and sat next to me on the bench. "Dax has made it down to Broadway and isn't hitting too much resistance. He should be here any minute. You ready?"

"Do I have a choice?" I looked over at Alex. "I would give anything to be able to lean back in one of those comfortable chairs on the train and fall asleep just like that." I rubbed my shoulder, trying to massage away the pain. "I'm done. I've got nothing left."

"You're not done. I knew it from the first time I met you. You're a fighter, and not just with the immunity from the parasite. That's genetics. You have the will to push through. When I got knocked out of the fight, you didn't give up. You ran into danger so you could save the girl sleeping next to you." Celwyn stroked Alex's hair. "No. You're not done. Not even close."

"You sure know how to flatter a girl. Do I have beautiful eyes, too?"

Celwyn shook his head. "Actually, I never noticed."

I did my best to try to smile, but settled for a nod.

"I need to talk to you about something. Paloma's right, you know. You're special, and we desperately need new Knights. You can come with me…" Celwyn paused. "If you want."

"I don't know what I want." I looked at Alex. "Maybe I just want to live a normal life."

The popping sounds of machine gun fire interrupted our conversation. Celwyn turned to watch the row of glass doors leading from the Station into Broadway.

"Dax is coming. Once he's inside the Station, Paloma's going to blow the doors. Then we have to go. Be ready to move." He nodded toward Alex. "She needs to wake up now."

I nudged Alex awake. Celwyn retreated towards the entrance to Broadway where the other soldiers waited, guarding the doors. A new group of soldiers burst into the Station, led by Dax, who had ditched his rifle for two giant knives that resembled machetes, one in each hand.

"All clear," Dax said tiredly.

"Move! Everyone back!" Paloma shouted.

Celwyn ran towards me while the other soldiers scattered. "Behind the bench," he instructed, then joined us.

Through the gaps between the slats, I saw Paloma standing out in the open, on the loading platform for the train, holding a device in his hand. He paused, as if waiting for whatever was pursuing Dax.

"Blow the bloody doors," Celwyn muttered.

Finally, Paloma turned and sprinted towards the train, ducking inside. Behind him, an explosion ripped through Broadway, sending a fireball of flame and smoke into the Station, shattering the glass on the doors as debris piled up against them from the inside. The grand entrance to Idrissia's premier Line City, the Silver Castle, crumbled into a pile of rubble.

Paloma ducked out of the train and began waving soldiers forward.

"Move it. Hurry up before that airship comes back around and sees you." The line of people moved forward, but didn't enter the train. Instead, the few remaining living occupants of the Station formed a single line to climb down a ladder at the edge of the station. Once there, everyone stepped into a maintenance opening for the giant water pipe connecting the Castle to the desalinization plant on the coast of the Pacific Ocean.

I followed, but stopped to peek over the edge of the opening, down the ladder, into the pipe. Inside, the water only came to their ankles, the flow temporarily shut off by an emergency valve in the Station, and the ceiling of the pipe far out of reach for even the tallest soldier standing on his toes. We wouldn't drown in the cavernous tunnel of steel, but getting out would require faith that we would find another maintenance ladder like the one we were about to use to get inside.

"I would rather take the train," I said to Celwyn.

"It's too dangerous with that airship out there," he replied. "We just need to buy time. Once the sun rises, we can use another maintenance hatch and go for help at the closest town."

"How do you know they won't follow us into the pipe?"

"No one is going to follow us."

Paloma stood on the train's loading platform, next to the ladder. He removed the device he had used to blow up the doors to the Station from his pocket and handed it to Celwyn before we reached the ladder. "Here. It's armed. You've got over a mile of range, but I wouldn't chance it. Blow it as soon as you're clear. You'll be protected in those metal pipes."

I looked at Paloma and then at Celwyn, a confused look on my face. "I thought the Knights were the only ones planning to destroy the City?"

"If anyone brings down the Castle, it's going to be me." Paloma said confidently. "I laid charges as soon as I arrived."

"Then why aren't you going to do it? Why give it to Celwyn?"

Paloma looked at Celwyn, sighed and a look of sadness crossed his face. He ignored my question, choosing instead to yell at someone else. "Dax, you got the guns mounted?"

"Yes, Captain." Dax poked his head out from the train. "I got both fifty calibers ready up top."

"Good. If we're lucky, we'll shoot that bastard Tarek out of the sky." He turned to Celwyn. "If not, I trust that you will get your vengeance after I'm gone. Either way, I'll still get to see his precious Line City and all of the rich newbloods he has hiding out in the Heights blown to bits before I die." Paloma looked at Celwyn sternly. "And either way, you'll live to tell the Order what happened here. You will tell them that your old captain was right, and maybe their eyes will finally be opened to the truth. They'll realize that war is upon them, and there is no peace to be had with the vampires—no more Accords to be struck." Paloma's expression softened and he puffed out his chest. "History will record that here, at the Silver Castle, I struck the first blow in the final war against vampires and restored the Order to its true path."

"You ain't going to make it into the history books if you stick around here talking," Dax said. The bearded mercenary took a puff on the cigarette hanging out of the side of his mouth, then flicked it to the ground. "That debris won't hold them long. Those shades will dig through it, and we all need to be gone when that happens."

"You're right as always, my friend," Paloma said. He turned to Celwyn. "Go. I'll give you ten minutes head start, then we'll leave, too. Once I give you the word we're clear, you knock down the Castle." He paused, then spoke firmly. "No matter what."

Celwyn nodded, then pushed me and Alex toward the ladder. "Time to go."

Paloma and Dax boarded the train, and the doors hissed closed behind them. I watched through the windows as they ran toward the front of the train where two large guns protruded from the top of the front car.

I looked at the device still sitting in Celwyn's hand. "This is what you wanted, right? To stop the spread of the parasite?" I paused. "You know that will include Saul."

Celwyn dropped the device into his jacket pocket. "It has to be done. I've been telling you that all along. Like you said, maybe Saul shouldn't even be alive."

I knew Celwyn was right. The vampires Tarek had bred in the lab next to my hospice, and the thousands of shades still roaming the Castle, could not be allowed to escape. But I refused to lump Saul in with the others. My friend never gave up on me.

And I wouldn't give up on him.

"Let's go," I said to Alex. Celwyn turned to make his way down the ladder first so he could keep an eye on the girl when she followed him down onto the landing. I turned to put my foot on the ladder, then slipped the necklace with my wedding ring out of my pocket and looped it on the top handle of the ladder.

The small gold band twirled on the chain, and I froze. Leaving the ring left me with nothing to remember my husband. Every possession remained behind in the Castle except for the Leatherman I gave to Alex and the ring hanging in front of me.

I made my decision quickly, turning to put my other foot on the first rung of the ladder. If Saul somehow made it this far, he would have a path to follow to safety. I owed him that much. The ring I left hanging on the ladder would mark life and no longer serve as a reminder of death.

All three of us climbed down to the maintenance entrance to the water pipe on the subfloor of the Station. I grabbed Alex's hand and stepped into the dark metal tube, instantly submerging my shoes in the water. Suddenly, I felt cold and tired. The throbbing pain in my shoulder intensified.

Celwyn closed the maintenance hatch, making a loud clank, then tapped the side of his helmet. "Paloma, we're all in the pipeline."

With the hatch closed, the sounds of the world outside disappeared. The long march to freedom had begun, and so had the countdown to the destruction of the Silver Castle.

CHAPTER THIRTY-FIVE

"I'M SCARED," Alex said.

"I know, but this is the way out. Just a little bit longer and it will be morning and we can get out of here." I promised what I thought I could.

We walked forward, following the bobbing headlamps from soldier helmets. The collection of battery-powered LED lamps fought a losing battle against the thick darkness surrounding us, permeating the inside of the six-inch-thick metal pipe, sealing us off from any glimpse of real light from the outside world. Just when we had finally been rescued from the darkness in the bowels of the lifeless Castle, we were now thrust right back into blackness. And the moldy smell reminded me of the whiff I always caught when I first turned on the tap water in Los Angeles.

And the moldy smell reminded me of the whiff I always caught when I first turned on the tap water in Los Angeles.

It was almost too much to bear.

After a short walk, the forward movement stopped abruptly. In front of us, the pipe sloped softly downward, running parallel to the train tracks that dropped from the fifth story height of the Station down to the desert floor. One by one, the others sat on the floor of the pipe and allowed gravity to do its work, carrying them downward like a water slide at an amusement park. Soon the three of us remained alone at the top.

Celwyn paused, listening to a communication in his helmet. "Paloma's left the Station. They saw movement in the Station. He said to blow it now."

My heart jumped. "Maybe it's Saul."

"Or maybe it's something not so friendly. If shades or one of Tarek's vampires get into these pipes behind us..." He looked down at Alex, who listened intently to our conversation, then back at me. "Don't make me say it. You know what will happen."

"You said you would give it ten minutes. It hasn't been ten minutes."

"We don't have any more time, Mel."

I grabbed Celwyn's hand before he could reach in his pocket. "Please give Saul more time. He's followed us the whole way. You know it's him."

Celwyn recoiled his arm and pushed my hands away. "I don't know that. You don't know that." He tapped the side of his helmet again, listening to the radio. "Paloma's under attack from the airship. For this plan to work, Tarek has to believe we're all on that train. He has to believe someone on that train blew up the Castle."

I nodded at Celwyn, then wrapped my arms around Alex. My shoulder burned with pain, but I squeezed nonetheless. Together, we sat down in the dark, murky water and pushed off with our feet until the bottom dropped out. The damp air rushed against our faces, along with an occasional splash of water. Below us, the lights from the others' headlamps grew brighter until we landed again on a flat surface. Several powerful hands reached down to help us to our feet.

Behind me, a lone light twinkled in the darkness at the top of the junction in the pipe. I found myself holding my breath, waiting for some sign that Paloma's device worked and Celwyn had destroyed the Castle.

The light suddenly began moving, sliding toward us inside the pipe. The metal floor beneath my feet rocked back and forth. The entire pipe swayed and shook. A roar that sounded like standing next to a jet engine grew louder, crescendoing for almost a minute, then slowly died out.

Now sitting on the floor of the pipe, Celwyn stood up and adjusted his backpack. "It's done!" he shouted. "The Castle is gone."

For a moment, no one responded, first out of disbelief, then realization of the impact of Celwyn's words.

One woman began sobbing.

A soldier mumbled, "We're safe."

I looked around at the small crowd of survivors. We were the only ones left alive out of an *entire city*. The city was all gone—the people, the buildings...everything.

Slowly, a sense of excitement built among those lucky few of us huddled in the wet confines of the pipe. We had made it. We had actually made it.

One of the soldiers shouted into the radio on his helmet, "What do you see up there, Captain? Is the Castle gone?"

Everyone quieted down, waiting for Paloma's voice to respond. Instead, a different voice answered.

"The Captain is tied up at the moment," Dax said. He spoke slowly, then coughed. "But he's got a shit-eating grin on his face a mile wide." He tried to laugh, then launched into another coughing fit. "To answer your question, yeah, it's gone. Idrissia ain't got nothing left of their precious city.

"What about the airship?" Celwyn asked.

"That thing is too damned fast," Dax replied. "The Captain clipped it one time, but it hit us good, and it's coming back around. We're sitting ducks moving in a straight line."

"Dax. Is Tarek on that ship?"

Celwyn waited.

"Dax, is Tarek on that ship? Dax!"

The pipe shook again, this time a smaller rumble. The vibration came from the opposite direction, away from the Castle. A moment later, a blast of hot air washed over us, filling the inside of the pipe with the scent of burnt metal and smoke. In the distance, a faint flash of white light twinkled before being consumed again by the milky darkness.

"They killed the Captain," one of the soldiers whispered.

Another soldier replied. "The Captain knew what he was doing. He saved us. That airship won't stick around. Let's go. It's safe now."

I looked at Celwyn. "What do you think?"

He stroked his chin. "If something followed us into this bloody pipe, we're going to have trouble. And if that airship is still out there, we'll be dead if we step foot out in the open."

Two soldiers in the group began moving forward, not waiting on the rest.

"Wait!" Celwyn hissed.

Both soldiers stopped and turned to face Celwyn. The larger one opened his visor. "You're not in charge here. Our Captain's dead, and we don't know you." He turned to speak to the remaining group. "I'm tired of hiding in the dark where those things have the advantage. It's going to be light soon, and our safest place is outside. That's where I'm going. If you want to live, I suggest you come with me."

A lot of heads nodded in agreement.

"I'm not going to stop you," Celwyn replied. "But we should stay together. We're safer together, and distances can be deceiving. Whatever you think you saw, if an explosion did make an opening in the pipe, it could be miles away."

"Screw that." The large soldier closed his visor. "If you can't keep up, that's your problem not mine." He motioned to the others to follow him and started jogging away from us, his boots splashing through the puddles covering the floor of the pipe. Most of the others followed, leaving only three remaining behind, one young male soldier and two silver-haired women.

Celwyn walked up to the soldier who remained behind. "So why didn't you follow the others?"

"The Captain trusted you," he said. "And the three of you were the only ones to make it out of the basement alive, so I figure I'm safer with you. But...I'm not taking any chances." He pulled a wicked looking knife from a sheath hanging on his belt. He turned to me and Alex. "My name's Reilly, and this is Seneca and Val. I pulled these two out of a tough situation in Grid Seven, and they haven't let me out of their sight ever since. They refused to go down into the basement with the others. Pretty smart move in hindsight. "

"I'm Mel, and this is Alex," I said.

"Walk and talk. Those guys are right about one thing—we need to keep moving. And you can call me Celwyn."

CELWYN'S INTUITION on distance proved to be accurate. The bobbing headlamps and splashing sounds from the soldiers soon disappeared, leaving us behind to slowly make our way through the dark, humid pipe.

Reilly led the way in silence. Behind him, Seneca and Val walked shoulder to shoulder with Alex, praising her bravery and quizzing her on what she would eat first when she made it home.

"I think I would start with ice cream," Alex said.

Seneca, who appeared to have enjoyed plenty of ice cream over her many years, reacted quickly. "Ooh, what flavor is your favorite?"

Alex paused for a moment. "Hmm. That's hard. Birthday cake, I guess."

"Wow. That's one of those fancy flavors," Val chuckled. "We're just plain old vanilla type of gals."

"I like strawberry," I muttered to no one in particular.

I felt a twinge of jealousy, wishing that I could be a part of the conversation, but the throbbing in my shoulder made it difficult to concentrate on anything other than putting one foot in front of the other. Every step felt like climbing a mountain, further exhausting my already limited reserves of energy. And in the back of my mind, I feared letting my guard down for even a moment. Through the fog of pain, some remaining part of my dulled senses screamed of danger.

It went unspoken, but I knew Celwyn felt it, too. Every so often, he would turn around and peer into the darkness, suspicious we were being followed. We progressed that way for at least a mile until finally a soft glow of light appeared in the distance.

"Quiet," Celwyn whispered. He flicked off the light on his helmet and pointed at Reilly to do the same. The darkness engulfed us instantly, a shroud so thick you couldn't see your hand in front of your face. "Listen," he said.

Deprived of sight, my other senses heightened as we sat in the dark. The smell of acrid smoke wafted through the pipe. Something burned up ahead, but the humidity had dropped and I also detected a small hint of circulation in the air.

That was new.

Alex clung to my waist, and I could feel her squirming. With every slight shift in her feet, the movement disturbed the water standing on the floor of the pipe, creating a soft splashing noise that broke up the silence. I had become so accustomed to hearing the splashes of footsteps that I had begun to tune them out as background noise. But now, sitting quietly in the dark, it became possible to discern the source of each splash, and it became instantly clear that someone besides us was moving through the pipe.

The light on Celwyn's helmet turned on. "Move," he said firmly. "Someone is in the pipe behind us."

CHAPTER THIRTY-SIX

FLEEING from a predator is a primal function that transcends age or injury. Fight or flight. Live or die.

Adrenaline surged and the pain in my shoulder faded. In response to Celwyn's warning, millions of years of evolution kicked in, and somehow everyone in our group, young and old, found the strength to run.

We sounded like a herd of animals splashing through a stream, abandoning any pretense of stealth or caution. No one cared. The literal light at the end of the tunnel beckoned to us, and we weren't going to stop until we reached it.

Slowly, the pipe veered from its straight trajectory, angling us slightly downward and to the right, where a smoky haze hung in the air before a jagged opening where the pipeline had been ripped apart at one of its welded seams. Outside the opening, sporadic fires burned in what appeared to be wreckage from the mag lev train.

Reilly stopped, and we all crowded behind him near the end of the pipeline, peering out into the night. The relief of being out of the confined space washed over us.

We had escaped the Castle. And we could see again, even if only by moonlight.

"Any sign of the airship?" Celwyn asked Reilly.

"Nope," he replied. "But I can't see anything in this mess."

A car from the train lay on the ground upside down in front of us, a blackened carcass of metal surrounded by piles of debris, many of them still smoking from the fiery explosion. A twisted line of derailed cars bisected the pipeline, knocking out an entire segment. The train's raised cement platform, lined with powerful electric powered magnets, had been destroyed, leaving the train to plummet downward, barreling through the parallel pipeline before finally coming to rest in the desert.

I shivered as a wave of unease rolled over my body. Celwyn felt it, too, and immediately began looking for a way down to the ground from our elevated perch.

I grabbed Alex's hand. "Stay close. It's not daylight yet."

Celwyn leaped off the edge of the open pipe, landing on the sandy desert floor at least five feet below. Luckily, the impact of the train had not only split the pipeline in two, but also destroyed the trellis foundation used to keep the pipeline elevated and level next to the train. Our half of the pipe sagged downward without its support, making the distance to the ground more manageable.

Reilly followed, brushed himself off, and beckoned for Seneca and Val. Each one leaped down to the desert, landing in the combined arms of Reilly and Celwyn, catching them to break their fall.

"You're next, little girl," I said to Alex. "They got you."

Alex looked back nervously into the dark pipeline. "What about you?"

"I'm right behind you. Go!"

Alex backed up, then ran full speed toward the edge of the severed metal floor, launching herself into space. The two soldiers on the ground caught the girl, and Celwyn gave me a thumbs up sign, signaling my turn.

I turned and strained to look for movement in the darkness. Part of me hoped Saul had found my clue, followed our trail, and survived the destruction of the Castle. Another part of me wondered if Saul's death, along with the rest of the infected, would be for the good of us all.

The pipeline behind me remained hauntingly quiet, devoid of movement. I pushed any thought of seeing Saul again out of my mind, slowly turned and walked to the edge, and prepared to jump.

This was going to hurt.

Celwyn tried to break the fall by catching my good side, but the impact still sent shockwaves of pain through the wound on my breast. I doubled over, nearly losing consciousness, before finally regaining control.

"Being shot hurts," I said grimly.

"I know," Celwyn replied. "Trust me."

"You still feel something out there?"

"Yeah." His head scanned the desert in every direction. "I just don't know if it's behind us, or out here."

"So where to?" asked Reilly, listening to our conversation.

Celwyn pointed at a smoldering train car sprawled in our path. "We're going to hunker down there until dawn. And I'm going to climb up top and look for Tarek's airship."

"But the train's still on fire," Reilly said.

"Exactly," Celwyn nodded. "Vampires hate fire, and shades won't go near it. Get as close as you can without getting burned. Get those fires going, make torches, do whatever you can to light this place up."

"You heard the man." Reilly looked at Seneca and Val. "Let's go ladies. Pick up anything that will burn along the way. Seat cushions, pieces of wood. Grab it all. We're making a bonfire."

Reilly removed the machete-looking blade from its sheath on his hip and strode over to a small juniper tree growing near the rail line. With powerful strokes, he separated two gnarled branches protruding from the base of the tree, retrieved them from the ground, and returned to hand one to Celwyn. "Torches."

———

I THREW another seat cushion onto the fire we had built outside the overturned train car. Behind me, Alex sat cross-legged on the ground, near enough to be warmed by the flames, far enough to avoid the smoke which kept shifting direction.

Val began to take off her shoes, but Reilly quickly stepped forward and shook his head.

"Put them back on. We may need to move in a hurry."

The old woman grumbled, then placed her sneakers back on her feet.

"I'm with you," I said to Val. "My feet are wet, and I'm exhausted. I just want to get some sleep right here by this fire."

Reilly worked on a torch, wrapping material shredded from seat cushions around the end of his juniper branch. For good measure, he overturned a bottle of wine, dumping its contents on the end of the makeshift torch.

"Did you find any food in the train car?" asked Seneca.

"No, that one just held the liquor. We're lucky any of it survived that crash." He handed the half-empty bottle to Seneca. "You want the rest?"

Val snatched the bottle first. "Wouldn't be the first time I had wine for breakfast."

Seneca shook her head, then held a cell phone up in the air, walking in circles looking for a signal. "Dammit, I can't get anything."

"I already tried. It ain't going to work," Val said.

Alex stood up, pointing behind me. "He's back."

I turned around in time to see Celwyn running full speed around the side of the train car. He made it back to the bonfire we had hastily built up from nothing more than a smoldering pile of junk, bent over to put his hands on his knees, and fought to catch his breath.

"They're all dead. The soldiers who left earlier. From up top, I saw their bodies a little way up the dirt road that runs by the track. The glow from the helmets' night vision made them hard to miss."

"So they were fighting something when they were killed," Reilly said.

Celwyn nodded. "Yeah, most likely."

"And Tarek's airship?" I asked.

"I—I can't be sure, but I think Paloma actually knocked it out of the sky. I saw some wreckage up the rail line that looks like it could be his ship." Celwyn stood up straight. "But that doesn't mean Tarek and some of his vampires aren't still lurking around."

"Can one of those things actually survive a plane crash?" Reilly asked.

"I don't know," Celwyn shook his head. "Maybe. If it's old enough, strong enough. But it would still be hurt, just like us."

"Except he could heal faster," I said.

Celwyn slowly nodded affirmatively. "Especially if he just had a big, bloody meal."

Reilly looked at an oversized watch on his wrist. "It's five o'clock. It'll be light soon." He turned to Seneca and Val. "You stay right here by this fire until the birds start chirping. No running off." He threw another chair into the flames, shooting a burst of sparks into the star-filled sky. "You two made it this far. You can make it one more hour."

"Maybe less," Celwyn said. He held up his satellite phone. "Help is on the way."

"What kind of help?" Reilly asked.

Celwyn picked up one of the torches made by Reilly. "The kind of help that knows what we're up against and won't be afraid to fight."

He handed me his rifle. "You still remember how to use this thing?"

"Yeah. Point and shoot."

Celwyn smiled. "Don't forget the aim part. Remember, you've only got what's left in that magazine. Make it count."

Next, he reached one arm behind his head and removed his sword from the compartment in his backpack, placing it by his feet next to the torch. "Now we wait."

I stared at the flames, dancing and leaping in a mesmerizing performance, and I felt hopeful. The sun would rise. Daylight would break.

A crashing noise broke the silence as one of the seats thrown into the bonfire broke into pieces, consumed by the heat, causing the entire burn pile to shift. Alex jumped up in a panic and ran to my side.

I ran my fingers through her hair. "It's just the fire shifting around, honey."

Alex looked up at me. "I don't want to lose you, too."

"Good," I said. "I don't want to lose me, either." I gave her a hug. "We're both going to make it. And then we'll find a way to get you home. Find someone in your family."

"I don't have a home," she said matter-of-factly. "And my family is all dead. I want to go with you."

Her words filled me with a warmth that made me forget all about my pain, and the threats that still lurked in the darkness of the night. I bent down and kissed Alex on the forehead. "I would like that very much."

For the first time, I began to believe this precious little girl might really be mine. I closed my eyes and hugged Alex, listening to Seneca and Val softly talk by the fire. And again, I felt hope.

But it didn't last.

A breath of unnatural cold air tickled the back of my neck. My senses prodded me to attention, and I pushed Alex away.

A hideous sound echoed across the desert, breaking up the stillness of the cold night. The direction of the sound eluded me, but I recognized the guttural scream.

"Be still," I hissed at Alex. "Tarek is out there. And he's calling for help."

Celwyn already had the sword in one hand and the torch in the other. He held the branch of juniper with cloth hanging off the end into the fire, and it burst into flame. "Tarek is still alive." He circled in place, surveying the crash scene, searching for movement. "And he just sent out the Blood Call."

Reilly nervously shuffled his feet on the other side of the bonfire, splitting his attention between Seneca and Val. He turned to Celwyn. "Do you think anything got out of the Castle behind us?"

"I don't know. Maybe. And if Tarek survived the crash, other vampires may be alive, too."

Reilly exhaled and shook his head. "Shit. This night ain't never gonna end."

Something moved in the distance, beyond the fire, and my hope evaporated.

We weren't going to make it to dawn. Not without a fight.

CHAPTER THIRTY-SEVEN

"BLOODY HELL," Celwyn shouted.

I strained to see the figure, who continued to approach, but remained obscured from my vantage behind the fire. "What is it?"

Reilly laughed. "It's the loudmouth who left us in the pipe. He's been turned into a shade." He walked forward with his torch. "Karma is a bitch, ain't it?"

I quickly made my way to Celwyn on the other side of the fire and raised my rifle, aiming it at the soldier. Without a helmet, likely lost back on the dirt road where he should have died, I noticed the large man's youth. His round baby face, now gray, was topped by a wavy head of blonde hair, his good looks surprisingly unaffected by the attack that took his mortal life. One of his legs, however, revealed the source of his infection. The powerful thigh looked like it had been mauled by a bear, the black fabric ripped to pieces, and the flesh underneath it exposed down to the bone.

Celwyn placed his hand on top of my rifle and gently pressed downwards. "No, save the bullets."

He and Reilly each walked forward, surrounding the newly born shade, poking and prodding with their torches. At first, the shade instinctively recoiled from the fire, but it desperately needed to feed, and its hesitance subsided, leading it to become braver, testing how close it could get to the burning tips of the torches.

The next time the baby-faced shade moved near Celwyn, the Knight sliced its good leg with his sword, then stepped back quickly, throwing up the torch to block any attempt to attack. While the monster wailed in pain, Reilly approached from the opposite side and stabbed the shade in the back before quickly retreating behind a series of threatening waves of his own torch.

Their dance continued, slicing and dicing our former companion until the thing could no longer stand and its blood flowed from no less than a dozen deep wounds.

Finally, Reilly poked his torch in the shade's face, distracting it with a vicious combination of fire and insults while Celwyn circled behind and removed its head with a swing of his sword.

The shade's torso fell to the ground, and the baby-faced soldier joined the rest of his ill-fated group in death. In a moment of weakness, I found myself sympathizing with Reilly's anger, rationalizing that the stupid kid deserved a horrible death for running off ahead and leaving us alone. But then I looked around at our motley crew: two old women, a child, and me—a middle aged nurse, slowed by an injury, nearly worthless in a fight.

The young soldier had wanted to live, so he wrote us off. Most rational people would have made the same decision.

Lucky for me, Celwyn was far from rational, convinced we were genetically selected to save the world from a vampire threat, and him duty-bound to an organization I wasn't sure actually existed. And the bond among Reilly and Seneca and Val ran deep. They had clearly been through hell together, and both of the old women viewed Reilly as their guardian angel.

Reilly wouldn't turn his back on them any more than he would sell out his mother. They were his family—maybe the only family he had left in the world.

I knew this because I saw the crazed look in his eyes when he heard Seneca and Val scream, and I heard the pain in his voice when he joined them.

In the closing thralls of night, on the cusp of the first rosy tendrils of dawn, everything descended into chaos. Screaming behind me. Reilly shouting as he made his way forward to Seneca's side. The cold tingling on my neck intensifying to the point of pain.

Danger.

Alex.

————

I TURNED and raised my rifle.

Seneca's screams still pierced the night, her shrieks rising and falling in waves. Val was gone. Behind them both, closest to the fire, Alex sat glassy-eyed, frozen, staring into the train car closest to our fire. A trail of blood led from the fire to the hollowed-out door frame of the car, now corkscrewed and lying upside down.

"No! No! No!" Reilly rushed to Seneca's side with Celwyn on his heels. He turned to Celwyn, "You said they would be safe by the fire! Damn these monsters to hell."

Reilly started to move towards the train car, and Celwyn grabbed his arm. "Val's already dead. Turn around. Look at her. Seneca needs you here. *We* need you here. Our best chance is to stay together."

I huddled with Alex, anxiously watching the train car for movement. Looking down, I saw the blade of my Leatherman peeking out from one of Alex's hands where she clutched its handle in a grip so tight her knuckles had turned white.

"Good girl," I whispered in her ear.

Not a single window remained intact on the train car lying upside down in front of us. A chorus of sickening sounds wafted out through the night, the sounds of flesh being torn and the grunts of an animal consumed by hunger. The sliding doors, mangled by the wreck, had been easily kicked open by Reilly as part of his search for seat cushions to burn. Now, in the open mouth of the train car, a dark figure crouched with his back turned, hunched over Val's lifeless body. The thing ignored our presence, singularly focused on consuming its prey.

"Shoot it," Celwyn whispered. "Now, while it's feeding."

I raised my rifle and took a few steps forward, aiming squarely at the back of the thing's torso. The rifle sputtered and kicked with each pull of the trigger, releasing a flurry of bullets that all struck home.

The figure flinched with each impact, but never stopped its work.

I kept walking forward, my finger depressing on the trigger, spitting round after round from my rifle until it clicked empty and silence descended on the train car. *How many bullets had I shot?* Twenty? Maybe more?

Nothing could have survived such a barrage.

But after a few seconds of remaining still, the monster turned and rose to its feet. Its height filled the doorway of the train car, slowly assuming a human shape dressed in lightweight black body armor with the Thracian mark of Idrissia etched on its chest piece. The face remained shrouded in the shadow of the train car, but the long black hair and piercing red eyes revealed the identity of our attacker. I knew those features. They were ingrained in my memory.

Somehow Tarek had survived the crash of the airship. Barely.

He stepped out of the train car into the glow of the false light between darkness and sunrise. The handsome face I remembered was gone, replaced by that of a swollen bloody ghoul. His long hair hung in disorganized tendrils, stuck together in clumps of bloody goo. Deep gashes and bruises pockmarked his face, darkened from its prior rosy hue to the gray color of a shade.

I turned to Alex and squared my jaw. "Look at me. I never asked you what happened to your sister. Whatever it is, you did what you had to do to survive."

Alex broke eye contact and looked down.

"You did nothing wrong, and if we can't kill that thing, I want you to do that again. You run into the desert and hide. You don't come out until the sun is high in the sky. Follow the train tracks until you see a road, and then you follow it until you see someone. Promise me."

The young girl shook her head. "I don't want to lose you. I want to fight, too."

"I know, Alex. And one day you will. But not today. Stay close to the fire." I placed a kiss on her forehead and turned towards Tarek.

Reilly pushed Seneca back towards the fire, and the old woman grabbed Alex's hand. Celwyn and Reilly took up positions in front of me, furiously waving their torches at the approaching vampire.

Tarek raised his arms upward and let loose a guttural scream from his unnaturally stretched jaws, revealing a mouth full of razor sharp teeth still dripping with Val's blood. Black clouds filled his eyes, leaving only a small red dot in the place of his pupils.

I began to panic, then I looked up. The black skies had lightened to a pale blue with a tinge of pink on the horizon. A plan formed in my mind. We didn't need to defeat Tarek—we just needed to make it until dawn.

I looked back at Alex and mouthed *I love you*, then reached around my hip to remove a cannister from my belt. The gun around my neck no longer seemed necessary, so I pulled the strap up and over my head. The spent rifle made a clanking sound as I threw it down, hitting a piece of metal debris from the train lying on the ground. Tarek focused on me for a moment as I walked forward towards him, leaving the safety of the fire and stopping between Celwyn and Reilly.

My heart beat like a freight train, but I worked hard to keep my composure calm.

Celwyn quickly shot me a confused look, then returned his attention towards Tarek.

I ignored Celwyn and kept moving forward. "You're out of time, Tarek. Look around. You've lost. Dawn is coming. You may kill us, but you won't have time to go far. More Knights are coming, and they will hunt you down in whatever shadowy hole you find to hide from the sun. This desert will be your burial plot."

Tarek spit blood from his mouth and spoke, not in the vampire tongue, but in English, laden with a heavy accent. His words came with great effort and reminded me of Saul, struggling on the rooftop to speak in the early throes of mastering the parasite. "You smell like a Knight, but you reek of fear, so you are not one of them. You are a pretender. A fraud."

Rage filled my heart. Maybe I wasn't a Knight, but I was no longer just a nurse. I had changed. And most importantly, I was no longer afraid.

The vampire's bloodshot pupils flitted to Celwyn. "But this one, *he* is a Knight. I've seen him before. He knows that I'm not capable of mercy, that I am the hunter, not the hunted, and I will drink when and where I please like a lion drinks water from a spring." The eyes moved like a laser beam, returning back to me. "And I will leave both of your bodies next to Paloma, with the hearts removed as a warning to any other Knight who may search for me."

Tarek erupted in a laugh that sounded more like a coughing fit. And in that momentary distraction, I rushed forward and raised the cannister of pepper spray hidden in the palm of my hand. The idea of one of us attacking Tarek had apparently never entered his mind.

Sheep don't attack lions.

From about ten feet away, I pushed down with my thumb and the cannister spat out a powerful stream of noxious gel, fanning out into a cone pattern that painted Tarek's face with a red liquid. Ballistic pepper spray was powerful stuff, even for vampires, and it seemed especially appropriate that I would use a weapon that so closely resembled blood.

He clawed at his eyes and bellowed epithets in Thracian, instinctively staggering backward from the spray. I quickly turned and ran back towards the fire to escape what I expected to be a quick and vicious reaction.

And it came.

Tarek rushed forward, reaching wildly with his arms towards me while struggling to keep his eyes open. He closed the distance in less than a second, and his momentum would have allowed him to grab me by the neck except for the countervailing force of Celwyn's sword, swung like a baseball bat, knocking the vampire back. The Kevlar vest worn by Tarek absorbed most of the blow, but a deep gash appeared on Tarek's bicep, oozing a black liquid that resembled tar more than blood.

Reilly closed on Tarek from behind and thrust the fiery end of his torch against the side of Tarek's face. The residue from the pepper spray ignited, and the flames began to consume the skin on Tarek's face. His cheeks melted to the sounds of crackles and snaps like dry wood burning in a camp fire. But the vampire never faltered. Tarek fought back like a caged animal, grasping wildly, looking to find his attacker.

Reilly lingered a moment too long to savor his success and found himself caught by one of Tarek's long sinewy arms. He dropped the torch, and the the two of them went down to the ground with Tarek on top, his head still encircled with flames. Reilly valiantly attempted to escape from Tarek, kicking his feet and thrusting with his hips, but the vampire couldn't be moved. Instead, Tarek drove his face into Reilly's chest, and rubbed it from side to side, wiping clear the burning pepper spray. Reilly's shirt melted, and then his flesh as the flames spread.

For a moment, both Tarek and Reilly burned together, wriggling on the ground until the fire died out, along with Reilly's screams.

Reilly never moved again, but Seneca quietly circled around and picked up the machete dropped by her friend and protector. The old woman moved like a whisper while Tarek straddled the now-dead body of Reilly, his vision obscured by a mixture of pepper spray and blood as he ravenously fed. And when the vampire regained his senses and attempted to stand, he received a blade plunged deep into his armpit, the only area not protected by his vest.

Seneca never said a word. She didn't run away or even attempt to avoid what she knew would come next.

Seneca stood her ground, even as Tarek plunged his fist into her abdomen and ripped her body into pieces. The old woman fell with a look of peace on her face while Tarek licked his hand, sucking up the juices from her entrails.

I quickly scanned the sky. The eastern horizon was a few shades lighter.

Tarek roared over the two dead bodies and turned to face us. Charred chunks of rotten flesh hung loosely from the bones on his face, and his eye sockets were nothing more than dark cavities. Tarek sniffed the air before finally leveling his hollow gaze in our direction.

Every nerve in my body tensed, preparing to fight. Adrenaline surged into my bloodstream, numbing the pain that plagued my worn body. Everything hurt, but I no longer cared. I would fight to survive. I would fight to protect Alex.

But just as quickly as the vampire focused his sight in our direction,

Tarek looked away, staring out into the desert. Then, Tarek returned to his feeding, tearing open a hole in Seneca's neck with his razor-sharp teeth. He didn't merely consume the blood. Instead, he ravaged the body like a wild animal, tearing chunks of flesh from the bone. It sickened me to hear the cracking and slurping sounds of eating.

"He's blind," I hissed to Celwyn. "And distracted."

Celwyn nodded his head in the affirmative, then held up one outstretched index finger in front of his lips.

He then looked up into the sky and pointed.

Birds chirped and a pale blue sky greeted us overhead, finally replacing the darkness of night. On the ground, I saw both a welcome and unnerving sight—shadows. Dawn had finally broken, but the derailed train car behind us blocked the new light of the morning sun from reaching our position.

For now, Tarek remained protected by the shadows, but he was blind, weak, and preoccupied. To escape, all we had to do was make it to the light.

I grabbed Alex's hand and looked at Celwyn. He carefully stepped around the fire and faced the desert with me and Alex at his side. In the distance, no more than twenty yards away, sunlight beckoned us, its fingers stretching towards our position, pushing back the shadows cast by the overturned train car.

We both took one more quick look back at Tarek to find him still leaning over Seneca's corpse.

Then we ran.

CHAPTER THIRTY-EIGHT

A SUNRISE INSTINCTIVELY BRINGS HOPE. Its warmth drives away the bitter cold of the night. Its rays illuminate the world, removing the sense of vulnerability that accompanies the dark. And somewhere down deep, in our primal programming, every human knows that daylight brings a reprieve from the monsters in the world that only come out at night.

The three of us ran away from the sprawling wreckage of the mag lev train, sprinting across the dirt and rocks toward an imaginary line in the dirt where light met shadow. We ran away from the dark. We ran away from a monster.

We ran towards hope.

Alex fought to stay by my side, the two of us kicking up clouds of sandy grit with every desperate step. I dragged her forward, forcing her to match my stride, and the girl never said a word.

She never faltered.

Behind us, I felt Celwyn keeping pace. Out of the corner of my eye, I saw the tip of his sword rising and falling with every stride, still in his hand.

I never looked back.

We covered ground quickly, and the sunlight felt almost close enough to touch. The boundary of the shadows neared, a literal finish line projected in the sand in a race against death.

And that was when Tarek struck.

One minute the desert loomed in front of us, and the next we ran into a wall of pain. The vampire didn't catch us from behind. Instead, Tarek appeared in our path. He was just there, moving so quickly that he might as well have materialized from thin air.

Our momentum carried Alex and me straight into a powerful backhand swipe that felt like a high-speed car crash. Tarek's blow instantly propelled us high into the air, throwing us backward like rag dolls. I lost Alex's hand and curled up into a fetal position only a second before my body slammed against the rock-strewn ground and rolled, gathering bruises and scrapes along the way before finally stopping.

The world spun and a ringing sound filled my ears. Slowly, I picked my face up from the ground and spat out a mouthful of dirt. My brain began processing my situation, pushing away the fog and confusion of shock.

Alex...*Where was Alex?*

"Alex," I croaked. "Alex!"

A low-pitched groan came from my right. I spun my head.

There, Celwyn lay unconscious, crumpled against an outcropping of boulders, hair matted with blood. In the chaos, his sword had somehow landed in the dirt, blade first, and stuck. Its hilt rose from the ground at a forty-five-degree angle well outside his reach.

But not mine.

I pushed both of my hands against the ground, willing myself to stand. One leg slid painfully across the ground, and I made it up to one knee. Before I could rise to my feet, something strong hit my back and drove my face back into the dirt.

An icy wind blew across my neck and the metallic smell of blood filled my nostrils. I struggled to move, but Tarek pinned me to the ground.

Death had found me.

In my final moments I thought of Alex, and wondered if she still lived. If I could buy her only a few seconds, maybe she could make it to the safety of the sunlight. Maybe my death could matter.

Every inch of my body ached, and my strength was gone, but I kept fighting. The sunlight was so close. I just had to buy Alex time.

"Run! Alex, run!" I shouted. At the same moment, I launched myself forward along the ground, reaching for the sword.

My hand never came close to the hilt. At the first sign of movement, Tarek grabbed my hair and yanked me back. My head slammed into the ground, and the world began to spin again. I fought to remain conscious, ignoring the high-pitched whine buzzing in my ears.

That screech turned into a scream. Was it mine? I wasn't sure. Perhaps I was listening to the sounds of my death as I left my body for another plane of existence.

But something in my mind clicked, and I recognized the source of the scream. It was Alex.

Suddenly the pressure on my back evaporated, and I heard another noise, this one louder. I turned and pushed up on my elbow. Behind me, Tarek sat on his knees in the dirt, wailing in his vampire tongue. The handle of a Leatherman knife protruded from one side of the vampire's head, its blade buried beyond sight. A few feet away, Alex stood motionless with a look of satisfaction on her face.

I grabbed the hilt of Celwyn's claymore, still sticking up from the ground, then used its leverage to slowly push myself up onto a knee. Words were harder. I fought to speak.

"Run," I whispered to Alex. "Into the sunlight. It's not far."

Another deep breath stopped the world from spinning. I swallowed and focused on speaking. I looked straight at Alex and this time the words came out loud and clear. "Alex, run!"

Alex looked at me with steel in her eyes. "No. Not without you."

I gathered my feet underneath me and pulled the sword from the ground. Weapon in hand, I turned toward Tarek still writhing on the ground, trying to to remove the blade from his head. Before I could even take a step, the vampire suddenly freed the Leatherman. He whirled towards Alex and plunged the knife into her chest so quickly she never even flinched.

Time stopped.

I saw the light go out in Alex's eyes.

Her body collapsed backwards, and lay motionless on the ground.

Tarek turned around and I witnessed the face of pure evil. The pupils in his eyes glowed again with a dim red light, and his angular facial features had reformed to near-perfect condition. His feeding had strengthened him, providing nourishment to the parasite living inside. A terrifying vampire stood before me, nothing more than a killing machine, devoid of any sympathy or remorse.

This monster had taken Alex from me, and I hated him for it.

Rage rose up inside me like the waters of a warm bath, removing every pain and thought.

Except one.

I was going to kill Tarek.

I lifted Celwyn's sword and lunged at the vampire, driving the long blade into his chest. A scream erupted from my mouth, but it sounded more like a wail of anguish. The pain of watching Alex die erupted out of every fiber of my body.

The tip lodged deep in the Kevlar vest, stopping it from striking home in the vampire's chest. But I didn't mean to kill him with the blade.

I bit my lip in determination, then I dug my feet into the ground and started pushing forward. Tarek swiped at me with his arms, but the long sword provided just enough length to keep away his attacks. Before he knew what was happening, I had covered several yards.

The line separating sun from shadow had been steadily inching closer during the fighting. Without Alex, the goal of crossing that line meant nothing to me.

I now had a different objective in mind.

While crossing from shadow into sunlight bought me life, it meant death for Tarek. And he knew it. The monster dug in with his feet and stopped my progress. He cursed at me in his horrible language and began to push me back, away from the burning tendrils of the morning sun.

I squeezed the hilt of the sword with both hands and lowered my shoulder, using every ounce of my remaining strength to push towards the sunlight. But Tarek's superhuman strength easily exceeded mine.

He plowed forward and my feet slid backwards in the gravel, making it impossible to gain traction.

My backward momentum increased, and I stumbled over a rock. I strained to hold onto the sword and fell to one knee, but someone caught me. Someone strong.

A pair of arms lifted me to my feet and I saw a look of fear cross Tarek's face.

"I've got you." Celwyn grabbed the hilt of his sword with both hands, intertwining them over mine. "Let's kill this bloody bastard."

Together, we pushed Tarek backward, steadily driving him towards the edge of the shadows. The entire way, Tarek shouted at us in the guttural tone of the vampire tongue, thrashing and straining to free himself.

We slowed as Tarek approached the sunlight. The vampire turned to look at the source of his impending demise, then desperately began to howl and shout the words of the Blood Call.

"No one will come to help you, Tarek." Celwyn said sharply. "You're going to die in this desert. I will take your life, just like you took the life of my wife Jessica and—" Celwyn's nostrils flared and he erupted in an anguished scream. "And my son! His name was Sam. Let their names haunt you forever!"

My body felt broken, but my voice still functioned. So I screamed my head off, joining Celwyn's furious shout of rage. And it worked. For a moment, the pain faded away and I felt strong. Together, we pushed Tarek into the sunlight and his body burst into bright red and orange flames. The sun's rays sliced through Tarek like laser beams, leaving nothing but a smoking pile of clothes—and a Kevlar chest piece with a claymore sword sticking out of the front.

I closed my eyes and walked into the sunlight. The warmth of the morning rays washed over my body, and I cried. The emotion poured out of my body, distilling into tiny streams of water exiting my eyes. Somehow, the night was over, and I had survived. That brought me immense relief. And with every breath, the rage subsided, restoring clarity to my mind. And that brought back the pain, quickly followed by despair.

Alex. My poor little girl.

Celwyn grabbed me by the shoulder and turned me around. "Look."

A group of hooded figures stood in the shadows next to Alex's body. An old man with white hair knelt by her side, caressing the girl's golden hair.

Saul had come.

CHAPTER THIRTY-NINE

"THE GIRL IS DYING, but she's not dead," Saul said softly. "Not yet."

Alex lay on her back in the shadows on the ground, eyes closed, blood caked on her lips. The Leatherman still protruded from her chest, poking through a shirt stained dark red.

"Maybe we can save her." I looked at Celwyn. "Call for help. We can get her to a doctor."

Celwyn looked down and spoke gently. "We can't remove that knife out here without surgical tools. If we do, she'll die instantly. And if we don't, she will still die, just more slowly. The Knights are on their way, but she doesn't have time. There's nothing we can do. I'm sorry."

Saul spoke again. "Melanie, I can hear her heart slowing. If there is something you want to say, speak it now."

I knelt down and took Alex's hand in mine. It felt cold, but still held a trace of warmth. "Alex, I don't know if you can hear me." I began to cry again. "You saved my life. You're such a brave girl. I never had my own daughter, but if I did, I would have wanted her to be just like you."

With my other hand, I caressed Alex's hair then kissed her on the forehead.

To my surprise, Alex's hand softly squeezed my own and a moan escaped her lips.

"Do something!" I shouted at Celwyn. "You have to have one of those fancy bandages or some other thing you can try?" I looked pleadingly at Celwyn. "Help her. Please. I don't know what to do."

"There's nothing I can do," Celwyn replied.

"No. Not good enough!" I pounded my fists on the ground. "I won't let her die. Not here. Not after she made it so far."

A thought began to creep into my mind.

A terrible thought.

Saul put a hand on my good shoulder. "Melanie, it's not your fault."

I grasped Saul's hand tightly, then used it for leverage to stand up. "No, it's that monster's fault. And I'm not going to let Tarek take her away from me." I paused and looked into Saul's eyes. "You're going to save her."

Celwyn knocked Saul's hand down from my shoulder. "No! Don't even say it."

"It's the only way!" I shouted.

Celwyn was right, of course. The thought of turning Alex into one of those *things* filled me with disgust.

Would a cursed life be better than death? Who am I to make such a decision? I'm not even her real mother.

But in that moment, I didn't care. I was selfish. I wanted Alex to live.

"Are you certain about this, Melanie?"

I looked at the men and women surrounding Saul. Each of them was once a shade, nothing more than an infected animal. Now, they followed Saul and at least outwardly appeared to be in control of their humanity. They seemed…*alive.*

Celwyn raised his sword and moved to block Saul. "You can't do this. It's wrong."

I moved the sword down with my hand, and spoke softly. "Celwyn. If you had the chance for your wife—or your son—to live, would you have taken it? Would you have done *everything* to allow you to spend one more day with them?"

He sighed and lowered his sword. "I don't know what I would have done. But that doesn't make it right."

"How do you know?" I turned to Saul. "How do you *know* that she won't turn into a monster?"

"I don't know what she will become because I don't know what is inside this girl's heart. But if she is what you believe she is, then she will be that way again. The parasite can be mastered. I can show her the way. My bloodline will be different."

Celwyn shook his head. "Death is not a choice. And if it was, you shouldn't make it for someone else."

He was right about the last part. I had no right to make this decision for Alex. It should be her choice. I strained to focus on what Alex would want, and all I could see in my mind was the image of the steely-eyed girl who saved my life when she could have run away.

Alex fought her way through the gates of hell and persevered until the very end. And in that moment, she reminded me of someone. Someone who had also fought against all odds to survive, even though everyone around him died.

I turned to Saul. "Back in the hospice, Celwyn asked me to kill you, but I didn't."

"Yes," Saul replied.

"Did I make the right choice?'

Saul paused. "Ah. I see. You want to know if I regret what I have become." He looked down. "And what I have lost."

"Yes."

"Before I changed, I was a religious man. I believed in a creator and a reward in the afterlife. But I still desperately clung to life. It's such a precious gift—life—and the paradox is that it can be so easily ended. Life is...fragile. Now, I don't feel so fragile. But I am still me. No less alive, no better or worse, just different." Saul took my hand. "Yes. You made the right choice. And I will forever be in your debt."

I looked at Celwyn. He shook his head disapprovingly. "It's wrong," he said flatly. "And if you do this, she will have to go with Saul. As he said, she *will* be different. She'll be one of them, and that means they *will* be hunted."

"Maybe," I replied. "But at least she'll be alive."

I nodded to Saul. "Do it. Quickly, while there is still time."

Celwyn made no move to stop him.

The old man leaned down and gently pushed Alex's hair away from one of her shoulders, clearing a small patch of pale white skin. The act resembled a kiss, a peck on Alex's neck that lingered perhaps a bit too long. His kiss left a small puncture wound where his teeth had broken the skin, and Alex's body immediately began to convulse.

"Blood of my blood," Saul said quietly.

Saul's companions murmured the same words, as if it held some magic power or enchantment.

The old man removed the Leatherman from Alex's chest and offered it to me. I shook my head.

"No," I said firmly. "It belongs to her."

Saul placed it in his pocket. "I'll make sure she has it." He picked up Alex, and cradled the girl in both arms. Her face already seemed to be turning a light shade of gray. "The first part is tough. It's best if you don't see it. And the sun is up. We need to get under cover quickly."

"Where are you going?" I asked.

Saul looked at Celwyn suspiciously, then faced me. "I don't know. And it's best that you don't know either. I promise I'll keep Alex safe, and that you *will* see her again."

Led by Saul, the small group of vampires backtracked through the debris field, clinging to the shadows. They moved quickly, and, within minutes, they entered the other end of the giant pipe leading to the desalinization plant in Long Beach.

———

I SAT in the sun next to Celwyn, leaning against a boulder. Even though Tarek was dead, I couldn't bring myself to leave the protection of the sunlight.

"You know, all I've heard for days is 'the Knights are coming, the Knights are coming.' First, they were going to kill everyone in the Castle, and now they're going to rescue us? I'm starting to believe you're delusional."

Celwyn grimaced. "Yeah, well, some days it doesn't seem real to me, either."

The pain from the gunshot throbbed through my body. "It hurts," I said simply.

"Where?" asked Celwyn.

I paused thoughtfully. "Everywhere, but especially the gunshot. Never been shot before." I looked at Celwyn. "I need to ask you something."

"What?"

"If we get rescued by the Knights, I assume you will tell them everything, right? I mean, these are people you trust?"

"What are you asking me?"

"You said you wouldn't hunt down Saul. But what about the other Knights? If you tell them about Saul, they'll go after him. And if they go after Saul, they'll be going after Alex."

"You can't ask me to lie."

"No, that's not what I'm saying. It's just that, you know Saul. He's different. They're not real vampires. They're not...monsters."

Celwyn shook his head. "And that's exactly why the Knights have to know."

"I don't understand."

"What happened here has changed everything. The Accords have been broken for the first time in thousands of years, and I'm not sure what that means. Probably war." He exhaled sharply. "But Saul—and what he's become—might be even more important."

"They'll be afraid of him. They'll still try to kill him."

"And I'm not sure they would be wrong." Celwyn sat upright and his eyes narrowed as we spoke. "When I first joined the Order, they taught us a lot of things about vampires. I mainly focused on physical training and what I needed to learn to be able to kill them, but I remember some of the things I learned about how they are made—it's a big deal. It's damn near a religious ceremony for them, handled by the Mothers, a bunch of secretive witches. Tarek was trying to shortcut that process and had the best scientists money could buy. Whatever he came up with in that lab in the Castle still took months. But somehow Saul mastered the parasite in less than a day."

Celwyn exhaled sharply. "Mel, no one, and I mean *no one*, has ever evolved from a shade into a vampire that quickly, and certainly not alone, without help. But even scarier is that whatever makes him different can be spread to others. He's starting not just a new bloodline, but a new Bloodline."

The things Celwyn said seemed so abstract, so irrelevant. My body ached and my throat felt like it was coated in sandpaper each time I swallowed. "You're worried about saving the world. I just want to make it out of here. We can talk politics later."

Before he could respond, the distinct *thwup thwup thwup* sound of a helicopter rang out from the direction of Los Angeles. Celwyn's watch buzzed with a message, and a faint smile creeped into his face.

"Let me guess. The Knights are here."

"Hmmph. So I'm not delusional after all."

I allowed myself finally to smile. "The answer to that question is still very much up for debate."

Celwyn stood, pain pinching his face, and began waving his arms. The sounds of the helicopter's blades became louder and louder until one roared over our heads. It circled over our position and was joined by a second and a third.

Soon, the noise of vehicles joined the sounds of the circling helicopters and a convoy came into view, driving along the service road that paralleled the pipeline. At least ten military-looking vehicles roared to a stop near our position just outside the debris field from the crash.

Soldiers poured out of the vehicles, all wearing gray body armor with a rifle in their hands and the hilt of a sword visible on their backs. One of the helicopters landed on the desert floor next to the convoy and a middle-aged woman with long, flowing black hair tinged with gray emerged from a sliding door, then gracefully leaped down onto the ground. A trio of soldiers leaped down behind her and struggled to keep up as she strode across the desert towards us.

Celwyn fidgeted and began to pace. "I can't believe she's here."

"Who is she?"

"Petranela Calatrava. She runs the Order. She's got a direct line to the Pope himself."

I rose to my feet to stand next to Celwyn. I figured if he thought she was important, maybe I should, too.

The woman stopped a few feet away from us and made a quick tap on her chest with her right hand balled into a fist. Celwyn did the same.

Her uniform was simple and gray like the other soldiers, but it had small differences. A white cross was emblazoned on her right shoulder. A scabbard for a sword hung on each hip instead of a single one on her back. She didn't carry a rifle, and I began to think she didn't need one.

She studied both of us for a few seconds, then motioned to one of the soldiers behind her. "Get them some water." She turned back to us. "We received your transmission, Celwyn."

He nodded. "Warden Calatrava."

She looked around at the crash site. "Do you know how many infected are still running around out here?"

Celwyn paused, and my heart skipped a beat before he answered. "The people, the infected, everyone's dead, including Tarek." he replied. He looked back over his shoulder at the Castle. "We're the only ones left."

"I hope you're right," she said grimly to Celwyn. Then she turned her attention to me.

"You must be Melanie. I understand you are immune to the parasite."

"Yes," I said.

"You have no idea how special that makes you. We need to talk, but I imagine this has already been difficult for you in a lot of ways, and I won't complicate matters right now." She paused and stared at my shoulder. "You've been shot."

I nodded.

She turned and motioned to a man behind her. "Get them both to the helicopter and fly them back to the Joshua operating base. I'll stay here with the trucks and make sure everything gets cleaned up."

I followed Celwyn into the helicopter and everything felt so surreal. I made it. I really made it.

I fought vampires with a sword. I shot a gun.

But I also saw good people die.

My new life lay buried in the ruins of the Silver Castle behind me. And a little girl remained somewhere out there with Saul.

The seat on the helicopter felt like a bed in a luxury hotel. I leaned my head back and closed my eyes. And for the first time in a long time, I allowed myself to sleep.

CHAPTER FORTY

"WAKE UP, SLEEPY HEAD."

My eyes slowly adjusted to what seemed to be the brightest lights I had ever seen, and Celwyn's face came into view.

"I'm a nurse," I said. "I'm not used to being on this side of the bed."

Celwyn chuckled. "Let's see how long they can keep you down. I suspect it won't be long."

I surveyed the makeshift hospital room that included an IV bag and a computer monitoring my vitals. The helicopter had dropped us off at a nondescript warehouse that had been taken over by the Knights as a temporary base. After being whisked inside, a medic prepped me for surgery and that's the last thing I remembered.

"How long have I been out?"

"About six hours," Celwyn replied. "They patched up the bullet wounds. That exit point had gotten pretty nasty."

"How's your face?"

A bandage wrapped around Celwyn's cheek, from his chin to above his ear. "The shades in the Castle took a bite out of me, but I'll be fine. One more for the scar collection. How do you feel?"

The pain in my shoulder had dulled into the background along with everything else. I glanced at the IV pole and noticed the morphine drip. "Actually, I feel great. But I think that's because I don't feel anything at the moment."

Celwyn sat down in the chair next to the bed, and began fidgeting. "Calatrava is going to come talk to you. She's going to ask you to join the Knights."

"Yeah, I expected she would give me a sales pitch since I'm immune."

"So what are you going to say?" Celwyn asked.

I shifted upright in the bed. "Honestly, I don't know. What do you think I should say?"

He looked down. "It's a big decision. I can't make it for you."

"Well, you're no help." I wasn't being coy. I really didn't know what I wanted. Part of me wanted to forget about Idrissia, vampires, and the Knights. I could find a nice quiet nursing job somewhere and hope the Knights could hold off the forces of evil without me.

But how could I go back to just being a nurse after what I had experienced? I knew what lurked in the darkness. And somewhere out there, Saul and Alex were making their way as vampires, trying to survive without becoming monsters.

Would it last? Would she become a monster, and if not, would the Knights hunt her anyway? Could I live my life without even trying to make a difference?

Someone knocked at the door, and Celwyn stood. Calatrava entered the room.

Celwyn nodded in her direction. "Warden Calatrava."

"Knight," she replied before turning towards me. "And how are you feeling, Melanie? Better I hope."

"I'm feeling great now," I replied. "But I suspect things will change when the morphine stops flowing."

"I'm sure it will. But I know a Knight when I see one. And the woman I see wouldn't be bothered by a little pain." Calatrava stood at the foot of my bed, and I got a close look at her features. She was tall and lean, but older than I first thought. Her long black hair was now pulled up into a pony tail behind her head. Her fierce blue eyes commanded my attention, but they also filled me with a sense of discomfort. I could match her gaze only briefly before looking away, as if avoiding looking directly into the sun.

"Celwyn has told me how you helped him, that you fought Tarek. Just so you know, someone other than a Knight hasn't killed a vampire in hand-to-hand combat in over two centuries." She smiled. "I'm impressed."

"I had some help," I replied. "And I fought because I had no choice, not because I wanted to impress anyone."

Calatrava began to pace at the foot of my bed as she spoke. "You strike me as a smart woman. You know what I am going to ask of you, and you know why I must ask it." She paused and stared at me with those commanding eyes. "You are uniquely suited for a duty that most would never dare to perform—and one that sadly seems more important than ever at the moment. You said you fought because you had no choice. But we both know that's not true. You're a protector. All good Knights are. So when you fought Tarek, who were you protecting?"

I felt the temperature in the room rise as color filled my face. *Did Celwyn tell her?* If I looked at him, she would see, and she would know we were keeping a secret. Those damned eyes saw everything.

"I fought Tarek because if I didn't, I would be dead. And Celwyn would be dead, too. We protected each other."

Alatrava looked at Celwyn, who maintained a poker face. No doubt the bandages helped.

"Ah, I see," she said. "Any good Knight should have their partner's back." She returned her gaze to me. "You know it's extraordinary how quickly a bond can be forged in the heat of combat. Often, those bonds can seem strong, like they will last forever, but the true test comes once the pressure subsides, when the passion of battle is replaced by the tedium of peace. Will it be the same then? Hmm, hard to know."

"Look, whatever you think I am, you're wrong. I'm just a nurse. You have hundreds of trained soldiers who can fight better than me. I barely learned how to use a gun two days ago. What difference can I make?"

"Melanie, there was a time when the Knights were legion. Thousands of us battled the infected across all seven continents.

Thankfully, the war ended with the Accords, and the vampires have largely remained compliant since the Middle Ages, their numbers small, hidden away from sight. And because our enemy's numbers were small, we became content with our numbers becoming small."

She turned away and lowered her head. "And I fear that mistake will lead to our demise, and perhaps the destruction of the human race. They can scale up quickly while we cannot."

"You sound like Paloma now," Celwyn said. "And you ran him off for saying these things."

"His methods were flawed, but his logic was sound. I only came to see it too late." Calatrava faced me again. "I will leave you to consider my offer, but remember this one thing, Melanie—history is filled with stories of a single man or woman whose actions changed the world. Being in the right place at the right time *matters*. Some call it providence, others call it fate. Some around here call it the will of God. I believe there was a reason Celwyn met you in the Castle, a reason that he stumbled upon the one person in a million who is immune to the parasite." She paused. "And I believe your story is only at the beginning, not the end."

She walked towards the door, but I spoke up before she could leave.

"I do have a question for you."

Calatrava turned around, confident that she now had me on her hook. "Anything. What would you like to know?"

"I understand the truce with the vampires, but the others who are infected—the shades—why haven't you ever tried to save them instead of killing them?"

She sighed. "Melanie, there is no cure. Many have tried. Believe me, if science offered a solution to this evil, we would use it."

"But the vampires have a way to help the shades control the parasite, right? The shades could become vampires, and some could be reasoned with. Some may even become allies."

"No. The number of vampires would grow. And they would all need to feed. This path leads to more death, not less. Make no mistake, no vampire will ever be a friend to humanity."

I nodded. "I understand."

Calatrava cocked her head and gave me one more inquisitive look with those piercing eyes before leaving my room.

———

I SAT with my backpack on the seat of the pickup truck parked at the edge of the Joshua base. The sun sank over the mountains to the West, leaving nothing more than a dim orange glow on the horizon. Soon it would be night, and now I knew what that meant.

Celwyn walked up to the truck wearing a gray Knight uniform like the others. "I can't believe you told her 'no.' No one says 'no' to Calatrava."

"Maybe more people should," I said.

He rolled his eyes. "Yeah. Like it's that easy. You've met the woman."

"She's not going to let you drive me to Los Angeles, is she?"

Celwyn shook his head slowly. "Nope. One of the other guys will be here in a minute. Apparently, I'm getting promoted. It's Captain now, and I have a lot of work to do."

"Ooh, Captain Celwyn. Aren't you important?" I paused. "You know, I just realized I don't even know your last name. If you take a woman out to kill vampires, you should at least tell her your full name. So what is it, Captain?"

Celwyn chose his words carefully. "My family immigrated to the United Kingdom from eastern Europe. We've been hunting vampires for a very long time. It's kind of what we do." He paused and looked down at the ground. "Except for my dad."

Now I was intrigued. "Don't hold out on me, Blondie. What's the full name?"

He smiled. "I can't tell you all my secrets. Have to save something for next time. If there is a next time—I mean, I hope there is a next time."

A long slow breath escaped from my lungs. "Oh," I said. "So, like you're famous. I get it."

"Not really, but I've got someone in my family tree a while back.

He's the famous one." He laughed. "You know the funny thing is that he wasn't even that great of a Knight."

"Oh, yeah, you're totally better." We both chuckled and it felt good. I would miss him. I would miss being *with* him. I shrugged my shoulders. "I guess there can be a next time."

Celwyn put one foot up onto the running board of the truck and leaned in close. "You're going to go looking for them, aren't you?"

"No. I wouldn't even know where to start." That was a lie. And a poor one.

Celwyn grabbed my hand. "Whatever you think you know about Saul, just remember this—you'll never be safe in his world. And I won't be there to protect you."

I squeezed his hand. "I know. I can take care of myself."

"Yes. Yes, you can, Mel."

He leaned in and pressed his lips quickly to mine. The kiss was forceful, but ended quickly. Too quickly.

Celwyn stepped back as the driver walked up to the vehicle. "You owe me a date, Mel Sanger, and I plan to hold you to it."

"You know where to find me, Captain," I replied. "The City of Angels."

"It's the devils that come out at night that have me worried. Stay safe, Mel."

Celwyn closed the door and the driver turned the ignition.

"I'm ready," I said.

The truck pulled away from the base and I watched Celwyn's form grow smaller in the rear view mirror. The truck's headlights illuminated the dark road ahead, and my senses reflexively sharpened. What was it that Celwyn had said? The Knights were the apex predators, not the vampires. I didn't need a fancy title and orders from someone like Calatrava to fight vampires. I could just be me.

I've always done my best work at night, and there's no reason why a hospice nurse on the night shift can't fight vampires, too.

Somewhere out there, Saul and Alex lived. I would find them, or they would find me. I really didn't care which happened first, but Calatrava was right.

My story wasn't ending. It was just beginning.

ABOUT THE AUTHOR

DL Barron took up writing during the pandemic, determined to use his suddenly available free time to pursue a life-long dream. He lives with his ridiculously patient wife and two overbearing dogs in Texas and is a sucker for a good conspiracy theory or compelling tale of the supernatural.

www.ingramcontent.com/pod-product-compliance
Lightning Source LLC
Chambersburg PA
CBHW020122120726
47903CB00007B/2061